To Mom
from Jan
December 25, 1982

I STILL
DREAM
ABOUT
COLUMBUS

I STILL DREAM ABOUT COLUMBUS

a novel by

Jack M. Bickham

ST. MARTIN'S PRESS   NEW YORK

Design by Laura Hammond

Library of Congress Cataloging in Publication Data

Bickham, Jack M.
  I still dream about Columbus.

  I. Title.
PS3552.I312   813'.54   82-5742
ISBN 0-312-40276-7   AACR2

First Edition
10 9 8 7 6 5 4 3 2 1

I STILL DREAM ABOUT COLUMBUS

1

Now I am old, and the place I live is more than fifteen hundred miles from Ohio. More than a half-century has passed. But I still dream about Columbus.

That crucial time in our lives began as high adventure, a golden, glorious time for all of us: my mother and father, my brothers and sister, and myself. Even today it seems unreal that the adventure could have so suddenly changed, making us feel our whole world was coming to an end. Sometimes the memories are so vivid, combining such joy and pain, that it appears impossible it could have been so long ago. On other days, seeing a stranger in my mirror, I wonder if it ever really happened at all. Could I have been that boy?

It was a blustery Sunday afternoon in October, 1927, when our parents bundled us up in our South High Street duplex for a ride on the streetcar. We begged to know where we were going, but they refused to tell us, like conspiratorial children.

"Perhaps we should give them a hint, Mrs. Riley?" my father asked with a wink as he put on his heavy dark coat.

"Oh, I doubt it, Mr. Riley," my mother said, tugging her scarf around red-blond hair. "They'll learn soon enough, don't you think?"

My father put on his wool billed cap, pulling it low over the curly hair on his forehead. "Well, perhaps you're right."

"Well, sir, I usually am."

"Ah, indeed you are, madam. Well, then, are we ready?" He examined us children, lined up and fidgeting like recalcitrant soldiers: Gail, my older brother, fourteen, almost as tall as my mother, with my father's dark hair and eyes and stubborn jaw, standing there with his hands in his coat pockets and glaring to show his disapproval; myself, just twelve, my hands hidden in the too-long sleeves of Gail's hand-me-down red-and-black wool jacket; Frank, eight, scuffing one shoe against the other so that both laces had already come undone; Mary, six, a blond doll with great blue eyes and red wool stockings that emphasized the black of her coat and high boots. "Everyone seems ready!" he said with pleasure.

Gail tried once more. "Where are we *going?*"

Pop chuckled and opened the front door. "Hurry, now!"

We trooped to the corner and waited in a brisk, cool wind. Heavy clouds hung low overhead, threatening rain. Another family of four came to stand at curbside with us, and then two lone men. Cars puttered by on the cobbles, making a great racket. Then the tall green streetcar could be heard, the overhead wires singing as it trundled up to our stop with a clanging and grating of steel wheels in the gritty tracks. We went out to the car and climbed on, Gail first, then me, Frank, my mother, and Pop with Mary in his arms.

The car was a long, drafty cavern rowed with wicker benches and seats, less than a third occupied. Pop motioned us on back and handed the motorman some change. "Two adults and four children, sir. And we'll be needing transfers."

That was too much for me. "Transfers! Where are we *going?*"

"Kenneth John Riley," my mother said with soft severity, mindful of the staring passengers, "be quiet and march."

I marched. Gail waited halfway back the car and let Pop indicate our chosen seats with a slight nod—a long wicker bench running sideways in the car where we could all sit side by side. If either Gail or I had been riding alone, we would have gone all the way to the open back, where you could fold down the seat used by the motorman when he drove the car in that direction. But of course you didn't do such things with your parents.

The streetcar jolted into motion. Gail sat glaring still, his profile so like Pop's. I was fair like my mother, and would be smaller, never achieving even my father's modest height. I often envied Gail that he would be almost five feet ten, like Pop, and would look so much like him. I think it bothered Gail, though, not only to have the responsibility of being the oldest but to know that he so resembled the greatest man in the world.

Pop sat on the far end, fanning out the transfers to count them. They were flimsy yellow sheets half the size of dollar bills that could be used for a connecting car line; they deepened the mystery because I didn't know we knew anyone that far away. But Pop seemed unworried. He put the transfers in his coat pocket, dug out a Chesterfield, tapped it twice on the back of his hand, and cracked a wood match to light it.

I sighed and waited.

The streetcar rumbled north with frequent stops. Light rain began to pelt the wide windows, and the street glistened. We rattled up Front Street along the river, approaching the enormity of Columbus's new and only skyscraper, the A.I.U. Building. This was Broad Street. Pop swung Mary into his arms again. "Come on, everyone."

We climbed out into the light rain, gawking at the building and other sights. Pop led us across the street to another car stop. We stared at other downtown sights until the car came along. The sign on the front said WEST BROAD—HILLTOP. My father motioned us out to the loading zone in the middle of the street.

"This is crazy," Gail muttered to me and Frank. "We don't know *anybody* on the Hilltop!"

The Hilltop, I knew, was new, the farthest westward development of Columbus. I had never been there, but knew it was a zillion miles away. Dutifully climbing on board the new streetcar, I felt a slight pang of nausea, the kind I got sometimes when I was too nervous. I sat down and practiced deep breathing to try to calm myself.

Any outing was an adventure for us. Although we did not consider ourselves poor, we had no car—those were for rich

people, or Uncle Jack (who was not very reliable)—and finan-
cially we watched our *p*'s and *q*'s at all times, as my mother liked
to remind us. Every so often we got to go to the show, but most
of the time we went to school and did our chores around the
house and played in our immediate neighborhood. And Mom did
the housework and some sewing for extra money, and Pop
worked at the radiator shop. Except for family get-togethers, we
seldom went anywhere else.

And yet here we were, rocketing out into the middle of
nowhere. No wonder I was nervous.

I watched Pop for some hint of what was going on, but he
ignored me. It was a temptation but I did not press him. Sometimes his hair stood straight on end, a warning for his temper. We
had learned not to press him too far. He had never turned a hand
on any of us in anger, but it was always possible that he might,
with sufficient provocation. He said once his own father had
beaten him and his brothers a lot, and he would never make that
mistake. Then, having told us that one night before Christmas
when we were being especially rowdy, he had pulled Gail around
roughly by the arm. *"But I swear, Gail Henry,"* he had said, voice
trembling as he held up a fist in front of Gail's frightened eyes,
"sometimes you tax me to the limit!"

Then he had turned away, and a few minutes later I caught
him standing alone in the living room, looking at the Christmas
tree, tears on his face.

"Pop?" I had said, shocked.

He turned, wiped his hand across his face, and grinned. "I
was just thinking, Kenny, of all the people who don't have as
much as we do during the holidays. Then, instead of being thankful, I lose my temper."

Sometimes he cried at the slightest provocation. He was
tough and sentimental, smart and naive, cynical and idealistic,
given to flights of lyrical Irish enthusiasm and bouts of the pro-
foundest mysterious gloom, loving and outward and then by turn
quiet and withdrawn. One thing he had going for him, he liked
to say, was that he could outwork any man alive. Sometimes,

seeing him walk slowly up the street in the evening gloom, gray-faced with exhaustion, we knew it must be true. We adored him.

If this strange streetcar journey seemed out of character for him, however, then for my mother it was incredible. Mom, after all, was the *serious* one. Her maiden name had been Prater. People in the family said there was a famous park in Vienna named Prater Park, and Mom's family had probably owned it once. Sometimes when she was exceptionally serious my father would ask her if she was wishing she had her park back.

What made that a joke was how poor her family had always been in this country. My father could joke about it because his family was no better off. But it was also a joke because Mom seldom had time for frivolity; she could laugh, and sometimes her laughter filled the house with its beautiful, happy sound. But she seldom took part in being silly, playing pranks, wasting time—as she saw it—with "nonsense." Sometimes all of us, Pop included, tried her patience with our repartee. This trip—taking us half-way across our known universe without explanation and with a sly smile, was Pop's style—but not Mom's.

The West Broad Street streetcar rattled across the river and headed out across the low-lying areas to the west, known as The Bottoms. Gail kept poking Frank and me and insisting we come up with some theory about where we were headed, and we kept frowning and trying to ignore him. Pop held Mary, and after a while her long stockinged legs dangled limp as she fell asleep. I tried to crack my knuckles without success. The streetcar climbed the long hill toward the Hilltop and then clattered along faster again, passing scattered small businesses, churches, houses. After a while Pop began craning his neck to see to the front. We came to an area along Broad Street where small shops lined the sidewalks. Much of the construction looked fairly new, in sharp contrast to the aged neighborhood where we lived on the south side. Then, seeing some landmark, Pop nudged my mother and got to his feet, hugging Mary to his shoulder. He walked to the exit door and pulled the cord to ring the bell that signaled the motorman we wanted to get off at the next corner.

The mystery deepened as we left the car in a fine, cold rain. Pop shepherded us close to wait for the car to go on by, then led us across the street. "Bundle up, everybody. It isn't a far walk."

"Who are we going to *see?*" Gail demanded.

"What makes you think we're going to see somebody?"

Gail writhed. "If somebody doesn't tell me something pretty soon, I'm going to bust."

"Well, son, if you bust, just cross the street first, okay? We wouldn't want some of you getting all over us."

"Gaw!" Gail said bitterly and stomped along in silence.

We walked south on the residential street. I noticed it was called Terrace Avenue. I had never heard of it before. The houses were single-family dwellings, most of them quite new and grand: two-story houses, frame, with big front porches and windows high up that hinted of big attics. Typical of the construction of that period, they stood much higher than the street, above little lawn terraces, so that we walked well below their level. This made them look even more enormous.

My father, still carrying a sleepy Mary, walked jauntily, a fresh cigarette in his lips. I had seldom seen him more perky. He walked like he owned the world. My mother, too, strode along with a smile on her face, as if she shared a great secret.

After walking a block or two in the icy rain, we came to a place where the street widened considerably, becoming two streets that surrounded blocks of narrow parkway between the lanes. Some new trees had been planted in the parkway, and some of the lots here were still vacant; others showed houses under construction, some showed occupancy and a few had For Sale signs in their raw mud yards. The parkway, making the space from house to house across the street even greater, added to my impression of wealth and dignity. In actuality, the lots were quite narrow, most of them fifty feet, and the houses tall and narrow to fit the lots; even so, they were built quite close together. But to my eye, accustomed to the south end, it looked like Rich People's Heaven.

We came to a house on our left that had a For Sale sign in

the yard and, beneath that sign, a smaller one that said Sold. The paving had been installed from the sidewalk to the porch, which was large with square pillars. The house was tall and narrow, mostly white frame with dark gray trim. It had a big front window looking onto the porch and a round window up on top, in the attic. It looked very grand.

Pop turned into the walk, leading us up to the porch.

"Nobody lives here yet," Gail protested, hanging back.

"That's right," my father said, putting Mary down on the porch. He dug in his coat pocket and brought out some keys on a ring that had a round paper tag attached. "Somebody will, though."

Stunned, we watched him walk to the front door, open the screen, and insert a key in the lock. The door swung open. He looked at us and his grin was so wide I thought it would split his face, reddened by the cold.

"Doesn't anybody want to see our new house?" he asked.

Mary, despite being sleepy, responded first. Her eyes widened. *"Ours?"* she chirped.

"That's right, punkin," Pop said, still grinning.

Mary ran inside. We heard her heels clatter hollowly on wood floors.

"Gaw!" Gail said reverently and went in after her.

Frank and I followed, Mom and Pop coming behind. By the time I stepped into the living room, Mary's voice was already sounding excitedly from upstairs somewhere, and Gail was talking a mile a minute, his voice echoing, from the back. "You mean this is *ours?*" he yelled. "I can't believe it! It's even got a dining room! Yow! Look at this! This kitchen is big enough to play ball in! Yow! Look at that backyard! Has it got a basement? Where does this door go? It *does* have a basement!"

"Mommy! Mommy!" Mary cried down the staircase. "Where am I going to sleep?"

Frank scurried off through a broad doorway to my right and into a great, vacant room with a shining wood floor that had to be the dining room. I stood as if rooted, shock tingling through my nervous system, simply staring. The living room seemed as big as our entire south side house. The walls had flowered wallpaper that was gorgeous. There was a brick fireplace, fake, with a radiant heater already installed. The golden glow of the new floor fascinated me. I could smell paint and plaster and varnish.

"Well, son?" Pop asked softly, a hand on my shoulder. "What do you think?"

"Is it really ours?" I asked.

"It sure is."

I was forced to revert to Gail's vocabulary for adequate expression. "Gaw!"

We explored. Mom and Pop walked from room to room, obviously familiar with the layout, watching our reactions. Mary ran continuously until Mom finally—gently—told her to slow down. Gail came out of the basement still talking a mile a minute and headed upstairs. Frank walked around slack-faced, dazed. I moved more slowly, but in no less amazement.

The house had four major rooms downstairs: living, dining, parlor, kitchen. The living room and parlor connected front to back on one side, the dining room and kitchen on the other. A hallway ran down the middle, and the stairs—down to the basement, up to the bedrooms—ran off this area. There was a pantry under one of the staircases. Pop said he would put a lot of shelves under there, for the things we canned.

The door to the backyard went out of the kitchen. There was a small back porch with latticework all around it. The backyard, bare earth, faced a muddy alley.

Upstairs were four bedrooms and a bathroom. Three of the bedrooms seemed huge to me. The smaller one, my mother said, would be Mary's. She and Pop would have the room on the right front, Frank and I would have the one opposite. Gail would have a room of his own in the back next to Mary's. Frank and I explored our room. It had two windows looking over the roof of the front porch to the street and two more on the side looking into windows of the house next door.

The bathroom was fantastic, with white porcelain fixtures and a tub with big claw feet and porcelain inserts, lettered *H* and *C,* on the faucets. The drain plug for the tub hung pristine on a nickle-plated chain that didn't even have any of the brass showing through yet.

The attic was the last area we explored. It was vast and wonderful, fully floored, with dust on the wide planks and the sound of the rain on the enormous, sloping roof.

"You mean," Gail asked as we all stood in the attic, "you really *bought* this?"

"Well, it's not all paid for," my father smiled. "But between us and Central Federal, we own it, yes."

"Gaw! I didn't know we had this kind of money!"

Pop's face turned sober. "It's a big reach for us. But we've saved. We got a good bargain. There's no reason why my job won't pay even better in years to come, and the country's economy is booming along better all the time. We're all going to have to scrimp a little. But we can make the payments and in a few years it will be all ours. It's certainly worth working hard and scrimping for, don't you think?"

"It's the greatest house I ever saw," I said.

My mother hugged me. "You and Frank will take care of your new room, right?"

"Even better than the one in our old house!"

"I'm going back to the basement," Gail said, heading down the steps.

"Me too!" Frank yelped.

"We'll all go," Pop said, chuckling.

Second inspection proved the basement was even more impressive than a first hurried glance had indicated. It was gigantic, the concrete block walls clean and gray, the floor unstained by water leaks. In one area were faucets and a floor drain where Mom could do the laundry, and at the far end was the huge coal-burning furnace, its spiderweb of white-coated round pipes going off in all directions. The small separate room that was the coal bin had a good, sturdy wooden door. Pop showed us where

he would set up his workshop and where we could play. Between
the basement and the attic, he told my mother, we would certainly have plenty of indoor clothesline space for once.

We climbed back upstairs, into the kitchen.

"We'll be moving before the end of the month," Pop told us.
"I've already checked at your new schools, and you'll transfer
fine. Next week sometime we'll try to get back out here in Uncle
Jack's car and show you the schools. They're nice . . . real nice."

"Will we move everything ourselves or what?" I asked.

"No, we'll have the movers for most of it. And some things
we can move in Uncle Jack's car."

"Are we going to plant grass and bushes and everything?"

"Everything," Pop said, and the grin came back. "We can
have a good garden out there, too. With a grape arbor. We've got
a lot of work to do to get everything shipshape, but we can
handle it, right?"

"*Nobody* is going to outwork us," Gail said firmly.

Mom waggled her finger. "And everyone is going to wipe his
feet every time before he comes in this house, and no putting
your hands on the walls. We're going to *take care* of this house."

We all nodded solemnly.

"We just wanted you to see it today," Pop said. "Now we'll
have to get back to the streetcar line."

"Did you close that attic door?" Mom asked.

He frowned. "I'll go check." He bounded up the steps.

"That thing out in the middle of the street will be great for
football," Frank said.

"Baseball, too," Gail pointed out.

"I think this neighborhood is going to have *everything!*"

Pop came hurriedly back down the stairs. "All set." His grin
faded as he stood there, and he began rubbing his left arm.

"Did you hurt yourself?" my mother asked.

"No." He rubbed the arm more and seemed distracted. "Just
a little pain, there."

"Joseph, you look pale. Maybe you should sit down a minute."

Despite the cold of the house, sweat had popped out on his forehead. He wiped his face with a handkerchief and then shook the arm loosely, like he did sometimes to warm up when we were going to play ball. "No. I'm fine. Shall we go?" We went out onto the porch. Pop gestured toward the parkway between the lanes of the street. "Did you gents get a load of that great place for playing ball? Wow!" He made a throwing motion. "Batter up!"

We trooped into the rain and no one gave any more thought to the moment at the bottom of the stairs. There was too much excitement, and after all, we all knew that Pop was indestructible.

2

We moved into our new home on the Hilltop during the first week of November. The builder had put only a few bushels of coal in the coal bin against the possibility of having to fire the furnace, so when we pulled up on South Terrace behind the moving van in Uncle Jack's big Buick, our first load of coal—five tons—had already been dumped at curbside. It was a clear, sunny, crisp day after a night of rain.

"You know what they say about making hay while the sun shines," my father said as we climbed out of the Buick. "I think you boys better get after that coal."

"We want to help move in!" I protested.

He gave me a look, forehead wrinkling. "What?"

"Nothing," I said quickly. "Only—where will we get the baskets?"

Uncle Jack shifted his cigar from one side of his mouth to the other. "Tell you what, Kenny. You and I will go hunt for some." My father nodded agreement. "There are some planks out back. Gail, you and Frank lay them out so you can walk across the mud to the side chute window."

The last thing I wanted to do was leave again as the burly moving men were just opening the back of the big yellow truck to reveal our belongings, but Gail and Frank obediently started for the back of the house after the planks, and Uncle Jack climbed back behind the wheel of the car. I had no choice but to climb up on the broad front seat beside him. I caught a glimpse of my mother and Mary entering the house, and my father propping the front door open. Then we were driving away.

"Well, it's a mighty big day," my uncle Jack observed. He was a big man, both taller and heavier than my father, wearing bib overalls, a red flannel shirt and hunting boots, and a leather cap with the ear tabs turned up. "I hope you realize, Kenny, how hard your parents have worked for this."

"I know," I told him. "And we're going to take good care of it, too."

Uncle Jack turned onto Broad Street and drove slowly, looking for a grocery. "I guess it won't be too bad. You can walk south and get out into the country in a few minutes. Joe can live with that."

I studied his expression. "What do you mean, live with it?"

"Well, you know how we all love the country. I think Joe— your dad—has always loved it most of all of us. But . . . " Uncle Jack sighed. " . . . you can't always have everything, I suppose."

"You mean Pop doesn't *want* our new house?"

"Of course he does. It's a big responsibility, of course . . . that debt. But he'll handle it. I just meant . . . well, you know how all of our family was raised on a farm. It's hard to have to live in the city. But I guess there's no alternative. A man has his job . . . has to live close to the streetcar tracks."

It was my first inkling that our new home might not represent as much a dream to Pop as to the rest of us. I knew about his family, certainly: his parents had lived in Logan County, not far from Indian Lake, and had always farmed; he and Uncle Jack and Uncle Jim had lived their youths outdoors, working or hunting and fishing. But Gramaw Riley had moved to Columbus after Grampaw died a long time ago, and it had never occurred to me that my father or his brothers might still look back fondly on their rural roots. We had always hunted in the winter and fished in the summer; I had never sensed that Pop felt any deprivation.

"If Pop wanted to live in the country," I told Uncle Jack, "he would have bought a farm."

Uncle Jack sadly shook his head. "Not to own, boy. Land has gotten too high. If you want to own something, you buy a fifty-foot lot in the city, unless you're a millionaire."

"Well," I said uncertainly, "I think we're going to be *real* happy in our new house."

"Here's a grocery," Uncle Jack said, wheeling to the curb. "Let's see about baskets."

The grocer had a big stack of orange crates and bushel fruit baskets out behind his store. He charged us a nickel apiece for four of them. With them in the backseat of the car and a twenty-five-pound chunk of ice riding on the front bumper for the ice box, we headed back to Terrace.

"Your dad feeling all right these days?" Uncle Jack asked casually.

"Sure." The question had been *too* casual. "Why?"

Uncle Jack shrugged. "No reason. I thought he looked a little peaked today. Maybe it's just all the excitement."

We got back to the house. Uncle Jack took his own tongs out of the car trunk and carried the ice inside while I handed Gail and Frank their baskets, making sure Frank got the smallest one with a broken handle because he wasn't big enough to carry much anyway. They had already changed to their grubbiest clothes. I did likewise and we got to work. We managed to keep a fairly continuous flow of coal going up the planks to the coal-bin chute. There wasn't really a chute, just a metal door that you tipped the basket against to tumble it into the room below. After a couple dozen trips up the slippery planks with maximum load, I found it hard to tip the basket into the hole without losing my balance.

"Try putting some of it inside, dope," Gail growled as I picked up gritty black chunks I had spilled beside the chute. He dumped his basket neatly. "Are you *ever* going to get big enough to pull your weight?"

"You just carry your share, buddy, and I'll carry mine!"

"If I left you your fair share, you'd be out here till about next Thursday!"

"Izzat so?"

"Yeah, that's so!"

"You wanna make something out of it?"

Gail sighed and rubbed a black smudge on his cheek. "No, stupid, just hurry up, will you?"

I hurried, angry. The mountain of coal seemed to get no smaller. Gail continued to mutter complaints while Frank worked stoically, face set in a dull mask, and I staggered around like a drunk at election under each load. The movers finished, closed up their truck, and departed. Clouds drifted over the sun and the air began to chill rapidly. We worked on. Some boys about our age strolled by. They studied us candidly. We nodded but didn't speak. They went on.

"I bet they think they're tough," Gail commented under his breath.

"They didn't look tough to me," I said.

"They did to me," Frank said.

"Frank, you could figure out a way to be scared of the Easter Bunny."

It began to grow dark. Lights shone in our new house, and in others along the street. We finally got the last lumps carried to the coal bin, and Frank went and got a bucket, a dust pan, and a broom. We carefully swept the street, putting the coal dust in the bucket.

"Look at you!" Mom exclaimed as we trooped in the back

way. "Straight upstairs! No—leave your clothes right there on the landing. Take turns taking baths."

"Go up in our *underwear?*" Gail protested.

"We'll all turn our backs," Mom said, an imp tugging at the corner of her mouth.

"Maw-*um!*"

"Just mind, young man!"

Groaning, we stripped to our long johns and trooped through the kitchen to the hall and the stairs. I saw that Mom already had a lot of our dishes put away in the new cupboards. In the parlor, Pop and Uncle Jack were moving furniture. After a small donneybrook upstairs because Mary was in the bathroom, she was evicted and Gail went in. Frank and I sat in our new bedroom, using packing boxes for chairs. Our bed hadn't been put together yet. The room was almost dark.

"Boy, it's a nice house," Frank said soberly.

From down in the basement came the chain-rattling sounds of dampers being adjusted on the furnace. Then we could hear Pop shoveling in coal. I shivered. "It'll be even nicer when it warms up."

"It's a big furnace. I bet it'll keep us real warm."

"I bet so too."

Frank looked at me.

"What?" I asked.

"What do you think about this new school and everything?"

"Well, I guess it'll be fine. Pop said it would."

Frank looked unhappy. "I liked the old school."

"So did I."

He continued to watch me. "Are you scared at all?"

"Scared?" I echoed. "Naw!" Then I thought better of it. "Sure. A little. But not much. I mean, not *too* much."

"We don't know where anything is," Frank said. "The store or anything. Not even the school. And those guys looked tough to me."

"Frank, don't worry about it. You worry too much!"

"I can't help it," he said unhappily, his eyes on a private horizon. "I worried about the Kerrigans down there, and now I'll worry about those guys we saw today. I worry about that new school. What if the teacher doesn't like me?"

"Gaw, Frank! Relax a little, will you? Everything is going to be fine."

Over the sound of gurgling water, Gail called down the hall to us: "Okay, you guys. Next!"

"That's you," I told Frank.

He got up with a sigh. "I just bet he left a ring."

By the time I had had my bath and was dressed, the house was much warmer, fine, dry heat coming up out of the floor registers. Downstairs, newspapers had been spread on the grand new floors and pieces of sheets tacked up temporarily at most of the windows. My mother served us our first meal in the new house, cornmeal mush and steaming tea. The fragrance of the food mixed with the riper odors of wet plaster and concrete beginning to sweat out of the walls and basement as the house warmed. Uncle Jack ate with us and then departed, saying he would bring the family back tomorrow—Sunday—after church. When we all went to the front door with him, we saw that it had started to snow—fat, wet flakes already beginning to coat the earth. He tooted the horn of the Buick cheerily as he drove away, back wheels spinning a little.

"That Jack," my mother sighed.

"He was a big help to us today, Jen."

"I know." She leaned against him.

He embraced her.

"Boy," Gail piped up. "Mush for supper and now mush for dessert!"

Grinning, Pop let Mom go. "Gail, go shake the grates. But not too hard. Then come on upstairs. We've got beds to put together."

"What are they going to do?" Gail demanded, pointing toward Frank and me. "Nothing?"

Pop's forehead wrinkled as it had at me earlier in the day. There also came a certain look to his eyes. The fact that he had never really whipped us did not make him any less formidable. Gail had just stepped over an invisible line.

He recrossed it swiftly. "Yessir," he muttered, and hustled for the basement door.

"Mary," Pop said, "you help your mother in the kitchen. Frank, you come with me. Kenny, you can unpack those things and put them on the dining room table."

We all obeyed. We worked late. When finally it was time to sleep, I lay wide awake in my bed across the room from Frank. The falling snow made everything outside the house very still. I wondered if anyone else was awake.

Finally, unable to sleep, I got up and padded silently into the hall. The new floor felt glossy clean under my bare feet. The furnace was burning low, the house chilling rapidly. I went downstairs.

The light from the streetlight shone over the snow, making our living room silvery bright. I was startled to see a small figure in one of the chairs. It was my sister Mary, barefoot and wearing only her nightgown.

I went in and knelt beside her. "Hey, what are you doing up?"

She rubbed knuckles across her eyes. "I couldn't sleep."

"I couldn't either." I hugged her. "Not scared, are you?"

"Yes."

"No need to be!"

"Everything is *different!*"

"Of course it is. But different doesn't have to be bad. It can be good. There's nothing for you to worry about."

"Oh, Kenny, will you always take care of me and be nice to me and not be mad at me?"

"Why, sure I will, sis!"

She smiled and slid down off the chair to embrace me. Her slender body was cold to the touch. "Then I'll be a good girl and go to bed," she announced and ran off.

I stayed in the living room a few minutes, smiling to my-self. Although there were times when my little sister and I went days without saying more than a few words, there had always been a special bond between us. It made me feel better to know I had somehow helped her get through this lonely first night.

After a while I went back up to the bedroom where Frank slept on. Perhaps, I thought, he was the only one who was not awake. I thought of Mom and Pop and how much all of this must mean to them. Then I thought of what Uncle Jack had said about my father perhaps wishing to live in the country, but giving that up to meet his responsibilities. I hoped he was happy tonight.

After a long time, Frank spoke my name from the other bed. But by that time I was almost asleep, and I did not answer him.

3

In the morning we got up to a snowy world and walked to eight o'clock Mass at our new parish church, St. Aloysius. I was relieved to learn that it wasn't such a long walk, and the church was very large and new and impressive, facing Broad Street, with a brick school building and wooden annex close by, separated only by a gravel playground. The parish priest was old and sang the Latin in a high-pitched nasal voice. The organ in the loft at the back was the biggest and most beautiful I had ever heard. My mother went to communion but the rest of us didn't. Mary had not had her first communion yet and I had committed at least two mortal sins, getting mad at Gail and telling Mom I had brushed my teeth once when I had only gone in and wet the toothbrush. I didn't know why Gail and Frank didn't go; to speculate about that, Sister Leocadia had told us, would be another mortal sin.

Pop was not with us, of course. He was not a Catholic and would never attend, even on Easter or Christmas. He always insisted that we go and work to be good Catholics—in that way he was at least as stern as our mother—but something personal had happened once between him and the church; the mere mention of his going with us made his mouth set in that angry, stubborn way.

All the children who attended the eight-grade parochial school attended the mass in a body, entering class by class with their nuns. There were a lot of them. They marched in silently, each class's nun behind her group, and stood by their pews. The nun clicked a wooden gadget that looked like a clothespin attached to a rubber nipple, and they all genuflected together and entered the pews. It was impressive. Fidgeting during the long sermon, I was relieved to notice that some of my prospective schoolmates did some horsing around without getting caught.

After mass my mother left us standing in the vestibule while she went out and pursued one of the nuns. When she came back she was smiling and had some forms that had to be filled out.

"You can all attend here this year, starting tomorrow," she announced. "Gail, you won't have to go to the public junior high the rest of this year after all. You can finish the eighth grade right here. So you'll all be together. Isn't that nice?"

"I don't wanna go here," Gail said. "I've heard enough about sin and all that junk."

"Gail Henry, mind your tongue! God will strike you dead!"

Back home we found Pop in the basement setting up his workbench and tools. His job downtown was with a radiator and fender shop, where he repaired radiator cores and straightened and refinished damaged automobile sheet metal. He knew everything about cars. But he had also been a carpenter, a roofer, a painter, a plumber and a stonemason. He knew everything about everything and had a lot of tools, many of them very old and inherited from his father. Hammering his heavy workbench back together and putting tools in the drawers of his cabinet, he looked serious and happy, a cigarette dangling from his lips and his little wool cap perched on the back of his head.

"Can I help?" I asked after I had changed clothes.

He paused a moment, frowning. "Yeah," he said finally. "You see the tools in this box? Use this rag and the oil can; carefully wipe each tool with the oily cloth and then put it in this drawer, here. Okay?"

"Okay," I said eagerly. Kneeling on the cold cement floor, I squirted a lot of oil on the rag.

"Not too much oil, son."

"I want to make sure I get everything covered. It's to fight rust, right?"

"Yes. But you don't want every tool so slippery you can't use it."

I rubbed the rag over a pipe wrench.

"Make sure every inch is covered," Pop added.

I forced myself to slow down. Shinnying on my knees, I carried the oily wrench from the box to the drawer and respectfully placed it inside.

Pop noticed. "You could move the box a little closer."

"Yessir," I said, grabbing hold of the big wood box. I heaved. It didn't budge.

"A little heavy?" Pop came over from the bench and grasped the box. He tried to lift it and it barely moved. His mouth tightened. "That *is* a little heavy." Planting his feet, he got a better grip and lifted. Cords stood out in his neck and slender arms. In a single convulsive movement he readjusted the box. Filled with heavy tools, it had to have weighed well over two hundred pounds. "There," he said, smiling.

We worked silently for a while. He put out his Chesterfield and whistled tunelessly through his teeth.

"Pop?"

"Uh-huh?"

"Would you have rather moved to the country?"

He gave me a piercing look. "What makes you ask a thing like that?"

"I dunno. *Would* you?"

He thought before replying. "Well, I grew up on a farm. My dad was a farmer, and his dad before him. But we had that hotel for a while up on the lake, so it's not like I never lived in town."

"But would you rather live in the country *now?*"

"Son, you can't always have everything you want."

I looked away. It was not the answer I had hoped for.

He seemed to sense my anguish. He put down his hammer and reached for a cigarette, tapped it on the back of his hand three times, lit it. "Look at it this way," he said. "We've got a darned nice new home here. It's more than most people have. We all ought to be proud of it. The yard is big enough for a garden, and I can get to work on the streetcar. You're going to go to good schools."

"But what about *you?*" I demanded. "What did *you* want?"

He looked genuinely surprised. "Son. A man doesn't go around worrying about what *he* might want. Not when he has a family. A man meets his obligations. That's number one." He paused and took a deep breath. "Oh . . . I suppose if I had it to do all over . . . it would have been nice to figure out a way to finish high school . . . go to college. I would have liked to be a doctor. Ever think about being a doctor? Helping sick people? I could have been a good doctor."

"You would have been great," I told him.

He smiled. "But that's water over the dam. As long as a man has his health and a steady job and can meet his obligations to his family, that's all that counts. And I'll tell you something else: there's a hell of a lot about most religions that would make more sense to me if they paid more attention to the basics, what I'm talking about here."

"Did you ever go to church when you were a kid?" I asked.

"Sure." His smile was a bit derisive. "Methodist. Lutheran. Holy Roller. We went to all of them."

"Why did you quit?"

"Your gramaw didn't. She still goes from one church to another."

"Why did you?"

"Because in my opinion they all came down to the same thing: 'give us your money and act like a damned hypocrite.' "

"The Catholic Church isn't like that."

He started to say something, then thought better of it. Finally he said, "Well, that's probably true."

"But you never go with us."

He sighed. "When your mother and I were going to get married, we went to see the priest. He started right off telling me what I *would* do. I would get baptized over again. I would study the instructions. I would take communion. I would raise you kids Catholic. I would—well." The derisive look came again. "I walked out. Probably shouldn't have. No use crying over spilt milk. You've got the government telling you what to do, the police telling you what to do, your boss telling you what to do. I don't need any church telling me any more of what to do. Sorry."

I didn't know how to reply. I resumed oiling tools and putting them in the drawer. It troubled me—not his stubbornness, which I already knew and loved, but the idea that he was so isolated from the church that was so much a part of the rest of us. There were times, to be sure, when some of the things the nuns told us about sin sounded awfully stupid to me—like if God was like *that*, who would want to go to heaven anyhow?—but I recognized that such thoughts were the work of the devil. It troubled me that this man who knew everything and was so wise had this chasm between himself and the rest of us. Didn't somebody have to be *wrong* here?

He seemed to sense my discomfort. Grinning, he reached over and tapped the bill of my cap, making it tip forward on my face. "Say, did I ever tell you about the two Irishmen in the rowboat? Well, the first one, Paddy, broke the oar. So the second one, Tom, said to Paddy. . . . "

Our new house was a very special occasion, and special occasions were marked by a gathering of the family. So by noon, the relatives began to arrive. Uncle Jack and Aunt Sal came, bringing their two girls, Phyllis and Milly, and Gramaw Riley. A little later Uncle Jim and Aunt Gertrude arrived along with their three kids and Gramaw Prater. It occurred to me that we would make a grand impression on our new neighbors with both Uncle Jack's Buick and Uncle Jim's Essex parked grandly in front. Then Uncle Bob and Aunt Helen walked up the street from the streetcar line, and the gang was just about all there. The house filled with friendly voices. Those who had come by car brought covered dishes. At two o'clock we sat down to a holiday-style meal: spare ribs, mashed potatoes, green beans, meat loaf, egg salad, green gelatin salad, fresh-baked bread, milk, coffee. For dessert, Gramaw Prater had brought two mincemeat pies and two pumpkin pies. No one could make pie quite like Gramaw Prater, even my mother. I disgraced myself by eating much too much and practically staggered from the table, joining the men in the parlor while the women attacked the mountain of dirty dishes.

Gail, Frank and I sat on the couch in the parlor and listened to the men talk. Uncle Jack said the snow had been heavier on the south side, and he had seen three wrecks on the way to the Hilltop. Uncle Jim, the older of the brothers who worked at a furniture store, said he was glad he wasn't driving the truck today. Uncle Bob, my mother's only brother, said the streetcars were running on time despite the weather. Uncle Bob smoked cigarettes constantly and looked haggard; I knew from overheard conversations that he was not working regularly after being laid off at Timken's.

"Things will pick up," he told the rest of us after the conversation had shifted to business conditions. "It's like President Coolidge says—there are bound to be some ups and downs."

"We're sure selling furniture," Uncle Jim observed.

"The roofing business is booming," Uncle Jack chimed in. "I'm talking to the savings and loan about borrowing enough money to put up a new building. I think the sky's going to be the limit in the next few years."

"There's no telling how big things will grow in the thirties," my father added, and the rest of them nodded agreement.

Uncle Bob got up and stretched nervously. "I need some exercise!"

"In this weather?" my father asked.

"Why not?"

Pop grinned. "Why not indeed?" He stood and went to the closet, and then everyone was on his feet, getting coats and hats. We went out to the front, and Uncle Jack pelted Pop with a snowball, and Pop hit Uncle Jim with one, and then Uncle Bob knocked Uncle Jack down the terrace and fell down after him, and then everybody started throwing snowballs at everybody. It was great snow for it, heavy and wet. Then Uncle Bob fell on the slippery sidewalk, which gave him the idea of sliding on purpose, and Pop joined in, running from the sidewalk next door to the slick place in front of our steps and sliding about fifteen feet. So then everybody started doing it, and pretty soon we were all covered with snow from head to foot, gloves soggy and freezing, water in our shoes, pants soaked through and icy. When we stomped around to the back door after a while to go in and warm up, the women all clucked at us like a flock of hens. It was wonderful.

In terms of getting acquainted with the neighborhood and our new school, I think it would be safe to say our results were mixed. The boys we had seen the first day lived a half-block down the street and their name was Rayburn—Ted, Tom, Jack and Hugh. They went to St. Aloysius too, and that was the initial cement for friendship. We also met the Smith twins, Sylvester and John; Billy Anderson; Frank Schroeder; the McCalls, Jerry, and Terry, and the Vincents, who lived kittycorner across from us in the biggest house and named their children in alphabetical order: Archie, fifteen; Betty, fourteen; Carolyn, thirteen; David, twelve; Ellen, eleven; Frances, ten; George, nine, and Harold, eight. Pop said it certainly had taken them a long time to figure out what caused it. There were also a great many smaller children and girls in the neighborhood, but they were of no significance to me.

The Rayburns quickly became our best friends. On some of the good days we played football out front. They had a tree house in their backyard. Their mother always had cookies. Gail rigged up a sheet across one corner of our basement and called that area *our* club, so that way we could offer them reciprocal visiting privileges for the tree house.

At school I promptly got myself into trouble with my teacher, Sister Domenic, and began wishing we were back in the south end.

Sister Domenic was perhaps fifty years old. I imagined she was about a hundred. Small and slender, with only the oval of her face revealed by the tight white bindings of her habit, she glared at the boys and addressed the girls in a sweet singsong that left no doubt about her favoritism. When I marched into the large, high-ceilinged classroom the first morning, she assigned me a desk directly in front of her.

"You're on trial, Mr. Riley," she told me in front of the class. "If you behave yourself, you'll get a different desk."

"Yes, sister," I singsonged.

"Don't talk back," she snapped. "All right!" She produced her wooden clacker from under the voluminous folds of her black robes and clacked it sharply. "Everyone rise!"

Feet shuffled as the forty-odd children in the room—boys on the right and girls on the left in the favored window-area desks —rose. Sister clacked her clacker again.

"Good morning to you," everyone started singing, *"good morning to you! We're all in our places, with bright, shiny faces —"*

I was horrified. At the other school only the first-graders, as part of their ritualistic degradation, were forced to sing this stupid song. I froze, lips sealed.

The song ended. Everyone put hand over breast and recited

the pledge of allegiance to the flag. Then we said an Our Father and a Hail Mary and a Morning Offering. *Clack!* Everyone sat down.

"Mr. Riley." Sister Domenic glared. "You didn't sing."

Feeling all eyes on me, I cowered and said nothing.

"Mr. Riley!"

I staggered to my feet, knocking my Zaner-Bloser workbook and Catechism to the floor. "Sister?" I said, strangled.

"You didn't sing!"

"No, sister."

"Don't you know the words?"

A lie seemed the easiest way out. "No, sister."

"Stay in at recess and I'll teach them to you."

"Yes, sister."

"Sit down!"

"Yes, sister."

We started with Catechism. Sister turned to page seventeen and called on a boy named Finley to tell us the first commandment of the Church. Finley rattled it off. Then she called on one of the girls to answer the easiest question of all, the one that headed every Catechism I ever owned regardless of grade level: "Why are we here?" The girl rattled off the stock response, as I still remember it: *"We are here to love, honor and serve God in this world, and to be happy with Him in the next."* Sister Domenic beamed as if the girl had just explicated an encyclical.

The stock catechism questions did not continue very long because it turned out that the bishop was coming later in the school year and our class was one of those scheduled for confirmation. Confirmation made you a Soldier of Christ. It was very serious. Sister Domenic told us about a child she had once had in class who had not taken confirmation seriously enough, and marched into church for the sacrament without sufficient memorization of the questions the bishop was likely to ask. God got wind of the student's bad attitude, sister said, and struck him dumb and turned his tongue black so he could never speak again.

The room got very quiet when she told us this.

She went on to explain to us that history was full of examples of bad children who committed mortal sins by not taking the teachings of God and the church seriously enough. She gave us a detailed account of a story I had heard before, about a boy (as usual) who took Holy Communion and then bit into the Sacred Host instead of letting it dissolve endlessly while stuck to the roof of his mouth. Naturally the Host, being the Body of Christ, started gushing blood. Then there was the one about the boy who for unknown reasons stuck his tongue out at the Host in the monstrance during benediction, and his face froze in that attitude so that eventually he starved to death and went straight to hell. Even if we somehow sneaked our bad attitude past God temporarily, sister said, our guardian angel would eventually file a report. And as far as confirmation was concerned, we should remember that the bishop had the power to excommunicate us on the spot if he didn't like our attitude. Sister then talked awhile about the exquisite agonies of hell, the fire peeling your flesh off and eating out your eyes, and it never ending, etcetera. Then we started geography and looked at pictures of cattle on mountainsides in Switzerland, which was an agricultural country.

When the hall bell rang for recess, the room emptied quickly and almost silently. I was left behind with sister. She closed the hall door and came over and glared at me. "Stand!"

I stood.

"I want you to try the song," she snapped.

Swallowing my humiliation, I choked out the first words. *"Good morning to you, good morning to you—"*

She rapped me hard across the top of the head with the clacker. "You *do* know the song!" she hissed.

"I just remembered it, sister!"

"You lied!" Sister Domenic's close-set eyes became black beads, and her pointed nose turned red. "You *lied* to me and to your classmates!"

"I forgot it! I just remembered it!"

"Don't tell more lies, boy! Do you want to fry in hell *forever?"*

"*No,* sister!"

"You have disgraced yourself before your classmates," she told me. "When they return to the classroom, you will apologize to them."

"I won't do it again," I said, hating myself for the cringing tone of my voice. "Please, sister—"

She rapped me on the head again, staggering me. "Stand in that corner!"

There was no help for it. I stood in the front corner, facing the wall. Writhing inwardly, I stood still as everyone filed back in and resumed his seat. Sister then delivered herself of a speech pointing out that there were few things in the world more despicable than a liar, because a liar tried to deceive both God and man. She then had me turn to face the class and apologize.

Every eye was on me. I felt two inches tall. The girls were giggling, the boys staring with a judgment I could not read.

"I am . . . very sorry," I said, strangled.

"*What?*" sister yelled.

"*I am very sorry!*"

"Sing the song!" she ordered.

I stared at her in new dismay. She *couldn't* ask me to endure this added humiliation. "Sister—?"

"*Sing!*" she thundered.

I would have died to avoid it, but I was trapped. My voice shaking, I sang the song all the way through its stupid verse. My mouth, when I finished, was so dry that I thought I would choke.

"Now sit down and say an ejaculation that God will forgive you!"

I went home that first day hating Sister Domenic and making plans never to return to St. Aloysius. But there was no avoiding it and back I went. The second day, I learned that my new class was far advanced on the times tables over my previous one. I got to write the five table on the blackboard twenty times during lunch. On the third or fourth day it was raining when we trooped in the annex with our lunch pails and bags, and somebody pushed me off the sidewalk into a mud puddle. So I got to stay after school for being rowdy. I was quickly becoming the class clown.

During the second week at recess I was standing, disconsolate, near the swings when a boy from the class named Buttleson came up to me. I had noticed Buttleson in class immediately because he was without doubt the ugliest kid I had ever seen. He had carrot-color hair that stood on end, eyes set so close they almost merged, a nose like a prune, and the most incredible array of buck teeth I had ever imagined. He seemed aware of the buck teeth and made an effort to keep his lips tightly closed over them. This so stretched his mouth that he looked like an ape.

"Hey, Kenny," Buttleson said, patting me on the shoulder. "Let's be friends."

"Why?" I asked.

"I like you."

"Why?" I repeated, more suspicious than ever.

"People used to make fun of me around here," he said, and then he unveiled that marvelous array of horizontal teeth in a glad smile. "But now you're here, they make fun of you instead. I appreciate it."

Not that it was really so bad. A couple of times the two biggest boys in the class, Olander and Jeffreys, decided they would terrorize me out behind the trash cans. But I told Gail and he looked them up at next recess and terrorized *them*. Gail, being an eighth-grader, was of course among the very elite, one of the biggest kids, and remote; but he always stood by ready to help, if with a slightly disgusted and world-weary attitude. And I had my duties, too; some kids took Frank's lunch one day and I came upon him crying, and gave him half my lunch and then found the boys and told them quietly what would happen to them if they ever bothered my kid brother again. Another day Mary fell and tore her dress, and I took her home, consoling her, and got her changed and back to class again. We all supported one another. I sometimes wondered how a kid without brothers and sisters could make it.

At home our adventure continued to improve. My mother

used all her spare time sewing—first making curtains out of flour sacks, so that soon most of the bare windows were covered. Then she got to work on rag rugs, spending every evening tying them inch by inch. Gramaw Prater brought a huge ball of rags and old socks, which helped, and Gramaw Riley contributed an entire oval rug, so that by Thanksgiving we already had the floors covered in two rooms and throw rugs in the hall upstairs.

It had been a momentous year from every standpoint. We were still talking about Babe Ruth's sixty home runs in a single season, followed by two more against the Pirates in the World Series. Everyone agreed there would never be another one like the Babe. He might surpass his own record, we thought, but no one else would ever come close.

Our sports conversations, however, tended to concentrate on the Dempsey-Tunney fight. People said the referee had given Tunney a long count. The Rayburns, who had a radio, said you could tell it had been a long count even listening to the announcer and the crowd. Since we had no radio, I had no way of judging. I kind of liked Dempsey, the way he tore in without regard for life or limb. I hated to think he had been cheated. But Tunney—Frank's hero—may have won fair and square.

It had been a year for heroes. There was Lindbergh. His feat, like that of Ruth's, seemed herculean, impossible. Our world was soaring and there was no limit to what any of us might do, especially if we were American. Gail went around whistling "The Varsity Drag" and "Mississippi Mud." Pop picked out the chords for "Girl of My Dreams" on his ukelele and added it to his occasional evening repertoire. Sometimes for a joke he boisterously sang some of the lyrics to "Where Do You Work-a John?" All the songs seemed happy, confident. It was the best time.

Late in the year the weather turned bitter cold. We had many snows and the wind howled. Every morning I awoke to the sound of Pop shaking the grates in the big furnace in the basement, getting the clinkers out of the firebox. Then he would rattle the chains that led to the damper-control mechanism. As the heat poured out of the registers every day, our house continued to dry out, losing its construction moisture. On the coldest days the walls beaded with water coming out of the plaster; sometimes it ran down the walls and made little puddles on the hardwood floors, which we hurried to mop up. On days when Mom washed and hung lines both in the basement and attic, the entire house had the tropical fragrance of a south-sea island.

It was harder for Pop, commuting so far to work on the streetcar, I think. He got home almost an hour later than he used to, trudging up the street in the gloom with his black lunch box. I often watched for him. On the days when he caught me at the window, his shoulders always came back, the smile came, and his step lightened. He never came in without a cheery whistle or wink or swipe at the bill of my cap. Then he would grab Frank up and swing him around. "You growed another pound!" And hug Mary, and then head for the kitchen where Mom invariably was preparing supper. My parents were the soul of propriety at all times, but I liked to sneak into the kitchen doorway sometimes and watch it when Pop had just gotten home and approached her. Often he gave her a little hug and kiss, perfectly proper. Sometimes, too, he smiled and rubbed his nose against the side of her face, while a sly hand stole to her flank. He knew it drove Mom crazy; whatever she was doing, she dropped it to push his hand away with a furious, soft, *"Stop that and behave yourself!"* But her eyes always told a different story. I was not quite wise enough to know what was going on there, but seeing it made me feel good.

After greeting everyone—Gail usually came in a little later from his store job—Pop would go upstairs to bathe and clean up before dinner. His work was filthy, and he came home gray with grease and oil. But when he came down to table, he was immaculate, his dark hair shining and still wet, his hands as clean as any surgeon's.

Pop made a point of his hands. Every night when he came home they were ringed with grime, the nails caked blue-black from his work. But he said no one had to be dirty, no matter what work he did. He took about a half-hour each night cleaning up, and I think twenty minutes were devoted to his nails. He had two little brushes and a penknife, and he worked constantly on them.

"Well, it was an interesting day at the shop," he often began after the food was on the plates. Then we would sit and listen as he regaled us with tales of Mr. Terwiliger, the assistant manager of the radiator shop, and his constant arguments with customers, or the latest escapade involving Terry Marshwak, who was not quite all there in the upper belfry but had a heart of gold. The stories were innocent, almost always funny—so that the people who came to the shop were real to us, and a part of our lives, too.

After meals often fell into a routine as well. Our father always helped with the dishes, clearing the table and drying and putting away. Gail and I took turns washing, but because Gail had his part-time job, my stints were much more common. My mother washed sometimes, too, but more often sat at the table and sewed while we cleaned up. It was then that household details were discussed.

"I see a sale on jars, Mr. Riley. It might be a good time to stock up."

"Well, Mrs. Riley, it might be, at that."

"Two dozen more jars . . . if we plan to do pear butter in the spring."

"I *hope* you plan to do pear butter again! How are we going to eat toast next winter if there's no pear butter?"

"I suppose that's true, although we could try straw-berries. . . ."

"Mrs. Riley, there are pear butter people in this world, and then there are strawberry people. The strawberry people are common. I doubt there's another family in all of Ohio that has a stock of pear butter annually to equal yours. Should we give up one of nature's finest things and join the common throng?"

Later we would all be in the parlor, Pop reading the newspaper, The Columbus *Dispatch*, while mother sewed again, or read a magazine. On rare occasions Pop would get out his ukelele and strum it and sing in his high, sweet tenor voice, "Beautiful Ohio" or "Frivolous Sal," which was his favorite. At holiday times we might join in on festive songs, but at no other. No one could sing as he did.

Sometimes we children had spats, of course. Gail sometimes lost patience with me, and there were evenings when Frank and Mary would bicker until Pop would look over the top of his newspaper, knit his eyebrows, and perhaps go so far as to clear his throat in a way he had.

"We have everything to be thankful for," he often told us. "We have steady work, food, a fine roof over our heads. We have each other and we have our health. No one has a right to ask any more than that. Just think of all the people in this world who would give their right arm to have what we have."

"Which reminds me of a story," he would likely say then, his face cracking into that crooked grin. "It seems these two Irishmen were going for a walk one day and it started to rain, and Paddy said. . . ."

"Daddy loves to tell stories," Mary pointed out to me once in the yard when she was tagging along after me as usual.

"He sure does," I agreed. "They're good, too."

"Do you like to tell stories, Kenny?"

"Well, not like Pop. I'm not good at it."

"I bet if you tried, you'd be *real* good at it!"

I grinned at her. "Maybe."

"Do you want to tell me a story?"

"I don't know any."

"Do you want me to tell you a story?"

"Yes, that would be grand."

"All right. Once upon a time there was this little girl, and she didn't have a sister. Sometimes she got real lonesome. But she had real nice brothers. One of them especially was nice. His name was . . . um . . . his name was Andy."

"Andy?" I said.

"Andy," she repeated. "And whenever the little girl felt bad or anything, Andy was always *real* nice to her." She beamed at me.

"Is that it?" I asked.

"Yep! How did you like it?"

"I think it's one of the greatest stories I ever heard."

"Do you? *Really?*"

"Really."

"Lean over," she ordered.

I bent down to her. She kissed me on the cheek. "There!"

"Do you know what?" I asked her.

"No. What?"

"You're great."

She giggled. "I know it. You make me that way." And ran away.

Late winter was mild, and on several occasions Pop took us —Gail, me, and Frank—hunting with him. Twice Uncle Jack came in the Buick and we drove far west, almost to West Jefferson. Other times we walked south until we got into the country and asked at a farmhouse for permission to hunt. Pop had a beautiful double-barrel twelve-gauge shotgun and Gail had a single-barrel of the same gauge. I had a very old ten-gauge that rocked me every time I fired it. Frank, being so young, just went along. It was glorious adventure but serious, too, because we were putting meat on the table.

The limit on rabbits was ten in those days. Gail and I always carried all the shells we could find. Pop never carried more than ten. He was uncanny. I never saw him miss. Late in the evening, we would walk back home, numb from the cold, and take our rabbits to the basement where we skinned them, picked out the shot, and soaked them overnight in cold salt water. We always cleaned and oiled our guns before calling it a night.

The expeditions started before dawn, and the night after one, there was never any trouble sleeping. Hunting was a day-long business. That was why we were so startled on our last expedition of that season when Pop called it off early.

We went with Uncle Jack, driving west and then south to a large farm that had many acres of corn stubble, with the charcoal slashing of big woods on beyond—promising terrain. Having secured permission at the brick farmhouse, we started out through the garden beside the barn and a rabbit hopped up and Pop shot it. We climbed the barbed wire beyond the garden and started down through the cornfield, five abreast, and hadn't gone fifty yards before both Gail and Uncle Jack had kicked out rabbits and shot them, too. By the time we worked that single field we had thirteen rabbits. Even I had gotten one.

For the next two or three hours things slowed down. Clouds scudded in heavier, and a chillier wind began to sigh. My legs started to grow weary, and the ten-gauge began to weigh me down. I was used to that; I always finished in a daze of fatigue.

At lunchtime we hunkered down in high, tufted grass between a cornfield and the edge of the woods and ate baloney sandwiches and cookies, and sipped sizzling-hot coffee from Uncle Jack's Thermos.

"Well, I think we ought to try the woods," Pop told us. As we climbed the next fence facing the woods, he added, "Did I ever tell you the story about the hunters that didn't know the difference between a fox and a rabbit?" Of course he had, but we pretended otherwise as usual. He so enjoyed telling it again that we all entered the woods laughing.

It was pretty hard going. The hardwood forest was densely undergrown with wild berries, what we called briar patches. Pop and Uncle Jack said this was wonderful because rabbits liked to hide in such patches. The trouble from my point of view was that this meant we always had to go straight through a briar patch, hoping to kick out a rabbit. The berry bushes in winter were long, tangled, strong as steel, and armed with millions of half-inch thorns. There was no way to pick your way through; you just had to plow ahead. I always wore at least two pair of pants, but they never provided enough armor. The stickers tore me to pieces.

By the time we had made our first pass through this particular woods, we had six more rabbits. I knew it was going to be a very long day; we never quit when the hunting was good.

At the end of the woods, however, instead of swinging around to start another pass, Pop walked over to the fence and sat down against a post. I saw him remove his leather cap and mop his brow. Uncle Jack went over and squatted to talk to him.

Frank came through the brush to my position. "What's going on?"

"I dunno," I admitted.

We saw Gail go over to join the men. Pop looked up at him and shook his head and said something. Frank and I hurried to join them.

"What's up?" I asked.

Uncle Jack looked strange. "Well, we've decided to call it a day."

"*What?*" I cried. "It isn't even three o'clock yet!"

"Shut up!" Gail said sharply.

I stared at him and saw a strange expression similar to Uncle Jack's. Then I got a chill that had nothing to do with the deepening weather.

I looked at my father.

He had his hat off. His face was bathed in sweat. He was a terrible color, his lips purple-blue. He seemed to be breathing very hard.

Seeing my attention, he managed a stiff grin. "Baloney didn't agree with me. Silly."

Uncle Jack pointed. "I'm going to go get the car and bring it around this back road. It's a lot closer that way."

Pop started to get up. "I can walk it, for God's sake."

"I know you can," Uncle Jack said. "But just sit still."

My father raised his eyebrows and settled back down.

"Kenny, come with me," Uncle Jack said. "You other boys stay with your father." He turned and started off toward the distant farmhouse at a killing clip.

"What's *wrong?*" I demanded breathlessly as we hurried across the corn field.

"Nothing," Uncle Jack said grimly. "We just wore out."

"There's something wrong with Pop!"

"Naw!"

I didn't argue at the moment. I needed all my wind to keep up. We crossed the field and went back up through the garden to the Buick and got in. Uncle Jack's hands shook a little as he backed out onto the road.

"He's sick, isn't he?" I demanded.

"Oh, he just got a little indigestion."

"No! He's never quit in the middle of the day like this! What's wrong with him?"

Uncle Jack sighed. "Well." He thought about it. "Maybe it's nothing."

"And maybe it's something else," I said, terrified.

"Our dad," Uncle Jack said, "had heart trouble. That's what finally killed him. He would be all right for a while, and then he would have a spell. Pain. Trouble breathing. He would have to take it easy."

"And you think *Pop* has heart trouble?" I demanded in horror.

"I don't know. He acted out there like Dad used to." Uncle Jack gave me a hard look. "We'll say nothing about it to him or your brothers."

Tears stung my eyes. I rubbed them away with my dirty gloves. Nothing like this was supposed to happen, and the enormity of my fear swallowed me up. *What if—!* I thought, and backpedaled from the unspeakable.

When we drove up the back road, however, Pop and my brothers were standing there beside the fence waiting for us. Pop climbed in with a crooked grin, and his color was coming back to normal. "I guess that'll teach me to eat two baloney sandwiches and ten cookies!"

In the backseat, Gail and Frank and I exchanged solemn glances. Uncle Jack agreed that we had probably all eaten too much. Then as we pulled away he talked as he often had before about our need for a good hunting dog. It all seemed normal again, except that we were heading home far too early and none of us could expunge from memory the way our father had looked sitting against that fence post. I could not ask my brothers how they felt at this moment. I tried talking about it with my pal, Tom Rayburn, but it didn't help much. A time bomb had started ticking under my world.

4

My father did not visit a doctor. "I'm never sick," he told us. "Why waste money on a case of indigestion?" I clung to the hope he was right, and during the spring and summer of 1928 it seemed he was.

We made many improvements, installing our grape arbor and planting pear, apple, and peach trees. The basement walls were given a second coat of whitewash, and Pop installed some more lights. We seeded our lawn with bluegrass and clover and it came up nicely. Mom insisted on planting some honeysuckle in back and privet in front, along the porch latticework. "Geez," Pop growled as we planted it, with a tone that implied considerably stronger emotion. "The stuff will grow like weeds and we'll be trimming it the rest of our lives." We found that the paint on the outside of the house was not all it should have been and had already started cracking here and there. So of course we had not only to repaint but to go over the entire house first with putty knives and wire brushes, smoothing every potential trouble spot, priming it with two coats, reputtying several windows, and then giving it two coats of oil-based white on the siding, blue-gray trim around the windows and doors, dark gray on the boards of the porch floor in front. It made our house look taller, somehow, and more stately, but I thought the job would kill all of us before Pop pronounced it satisfactory and made us spend about six hours in the backyard cleaning all the brushes and cans with turpentine until they were cleaner than they had been before we started.

"Gaw," Gail protested near the end, when Pop made him redo an old paint can. "It's clean enough."

Pop's head came up sharply, hawklike. "What did you say?"

"I said that's good enough. It's just an old can."

"It's *not* good enough," Pop snapped, and he was just as angry for the instant as he could be. "People judge you by the work you do," Pop lectured us as we continued. "Don't *ever* let me hear you say something like that again!"

Chastened, we worked in silence.

But Pop could play, too—like the evenings he joined Gail, me, and Frank for first bounce or fly, monkey move up. He always took it easy at bat because he could hit our pitches a mile. Every once in a while he forgot himself, or could not contain his exuberance, and hit one a block over the outfielder's head. More often he popped up on purpose, trying to put it just out of our reach so we would run like crazy and either just miss or make a spectacular catch.

"*Great* catch, Kenny! *Tremendous* catch! Lajoi couldn't have made a better one!" Or: "Nice try, son! You really ran that one out! My fault!"

I think he liked catching best of all, however, especially when Frank was pitching. He had a knack for arousing Frank's competitive instinct.

"Okay, Frank! Fire it in there, boy! It's Babe Ruth at the plate, now, and the count is one and one. Two men on and one out. Fire it in there, boy!"

And Frank would zap in a high hard one that I would fan.

"Way to be, Frank, boy! Way to hum! Way to shoot!" The ball went back to Frank with something on it, stinging his glove. "Okay! It's one and two on the great Ruth, now, one out, two on, and the crowd is screaming! Let's see what you're made of out there!"

And Frank would pause at the belt, looking around at the

imaginary base runners, and then throw again, a little sliding curve ball that I couldn't have hit with an ironing board.

"Okay!" Pop would yell, taking the bat from me as I headed for the outfield and Gail came in to hurl, Frank moving to catcher. "Let's see what this relief pitcher has to offer! It's two out now, two runners still on, the bottom of the ninth, we're leading the Yankees one to nothing! Seventh game of the World Series and who is it coming to the plate? It's Gehrig! It's Gehrig, the toughest pressure hitter of them all!"

And Gail would wind up and throw one so hard it sizzled into Frank's glove. Pop would watch it. "My God, I missed that one! It was a strike! Strike one!"

And Gail would wind up and throw the next one a little harder still. Pop would swing mightily and miss. "Strike two! It's on and two now, and the crowd is on its feet, screaming! Gehrig digs in, a mean look in his eye! Here it comes!"

And Gail would take a full windup.

"The runners are going!" Pop would yell.

Gail would fire the hardest pitch he had ever thrown in his life, a screamer, a ball down the middle with smoke coming out of the black tape wrapped around the strings, and you could already see Frank the catcher wincing, holding up his glove for it. And Pop would swing from the heels, missing it about three feet, going all the way around to his knees, falling over backward.

"My God, what a pitch!" he would gasp. "The Great Gehrig has struck out! Listen to the crowd go wild!" And he would get up and trot to the second tree in the outfield, sweating heavily, still chuckling to himself, having the time of his life.

And then go back on a long ball hit by Frank and take it in over his shoulder on the dead run like a pro, nothing to it.

"Lucky!" he would say with a grin, trotting in to pitch, and probably send us up a pitch with so much spit on it that you felt like you needed an umbrella.

"Pop!"

"It must be starting to rain out here!"

When we quit most evenings the last rays of the sun were

coming over the houses on the west side of the street, often bathing the front of our home in pink, magical light. Sometimes Pop would stop at the curb and just look up at our house.

"Isn't that a great-looking house?" he would ask softly. "Isn't that grand, boys?"

We always agreed with him because it was true.

Some nights we played hearts. More often, we did our homework while Mom sewed and Pop read the newspaper, perhaps smoking one more Chesterfield. He was a restless man, and he seldom spent the entire evening in his chair. There was always a hinge that needed adjusting, a faucet that didn't seem to turn right, something to do.

We followed the election campaign with interest. Everyone but Pop was for Al Smith right from the start. He was on the fence until sometime in August when we happened to be down on Broad Street and a big parade came by. It was the Klan, staging a bed-sheet march. Out in front they had crosses and American flags, the hooded officers (I suppose) coming next with signs that said things like America for Americans and Rome No! The rank and file came next, looking like Halloween spooks to me, carrying Hoover placards. Then came a band and finally some more spooks carrying an effigy of Al Smith suspended from a hanging tree.

Pop turned away, grabbing my arm in a painful grip as he propelled me away from the curb. His face was white with anger.

"That does it," he exploded. "If those baboons are for Hoover, I know who I'm for!"

"Gaw," Gail said. "They got a right to express a preference!"

"Is that what you call it," Pop demanded hotly, "when a bunch of loonies too cowardly to show their faces get themselves up in sheets and march down Broad Street with *crosses* and figures of a *lynching?* Doesn't it strike you, Gail, that there's just a little something wacky going on there?"

"Klansmen are patriots," Gail said stoutly.

"Was *that* patriotism? You'd better study your facts, son. This family is Catholic. If those loonies ever get through killing

Negroes and Jews, the next cross they'll burn will be on *our* lawn."

"That's not true," Gail said. "Not in Ohio. A couple of the Grand Dragon's closest associates are Catholics."

"Oh, my aching back," Pop said. He looked at me. "Do you believe that?"

I shrugged. "I don't know what to think."

Pop looked down at Frank and he shrugged, too.

Gail piped up, "I wouldn't even have that job in the store after school if it was true about Catholics. I *know* Mr. Harrison talked to the local Wizard about me."

"And what the hell kind of a country does that leave us," Pop asked angrily, "when a bunch of nincompoops in white underwear dictate to a businessman who he can hire? If they're for Hoover, then I know who I'm for. Oh, my aching back!"

By the time the nation voted that autumn, however, none of us really thought Al Smith had much of a chance. Billy Anderson said his father had said that the pope would be living in the White House if Smith were elected. A more common adult comment, as relayed to us through neighborhood kids, was that things were going well with the Republicans, so why change? It was the first election I had taken any interest in, and when the paper boys went up and down the street near dawn, yelling *"Hoover elected, read all about it!"* I was bitterly disappointed.

Pop sighed. "The country will go on," he said glumly. "It always does."

Looking back, I know that those last days of 1928 represented the final stages of our innocence. Nothing was said about my father's possible illness, and he went to work regularly. Mom occasionally took in small sewing jobs. We boys looked for lawns to mow in the summer, coal to haul in the winter. But we knew no sense of desperation. We were dirt poor; the hand-me-down clothes, the meals of mush or beans, and the careful counting of pennies proved that. But we knew we were far better off than most because we had our own house and never really went hungry. We were putting back a few cents each week in a bank account "against a rainy day," as our mother put it. The time would come, we confidently believed, when we would have a radio and perhaps even a car.

For Christmas that year I received some new long johns, three pairs of socks, and a yo-yo. I felt like a millionaire. I remember that Frank and I went together and bought Mom and Pop a tiny spun-glass ship for the mantle; it cost an enormous $2.11.

The new year began bitterly cold. We returned to school, Gail to West Junior High and the rest of us to St. Aloysius. During our second week back—I know it was a Tuesday—I recited poorly in history and had to stay after school to write *I will study my history* a hundred times. So both Frank and Mary got home well before me. It was past four when I trudged up Terrace, dragging my book bag with its broken strap and scheming ghastly revenge on Sister Domenic.

"Kenny! Kenny!" someone yelled frantically up ahead.

Looking up, I saw Frank coatless, running up the street toward me. His sweater flopped open and he had no hat against the cold and he looked wild-eyed.

"What's *happened?*" I demanded, catching his rush.

"It's Pop! They called Mrs. Rayburn on their new telephone and she came and told Mom, I guess Mom went down there awhile ago, and Mrs. Rayburn is at our house, Mary is crying and everything—"

"Wait a minute! Wait a minute!" I shook my younger brother hard, trying to make sense of his words. "Start over! What do you mean, it's Pop? What's going on?"

Frank gasped for breath. With a shaky hand he rubbed tears off his cheeks. "Mrs. Rayburn said they called from the radiator shop and Pop collapsed and he's at the hospital and nobody knows—"

I didn't hear the rest of whatever he said. I was off and running for the house as fast as my legs would carry me.

The night's light coating of snow had been cleared from our sidewalk and steps—work Pop had done before the rest of us were up this morning—but a film of ice on the concrete forced me to slow as I ran to the front porch. For once I did not pause to wipe my feet as I burst in.

Mrs. Rayburn was in the living room. Mary was with her but ran to me as I entered. "Oh, Kenny! It's horrible—Daddy is sick —"

"Hold on, hold on," I muttered, hugging her. I stared at Mrs. Rayburn.

"Now, Kenny, don't get hysterical," she said. She was a big woman with curly red hair and a stolid face. But her lower lip trembled. "We don't know anything yet, and it's up to you to be a man."

"I'm not going to get hysterical," I told her. "I'm *twelve.*"

"Of course," she said after a pause. "I forgot you were so old." She patted the sofa. "Sit by me and I'll tell you what I know."

It was not very much. She had had a telephone call about two o'clock from Mr. Craner, who owned the radiator shop where Pop worked downtown. Only a few days earlier, with installation of the Rayburns' telephone, Pop had given Mr. Craner the number for emergency use. Pop had gotten sick on the job—had thrown up and then lost consciousness, Mr. Craner said. Two other workers had taken him to Mt. Carmel Hospital in the truck.

"How bad is he?" I demanded, conscious of the effort it took not to cry.

"Why, nobody knows," Mrs. Rayburn said. "I came and told your mother and she put on her coat and left right away for the streetcar. I'm sure she's with your father by now at the hospital. All we can do is wait to hear from her."

"Why didn't somebody come to the school and tell us?"

"Your mother said not to. I promised to stay here—meet you when you got home."

I started toward the door.

"Where are you going?" Mrs. Rayburn called sharply.

I looked back at her. "To the hospital."

"No. Your mother said no. She left orders for all of you to stay here."

"I want to *be* there!"

"I just told you what your mother said. Kenny, until Gail gets here, you're the oldest. You have to accept responsibility for Frank and Mary and watching after the house."

Torn, I looked from her to my little sister's frightened, tear-streaked face. I didn't know what to do. I was scared half to death myself. "Has somebody gone to tell Gail?"

"Yes. I sent Frank. Did he find you on the way?"

"Yes, ma'am. Why didn't he come back for me sooner?"

"We didn't know where you were and kept waiting for you. Were you playing somewhere?"

"Stupid sister made me stay after school and write stupid history," I admitted bitterly.

Mrs. Rayburn sighed. "Well, you're here now, and Frank has gone to find Gail at the store. I need to get back home. They might call." She left the sofa and came across the room. She engulfed me in her arms. "You'll be a little man and stay here and watch after everything?"

"Yes," I said, muffled.

"I'll come back immediately if I hear anything," she promised, putting on her coat. She bustled out, closing the door firmly behind her.

Mary began crying again. She looked awfully little, sitting there on the sofa with her stockinged legs dangling. I took a deep breath and went to her, awkwardly putting an arm around her. "Quit that, now," I ordered in my most grown-up tone. I patted her. "We've got to be *big* now and wait and see what's going on."

"Oh, Kenny," she bawled, "what if Daddy is *dead?*"

"Don't be a ninny," I told her, although her words struck terror into my heart. "He probably just had a baloney sandwich. Baloney doesn't agree with him."

The thought seemed to cheer her up a little, but she clung to me as if there really were something I could do for her. I looked around the suddenly empty and enormous living room. *I was responsible.* I cast around desperately for the right thing to do. "Why don't we go see if we can find some cookies or something?" I asked.

In the kitchen there were some sugar cookies. Milk and other perishables were kept in a window box during the cold months, a crate mounted outside the kitchen window. I opened the window and got down a quart bottle of milk, a fresh one, its cap pushed four inches out of the top of the bottle by a frozen tongue of separated cream. I spooned the cream sludge off and gave Mary a glass of milk and several cookies. Sitting at the table with her, I took two cookies myself. They tasted like cardboard or communion wafers in my dry mouth.

"If Daddy is dead," Mary said, "we'll get thrown out of the house and we'll starve to death."

"Don't talk like that!"

"I can't help it! It's true!"

"In the first place, Mary, Pop isn't going to die. In the second place, we've got savings—"

The front door slammed and Frank, breathless and covered with tears, burst in. "I couldn't find Gail! He's making deliveries! I left a note! Have you heard anything—"

"What are you doing, running in here with snow on your feet?" I yelled.

Frank stared, shocked. "What?"

I pointed to the puddles forming under his shoes on the linoleum. "Mom will *kill* you! Get back to the front door and take those shoes off! Then get the mop and clean up that mess!"

"Pop is in a *hospital.*"

"*I* know that, dummy. Is that any reason for you to start acting like the wild man from Borneo? Do what you're told!"

Frank dumbly obeyed, and I congratulated myself. Something told me that whatever else might happen, we had to preserve normalcy at all costs. While Frank mopped up the water on the floor, I got out some more cookies for him and poured some more milk. Crossly I ordered him to sit down and eat. I had seldom bossed him around. But he did what I told him as if I had been giving orders forever.

"There's no sense getting all worked up over nothing," I told him and my little sister. "Gail will get here after a while. Mrs.

Rayburn is waiting by the telephone. Mom will call in a little while or else she'll come home—and chances are Pop will be walking right alongside her, making a joke about the whole thing."

"You really think so?" Frank asked sorrowfully.

"Sure," I lied.

Somehow I kept them busy for more than an hour. We washed the dishes and put them away. Then I made them go to their rooms and do homework. In the deathly silence of the house, I walked around and kept peering out through the front windows at the gathering gloom of night.

It was past five when Gail came. Frank and Mary fled down the stairs to greet him, acting hysterical again. I bawled them out again.

"Kenny is right," Gail said. He looked drawn and old suddenly, and his lower lip trembled. "We've got to be *big* now." He looked at me. "I think I'll go see if the Rayburns have heard anything else. Then we better think about supper."

He left without his coat, running down the street. Frank and Mary sat silently in the parlor with me. I turned on some lights, fighting my own fear. Within minutes Gail was back. Mrs. Rayburn was with him and she was carrying a steaming pot of soup.

"We haven't heard anything yet," she said cheerfully, taking us all into the kitchen. "But land's sake, that doesn't mean anything. No news is good news in cases like this, really. I'm sure your mother will be here any minute and tell us everything is just fine. Now. Get out those bowls, Gail. No, the big ones. Good. Frank, are there any crackers? Some bread, then. Good. Yes. Everyone sit at the table and let's eat this while it's good and hot!"

It was vegetable soup, thick and delicious. We spooned it in while Mrs. Rayburn, God bless her, kept up a constant stream of chatter about the weather, her telephone, school, the chances for an early spring garden. She opened a jar of my mother's pear butter and let us have that on bread for dessert. By the time we had finished, night stood vast and threatening at the windows.

"We'll just do up these dishes and then I think it's time for homework, don't you?"

Mary looked up at Mrs. Rayburn with those big eyes. "Are you going home now?"

Mrs. Rayburn enveloped her in a hug. "No, darling. I'm going to stay right here with you. You don't have to worry about a thing."

I exchanged glances with Gail and wondered if he felt the same hot flush of relief that I experienced with her words.

The evening seemed endless. We gathered in the parlor with our books. Mrs. Rayburn pretended to read a magazine, although she did not seem to turn the pages very often and kept glancing at the front door. After a while Mary colored some pictures with her crayon stubs and Gail stared into space. Frank wrote endlessly on something in his tablet. I accomplished nothing.

It was about nine o'clock when we heard the car. It pulled up in front and we saw from the windows when Uncle Jack came around and opened the passenger side and a bundled figure—our mother—got out. Pop was not with them. Icy dread struck its fingers into me as I watched the two of them come carefully up the icy walk.

They came in, my mother first, staring at us with eyes dazed by the sudden bright lights. She leaned against the wall and took off her boots, and Uncle Jack, pale, wiped his feet. We were all standing, waiting for them to speak.

Mom had been crying. She looked at each of us. "It's all right," she said softly. "He's going to be all right."

Mary started to bawl again.

Mom came in and sat on the couch, hands clutched over her knees. There were lines in her face I had never seen before. Uncle Jack, remaining standing at the door, looked years older.

"Now, what's happened," Mom said slowly, obviously picking every word, "is that your father has had a heart attack."

"Oh, no!" Gail groaned.

"It was a serious attack. But they got him right to the hospital and it looks like he's going to be all right."

"Is he hurting?" Frank asked. "Are they—"

"No, he's sleeping. He was sleeping when we left. And your Uncle Jim is with him, and in the morning Gramaw Riley will go. He's going to be just fine."

"When can he come home?" I asked.

Mother's lips set. "It's probably going to be a week or two at least."

"A week or two!" Gail exploded. "What about his job?"

"Well, Gail, that's just one of those things that will have to take care of itself for right now. The important thing is to get your father healthy again."

Uncle Jack walked into the room. "What you've got to understand," he told us, "is that your pappy is going to need a long time to recuperate. You don't have a heart attack like this and get back on your feet in a day or two. Or even in a month or two. So it's going to be . . . hard for a while. But the important thing is that the doctor says he's going to live."

No one spoke. The room was tomblike. Somewhere across the city, I thought, Pop lay in a ward with strangers. He had almost *died*. I remembered the hunting incident and what Uncle Jack had said about *their* father.

Everything was going to be different now. I knew that without being told. We had some life insurance—a man who came every week for twenty cents—but no other kind. Hospitals cost —my God!—hospitals cost *a lot*. And if Pop was going to be out of work a long time, where would the money come from? In an instant, our world had been knocked from its moorings. Mary had been right. We could be out in the street. We could starve. I felt a bolt of dread like none I had ever known.

"What we all have to do," my mother told us, "is go about our business just as normally as we can. I'll be going to the hospital every day, but I'll do that during school. Your father is going to live. That's the thing we have to remember, and thank God for it."

We all nodded. But her words made me see the real root of the problem. It went beyond losing our house and our food. Pop

would live, she said. Now. But he had almost died. He *could* die.
This was the heart of it. This was the knowledge that would never
allow anything to be the same again.

5

Pop came home on February 16, riding in a huge black Packard
ambulance. The driver and his assistant carried the stretcher up
the sidewalk and into the house, then up the narrow staircase to
the bedroom. Pop looked thin and pale, but he gave us his
crooked grin and a thumbs-up sign as he was brought in. Then
the men got him off the carrier and into bed and were gone.
After a few minutes, Mom opened the bedroom door and let us
in.

He was propped up in the bed on all the pillows, wearing
white pajamas. He looked older and his hair had turned mostly
gray, but the smile he had flashed in the living room was in place.

"This is a fine-looking crew!" he said.

Solemnly we went to the bed, Gail and me on one side,
Frank and Mary on the other.

"Are you feeling okay?" Gail demanded. "Do you hurt
. . . or anything?"

"Feel fine! Never better! Oh, I'm still a little weak. The
doctor says you get your strength back slowly in cases like this.
But I'm making progress. Don't you worry. I'll be my old self in
another few weeks."

"We were scared," Frank told him gravely.

"Say, listen, the old man was scared for a while there himself!
I was soldering a core in a radiator, see? 'Twenty-seven Chevro-

let. My arm was aching, but I didn't pay any attention. Then about the time I was finished and started to lift that thing and carry it back out of the shop, the pain hit me in the back. I thought at first I had hurt my back, stooping. But then it came through to the *front,* see? How many times have I said, 'my aching back'? I'll tell you what. I never knew what an ache *was.* Then I couldn't get my breath. I guess that's about when I passed out. It was something, I'll tell you!"

"But you're fine now," I told him.

"Why, sure!"

I leaned across the bed and hugged him.

"What's all this?" he asked gruffly, holding me at arms' length. "Tears in my big boy?"

I sniffled and tried to straighten up. "I guess we're just glad you're home."

"I'll tell you what: I'm glad to *be* home!"

Mom, who had gone downstairs, came back with a tray that had a water pitcher and glass on it. She put them on the end table and got a small chrome push-button bell from her pocket. She put it beside the pitcher. "I think we'd better let your father rest a little while now," she said.

"Aw!" Frank protested.

But Pop rested his head back against the pillow, and his color seemed less robust than it had only minutes earlier. "Maybe she's right, Frank, old boy. That ambulance ride was a doozie." He closed his eyes as if completely worn out.

We filed silently from the bedroom and downstairs. In a few minutes our mother came down to join us. Without plan, we had a council in the kitchen, the four of us children around the table, Mom standing by the sink.

"He's *real* tired," Gail observed.

"Sure," I said, "but he'll be fine now that he's home."

We looked at our mother for corroboration. A frown crossed her face and she seemed to consider alternatives. When finally she spoke, her voice was kept low. "I think the best thing is to tell you all the absolute truth."

"About what?" Gail blurted.

"Your father's heart attack was very, very serious. There was . . . damage to the heart. Now. Don't start crying, Mary, or I can't talk. The doctor says he can be fine—live a long time. But he simply can't expect to return to the level of activity he always had before."

"What about his job?" I asked.

"Kenny, Mr. Craner had replaced your father on that job before the first week was past. There *is* no job there anymore."

I was shocked. "They can't just give away his job!"

"Of course they can. They did."

"He'll get another one like it, then."

She shook her head. "No. The doctor says it's very doubtful if your father will ever be able to hold down a full-time job, manual labor, again. . . . Don't look like that! It's not the end of the world! We've already talked about it. He can do book work for some store out here on the Hilltop. Possibly do some repair jobs working out of his shop in the basement. It's not like he was going to be an invalid. And the rest of us can help more now that he's home. I'm going to be doing a lot more sewing . . . possibly some ironing, if I can get it. Gail, we have your job at the grocery. Frank, you and Kenny might be able to get more coal and yard jobs if you really try."

"We can get a *lot* more," I told her.

"Of course you can." She smiled and tousled my hair. "So. We'll say nothing of this little talk to your father. Everything is going to be just fine. I wanted to make sure, though, that you didn't expect any miracles. Be cheerful and thankful. We'll just . . . wait to see what tomorrow brings."

No one spoke right away. I watched Gail. He looked not only worried, but older. I felt sorry for him. He was the only one of us with a real after-school job; he had to feel the burden most heavily.

Mom got up and went to the stove to make coffee. Even by the time it was ready, we had not said a word.

Then a voice from the hall doorway startled us. "What is this? A family meeting without the head of the family?"

Pop stood there in his pajamas, robe and slippers, a Chesterfield dangling from the corner of his mouth.

"Joseph!" Mom cried. "You said you were worn out!"

He grinned at her. "A man can't stay in bed forever."

"But you weren't supposed to try those stairs for two weeks!"

"Baloney." He came to the table and sat down very carefully. "How am I ever going to start getting back to normal if I mope in bed all the time?" His skin was the color of old bed sheets and there was a film of cold sweat on his face. "Could I get a cup of that coffee? It smells good."

By spring he was better. On his good days he walked as far as Broad Street. Every once in a while when Frank and I got home from school and had no work, he walked slowly to the parkway with us and we played a little catch. He did not move very much, and his throws had no zing to them. We were in agony trying to get every throw right to him, to keep him from lunging a few steps.

"Well, boys," he said as we sat on the front porch steps after one such game, "I've got a sign to paint."

"A sign?" Frank echoed.

"Yep. I'm feeling better. I think maybe we can open a little radiator business right here at the house."

"We can help," Frank said.

"Well, Frank, I want you to concentrate on your lawn business. There might be quite a bit of money in that this summer if you push it a little." He paused and tilted his head. "If you *push* it. Get it?"

"Gaw," I groaned, catching the pun.

He chuckled and reached for a cigarette. "I'll try to teach you some of what I know, Ken. You're getting stout enough, you can do some of the lifting for me. You might get a trade out of it. Give you a job to work at until you've finished school."

"I might like to do it all my life," I told him.

"No. I want you to do more than that. With luck you can finish high school and go on to college. Things ought to take an upturn soon . . . we can save money for all of you to go to college.

You have to get your education. Pay for this house so we're secure and get you boys your education. Those are my priorities. Even with this . . . condition, we can accomplish that." His face grew grim. "We have to."

So in a day or two a sign graced our front yard advertising radiator work.

In those days the engines of cars shook so badly that the core of the radiator—the finned portions circulating the water—often broke or separated from the main body. A customer would pull his car up the alley and into the backyard, and Pop would take out the radiator and drag it down to the workbench in the basement, where he would clean and resolder it. It was hard work, skillful. I watched and helped a little, especially with dragging the radiators up and down the basement steps. On his good days Pop could have done this for himself; on his bad days—which came in no pattern and without clear cause—the soldering was almost more than he could handle. He liked to talk while he worked, and he explained to me how it was important to remove twist stresses from the core, have the metal clean, and use plenty of acid flux. I watched closely, admiring the competence of his hands.

Intense summer heat and humidity enshrouded the Hilltop early in July one morning when I staggered down the steps with the radiator from a Dodge sedan. Pop sat on his stool beside his bench, his soldering irons heating on a little gas burner. We had worked together in the yard, removing hoses and unbolting the radiator from its fittings, and I was already hot and out of breath. Pop looked a bit pale and he was breathing hard.

"Put her up here and let's see what we've got," he said.

I hefted the heavy radiator onto the bench with a convulsive effort. A few dribbles of rusty water spilled from the open neck and onto the floor. Squinting through the smoke from his cigarette, Pop turned the radiator and studied its bottom portion.

"Nothing too bad," he said after the inspection. "Looks like it just shook loose." He put his cigarette out and reached for a wire brush, and suddenly he lurched as if he had been hit. His mouth opened and one hand went to his chest. He began breathing convulsively, in distress.

"*Pop!*"

He waved me off. "Nothing," he managed to gasp. "Will pass —in a minute." He choked and gulped air. With shaking hands he supported himself on the edge of the workbench and slid off the stool. He went slowly to his knees and then to a sitting position on the wet black floor. His right hand was at his throat now and he breathed heavily, with enormous effort. His face had no color whatsoever.

Terrified, I started for the stairs.

"*No!*" he choked.

"I'll get Mom! I—"

"No. I'll be okay in a minute." There was a fierce purpose in his expression, one that brooked no opposition.

"Are you sure?" I asked.

He nodded and pointed toward the laundry area. "Drink."

I ran to the faucets with the tin cup we often drank from while working here. Taking the cup back to him, I saw that he was shaking too badly to hold it. I held it for him, spilling some of the water down both sides of his chin. That was when I realized I was shaking, too.

The water seemed to help. After another minute or two he stopped breathing quite so heavily, although the exertions of his chest were far from normal. He got unsteadily to his feet and I helped support him to the steps, where he sat down again, heavily.

"Think I better rest awhile," he said huskily. "Must be hotter than I think."

"Pop, if you can make it upstairs—"

"Of course I can make it upstairs!"

"Then go on up, Pop. Please. Lie down a few minutes."

He gave me an unbelieving look. "How am I ever going to get back in shape if I baby myself?"

"You can't get back in shape by overdoing it."

"Overdoing it! I haven't done anything yet today!"

Looking into his stubborn eyes, I almost wept. He had scared me so badly. For weeks I had shared the delusion with him that he was slowly getting stronger. There had even been days when I thought he was truly better. I had tried to ignore those other days when the work was obviously a strain for him. But now I saw that he was making no real improvement. This spell had been serious. I wanted to get him out of the basement lest he have a worse one and die before my eyes.

"We've got the Kuhlman car coming in after lunch," I told him. "That's going to be a hard job. Lie down a little while so you'll be rested up for that."

"What about this job?"

I hesitated, then spoke what I knew was the truth. "I can do this one."

"Go on! You've never done one in your life."

"I've watched. I can do it."

He was going to argue. But then something happened down there in his chest. His eyes went far away and his right hand stole to his midsection. He gasped several times involuntarily; then he began breathing deeply, forcing a semblance of control. I saw the fear in his eyes.

"Well," he said slowly, "maybe it's time you started learning a trade. Might be good for you."

"Yes," I said, indulging the lie. "And how can I learn unless I *try?*"

He stood shakily, brushed my hands away, and grasped the banister that led upward. "I'll sit on the front porch awhile . . . cool off. . . . Not a word about this to your mother."

"Yes, sir."

He glared at me. "I mean it. Not a word."

"Yes, sir!"

He went up the steps with agonizing slowness. I did not stir until he had gone out of sight into the kitchen and I heard his steps make the floor creak directly over my head. Then I turned to the workbench. The irons were red hot. There was the solder, the flux. Here was the radiator. In *his* hands a job like this would appear easy. I knew precisely what to do. I simply did not know if I could make my hands do it adequately.

There was nothing to do but try. Reaching for the wire brush, I began.

It was a job that would have taken my father twenty to thirty minutes. More than an hour later I was just finishing it up as best I knew how when the floor overhead creaked again and he came slowly back down the stairs. His color was just as bad but he was breathing normally.

"Well, well," he said with a little smile, shuffling over to the bench. "Let's see how we're doing."

I squirmed off the stool and let him have a clear field of view. He turned the radiator on end and squinted at my soldering. He tested the seams with a fingertip, turned the work this way and that.

"Sloppy," he pronounced finally. "Let me show you something." His hand trembled as he reached for one of the irons, but it became rock steady as he applied the point to the long seam I had just dressed. As he moved the tip of the iron, the rough and uneven seam I had so labored over became liquid again and magically smoothed.

"The tip has to stay very hot," he said, concentrating on the work. "That means you either work fast or have to reheat and lay a new bead. So you learn to work right along. See how I'm keeping the point right in the junction, with the body of the iron leaned ahead? That's the secret."

"Yes, sir," I said, learning.

He put the iron down. "There." He blew on the seam. "Looks a little better, doesn't it?"

"It looks *perfect,*" I said.

His faint smile came. "Well, not perfect but okay. Remember: a good-looking seam is probably stronger, too. All right. Do you want to test it?"

I nodded eagerly and reached for one end of the radiator. But he remained perched on the stool and it was clear he was not going to help me carry it across to the laundry drain as always.

So I hefted the thing myself and carried it over. There, kneeling, I ran water into the filler hole and slid the radiator onto some fresh newspapers and looked for the telltale signs of leakage. The radiator held. It was fixed.

"Done," I pronounced.

"You did a good job," Pop told me.

"It was a mess until you neatened it up!"

"Well, you'll learn. Your work would have *held.* It's just that it didn't look quite professional yet." He winked at me. "So do you want to have a hand at putting it back in by yourself?"

"Sure!"

"Okay." He reached for a Chesterfield.

The owner of the car was due back at noon, and for a while I was on the border of panic, not knowing whether I would have the job done in time. But Pop, who came out of the basement after a while and sat in a deck chair near the back door, did not seem concerned. He watched and said nothing. When I finished tightening the last hose and refilled the radiator and block, he came over and peered into the engine compartment as I started the motor to circulate water, the crucial test. Satisfied, he nodded and went back to the chair and waited until the owner came. Then he collected the money and nodded to me and we watched our customer back out of the yard and drive away down the alley.

"You did fine," Pop told me, putting a hand on my shoulder. "I think it's good for you to be learning this, don't you?"

"I sure do," I said proudly.

He patted me. "We'll just let you have a hand in some of it some days. There's no substitute for experience, I always say."

It was only later in the day, sweat stinging my eyes as I worked on the Kuhlman radiator, that I realized a benign hypocrisy had begun: my father could not admit—to himself or anyone else—that on certain days he was not capable of doing this work; the only way he could allow me to do it for him was to pretend that it was a favor to me, training.

That was all right, I decided. Maybe one day he would really get better. In the meantime, if there was delusion here, I needed it as much as he did. For him pride was at stake. For me: confidence in our future as a family.

The 1930s, everyone agreed, would be a wonderful era. And despite Pop's illness and the worry associated with it in our household, there was nothing else that seemed ominous about that summer of 1929. More houses were being built all around the neighborhood. The Rayburns bought a car. Uncle Jack expanded his roofing business. On days when I was not at work with Pop in the basement, I found lawns to mow, errands to run for money, ashes to haul, weeds to pull. Despite all this there was time left over for hikes into the country with the Rayburn boys and the Smith twins; shorter walks to the creek where we were not supposed to swim but always did; street baseball—usually first bounce or fly but sometimes two-a-cat—furtive cigarette smoking in the Rayburn tree house; sweaty speculation about Frank Schroeder's sister . . . and Billy Anderson's sister . . . and Betty and Carolyn Vincent; building a raft at the creek and going downstream, poling it all of a hundred feet before it broke apart on us and sank; fishing and seldom catching anything but crawdads; a family picnic all the way up on the Olentangy River with fried chicken and baked beans, Devil Dogs and grape soda; shooting marbles in a dusty ring in the alley; going to the Rivoli and saying you were eleven to get in for a nickel, stalking the horse-drawn ice wagon and waiting in the bushes until the ice man had carried a big chunk of ice in his tongs into someone's house so you could make a mad dash for the wagon and climb in the back under the wet black canvas and steal a piece of glistening clear ice off the shaggy wood floorboards; whapping the bread man's horse with your slingshot to make it walk down the street with the bread truck; exploring up and down Broad Street and even poking your nose into the bowling alley and pool hall (but never staying); and wishing, wishing, *wishing* for a bike.

Gails' full-time job took him out of much of this, and for some of it Frank was a bit too young. But I had it all: a golden time, a beautiful summer, a coda to a time of innocence both for me and for the country . . . the last summer of our youth.

6

In the fall we went hunting as usual, but it was *not* as usual because Pop did not last very long and could not go through the briars at all. After our second jaunt, Uncle Jim came by and brought us a surprise: a slender, low-slung, brown mongrel hound named Max.

"He's fourteen months old," Uncle Jim told us, "and he's already a trained rabbit dog. When you go out with a good dog, it makes it a lot easier. I've seen Max work; he scouts out in front and jumps the rabbits and runs them back at you; he's hell in a briar patch, boys—he goes in where fools fear to tread, and the rabbits come out running in all directions."

Max came over to me with his sad eyes drooping, his stumpy tail going a mile a minute. I petted him.

Mom said firmly, "We won't let him sleep in the house."

"He's a *hunting* dog," Uncle Jim said with a grin. "He doesn't need to."

Pop looked dubious. "I imagine he eats a lot."

"He earns his grub, Joe. When you go out hunting with Max, it's meat on the table."

Pop raised his eyebrows. "I guess we can try him."

Try him we did, the next Saturday. Churning through a light snowfall like a perpetual-motion machine, Max scared up twenty-two rabbits in less than three hours. For good measure, he pointed a few pheasants and treed some squirrels. On the way home in Uncle Jack's car he was still so excited that he bounded from one to the other of us, slobbering all over our faces. When we got home, Mom sternly made us put Max in his run in the yard. When the snow began falling again after dark, she went repeatedly to the back windows and peered out, sighing. In the morning when Frank and I got up to fire the furnace, Max was curled up on the the blankets at the foot of our parents' bed. On Mom's side.

From the time it happened I heard people talking about "the crash," but I didn't understand it. By February or March of 1930, however, I could begin to see that things were different even on my walk down Broad Street to St. Aloysius. Here a variety store had closed, and there a dress shop. There didn't seem to be quite as many cars out. I saw my first hobo, a sad-eyed middle-aged man in a dark suit that was sizes too big for him. Then Gail lost the after-school job. It was the three of us again, back to hauling the coal from curb side to house bin in fruit baskets. But now some of our old customers were doing this job for themselves.

In the spring we had a family conference. Everyone sat around the dining room table.

"We have some wonderful news," our mother said brightly. "Gramaw Prater is coming to live with us."

"Here?" Frank said, thunderstruck.

"Of course, here," Mom smiled. There was emotion and tension beneath the forced gay exterior. "I know it's going to be wonderful and we'll all love having her."

"I thought," Gail said slowly, "she lived with Uncle Bob and Aunt Helen."

"Well, she has," Mom conceded. "But Uncle Bob has . . . had trouble lately. They're giving up their house. So Gramaw Prater has to live here."

"Where?" Gail asked, watching her carefully. He was seventeen now, tall and lank, a man.

"What we're going to do is put some of Frank and Kenny's things in the attic—right at the top of the stairs where they'll be easy to get—and then you can move your bed in the room with theirs. Then Gramaw can have your old room. Won't that be nice?"

No one spoke. Frank and I waited for Gail's explosive protest. It didn't come. Instead he meditatively cracked a knuckle and spoke softly. "Where are Uncle Bob and Aunt Helen going to live?"

"They're renting a place up on Summit Street. Half of a double. It's small but it will be just fine for them."

Pop stirred. "It will take some rearranging all around, but Gramaw Prater has always been fun to be with. She has her pension; it's small, but she'll pay her own way here and give us all a lot of company. I know we're all going to be glad to have her."

"When is she coming?" Gail asked.

"This weekend."

Later, we rearranged our room so Gail's bed could be shoehorned in. Each of us would have a small dresser at the foot of our bed; Gail would share the closet in Mary's room. He was fuming.

" 'Glad to have her' my ass," he said under his breath, shoving the bed against the wall. "Why doesn't she stay where she belongs?"

"Grampaw is dead," I pointed out. "She has to live with someone."

"She could live by herself!"

"She probably doesn't have that much money," Frank said.

"So does she have to come and mooch off us?"

Gail's insensitivity shocked me. "Gail, she's Mom's *mother.*"

"So she takes *my* bedroom!"

"She can't just sit out in the street!"

"At the rate we're going, we'll all be out in the street before long. Pop can't work—"

"Pop is getting better," Frank said.

"Do you really believe that?" Gail demanded incredulously.

"He *is* getting better," I insisted.

"He's not. He never will. This is as good as he's ever going to get again."

I swallowed hard. "Okay, then. That's all right; too. He can hunt and fish and take walks and work around the house. As long as people bring their radiators—"

"People aren't going to be bringing as many radiators," Gail said, "because people aren't going to have as many cars. We're in a *Depression,* Kenny! Don't you understand anything? And our father is a sick man. We're going to be lucky to have enough to eat and a roof over our heads without Gramaw coming to add more trouble."

Before I could reply there were footsteps in the hall. Our mother came in and looked in some dismay at the bed arrangement. "I didn't know it would be quite this crowded," she said.

"It's fine," Gail said cheerfully. "Once you're in the bed, how much floor space do you need?"

Mom looked at him with troubled eyes. "I know how hard it must be for you, giving up your own room—"

"Listen," Gail said, grinning. "This is great! The brothers are back together again! And if I ever get sick of 'em, why, I'll just get some lumber and build myself a room in the attic."

Mom's troubled expression did not go away. "She's getting old, Gail, and Uncle Bob—"

"So now *we* get all the doughnuts and pies," Gail said with a chuckle.

Mom went to him and put her arms around him. "You're a good boy."

Gail hugged her. "We'll do fine, Mom."

Her eyes as she looked at him were overly bright. "Of course we will. Now get this cleaned up and come down to the kitchen, all of you. I made some cookies. They may not be as good as my mother's, but you can eat a few anyway."

She left the room. Max bolted in from the hall and leaped into the middle of my bed.

"Get that mutt out of here!" Gail growled, reverting to his other personality.

I hugged Max, who frantically slobbered on my face. "Gail, I dunno how many of you there are, but you'd *all* better get used to Max being in here. He sleeps with me these days."

Gail groaned and rolled his eyes heavenward. But I knew there would be nothing more said. Just like Max, his bark was worse than his bite.

Gramaw Prater moved in on schedule, bringing a surprising amount of old furniture. Some of it was jammed into her bedroom. A couch went in a corner of our parlor along with a gateleg table and two extra lamps. Her small desk went in the living room, and on it was placed her greatest prize and a source of great excitement for us—her radio. We had never had one in our house before. Gail, Frank, and I collaborated on getting a piece of wire out under the window, up the side of the house on porcelain insulators, and across the back of the lot to the pear tree. Then we sat on the floor in fascination as Gramaw tuned the set and let us listen to WJR. Tom Rayburn came over and listened with us.

Of all of us, Pop enjoyed the radio the most. Maybe it was because his heart kept him away from many people he had known at work, or perhaps it was his native curiosity. Through the spring it was he who most often turned the radio on in the evening, often rocking back and chuckling at some comedian's joke or leaning forward intensely, scowling, as he listened to the news.

Everyone said things were not as bad in Columbus as they were many places because Columbus had no single supporting large industry and had never boomed quite so high as some other cities in the twenties. But even in Columbus things were bad enough. The *Dispatch* showed bread lines. Wheat, once selling for $1.35, was at about 80 cents. By May people were saying the area needed rain. By June the word *"drought"* was being used over a great chunk of the Midwest.

"As long as people have cars, we'll be all right," Pop told me one day early in July. He had the radiator of a Packard on the bench and it was one of his good days, so he was doing all the work himself. "One thing about being in the repair business: the worse times get, the better your business becomes. That's because people have to repair the old instead of buying something new."

"Do you think the Depression will last much longer?" I asked.

"No, I think it's about bottomed out."

"I hope so," I said fervently.

The Depression had touched the family in other ways. Uncle Jack still had his roofing business, but there had been some awful setback and he had lost almost everything. He no longer had his grand Buick. His entire business now consisted of a Chevrolet truck that he worked out of and used for the family as well. Uncle Jack looked old. The quick smile was no longer there so often, and on his last visit to the house his big laugh had not boomed through the room a single time.

Uncle Jim, as far as I could tell, was in even worse shape. He had lost his job at the furniture store. He was working now at a dairy farm north of the city somewhere. Some days there was no work, he said, and he went to the city employment office and stood in line to see if there might be part-time work for a day or two at night as a plant guard or perhaps a street sweeper.

Uncle Bob and Aunt Helen were no longer in Columbus. They had gone to Detroit, where a job had beckoned. The job had been gone when Uncle Bob arrived, but he had found something else, as a janitor.

It hurt, thinking of Uncle Bob pushing a broom. I thought it was unfair. Pop said there was no question of fairness or unfairness now for people, only a question of survival. He said we were far luckier than most.

Every Friday was our payday. Gail and Frank came home for lunch—Gail was at another grocery and Frank set pins at the bowling alley—and brought their weekly paychecks. Our mother sat at the kitchen table with her ledger book and papers and the jar containing whatever money Pop and I had made during the week on radiators. Then she doled out change to Gail and Frank and me, set aside money in four cheese glasses for other needs, and put the checks and any remaining cash in a brown envelope. After lunch Pop and I walked to the bank to make our regular deposit.

It was the last week of July when our trip was thwarted.

While we were still a block away on Broad Street, we saw the crowd up ahead. People milled around the front of the bank building and some cars had parked in the street. There was a policeman nearby.

"What's going on?" Pop asked worriedly.

"Maybe there was a robbery!" I said excitedly and ran ahead.

But it was not a robbery. I knew that when I saw a couple sitting on the concrete steps of the building next door, their faces blank with shock. And I was surer when I saw another man crying and wringing his hands.

I wriggled through the muttering crowd to the front door of the bank. The blinds had been pulled. There was a hand-printed sign in the glass:

CLOSED
Until further notice

Pop came up on the edge of the crowd. He was badly out of breath. His eyes found me and then he read the sign.

"That can't be!" he gasped.

An older man turned bitterly to him. "Looks like it is, though, bro."

"What does it mean?"

"What does it always mean?" The older man made an angry slashing gesture. "Closed. Kaput. Finished. Out of business."

"But I talked to Mr. Parker, the president, just a week or two ago! He said this bank would *never* have any trouble, with so many loyal depositors—"

"It looks like he was a true banker," a woman said with shrill bitterness. "A good liar!"

Pop shoved past the others and nudged me as he came to the door. He started hammering on it with the flat of his hand. "Mr. Parker!" he called loudly. "It's me! Joseph Riley!" He hammered again, making the glass rattle. *"Mr. Parker!"*

The policeman came through. He tapped my father on the shoulder with his billy club. "That's enough, now, mister."

"You don't understand! They've got my money in there!"

The policeman's wide, expressionless face showed nothing. "They've got a lot of people's money, sir. But you can't make a disturbance."

Pop's face twisted. He held up the brown paper bag. "I wasn't even trying to take any money *out*. I was trying to put some more *in*."

"In that case," came a sarcastic voice from the back of the crowd, "brother, can you spare a dime?"

Pop turned to a well-dressed man in the front row. "They can't just close—permanently! They've got our money in there."

The man shook his head somberly. "That's just the point. There probably isn't any money in there at all anymore."

"By—my deposits!"

"Your deposits . . . my deposits. The same thing. They took our money, loaned it out. The people they loaned it to couldn't pay it back. It's gone." The man, with steel-gray hair and a handsome profile and an expensive suit, had been perfectly calm up to this point. Now suddenly big tears coursed down his face. "All gone. Very simple, really."

The crowd was growing. Evidently the sign had been placed in the bank window during the lunch hour, and word was just now spreading. A woman who had just arrived took a look at the front sign and collapsed in a faint. Others scrambled, trying to obey the officer's orders to "Give her air!." Pop, his eyes vacant, pushed through and started away. I followed.

"It's not right," he said slowly, as if to himself. "They can't just take your money and then close. Parker wouldn't lie to me . . . would he?"

"Maybe it's just temporary," I said. "Maybe they'll be open tomorrow."

He shook his head. "It's not temporary. This has been happening all over the country. But Parker *assured* me this bank was all right. I thought he was my friend." Pop seemed more dazed than angry. He was walking fast, the way he always had before his heart attack, and I had to stretch my legs to keep up. "What are we going to do? Our savings . . . the little we had . . . were all in there."

"Pop, slow down a little."

He seemed not to hear. "First the job, now this. What are we going to do? The insurance money was in there. The school money. Everything!"

"Pop, take it *easy!*"

He churned up our street. We met a couple of people hurrying the other way, as if to a fire. Pop seemed not to see them any more than he heard me. His face was brick red now from the harsh walk in the afternoon humidity, and he muttered to himself as he strode along at the same killing gait. "Pretend to be a friend . . . give out a pack of lies . . . what's a man to do when everything goes wrong. . . ."

We neared our house. Mary was on the front porch with Gramaw Prater, the two of them in the porch glider together. As my father rushed up the steps, Gramaw left the glider and hurried toward him. He entered the house. She followed.

"Daddy looks mad!" Mary observed to her doll.

I hurried into the house after the adults. From the kitchen came the sounds of raised voices—Pop's, angry; Mom's, frightened and inquiring. I went down the hall to find them facing each other over the table, with Gramaw in the doorway beside me, her hands clenched.

"—just what I said!" Pop was saying. "Closed—'until further notice.' Which means it's failed—gone under!"

"Oh my God," my mother said almost inaudibly.

Pop's fist slapped into his palm. "Well, I'll tell you one thing. They won't get this house! They'll never get this house! We worked and scrimped too long and too hard for that!"

"What are we going to do about the insurance and tax money?" my mother asked, her voice trembling. "We have some time, but—"

"I'll tell you what we're going to do!" Pop snapped. "I'm not just going to sit around and wait for radiators anymore! I'm going to put up a couple more signs out front. I can fix roofs. I used to be a roofer. And house painting. I can paint. I'll make a lot more money, that's all. I'm going to the basement right now and make the new signs."

"You can't," Mom said. "Your health—"

"Damn my health!"

"The doctor said—"

"I don't care what the doctor said! Listen, there's nothing all that wrong with my heart. So I hurt a little, get dizzy a little. So what? A little dizziness never killed anybody yet."

My mother went to him, clinging to his shoulders. "You're doing all you can already. You mustn't try doing any more. You could . . . hurt yourself—"

"What do you think I would have to live for if they came and put us out of this house?" Pop demanded, breathing very hard. "How could I ever face any of you again if—" He stopped, and a terrible look of surprise and pain crossed his face.

"Joseph?" my mother said.

Pop's eyes closed. He collapsed to the floor. A chair went crazily against the wall. In the instant of crazy surprise, I remember thinking that the chair must have knocked paint off the wall and the spot would have to be touched up.

Mom fell to her knees beside Pop, holding his face in her hands. "Joseph! *Joseph!*" She looked at him more closely and began to sob.

Gramaw Prater bent over the two of them for the merest second. Then she hurried to the sink and began running cold water, pulling towels from the cupboard on the left. "Kenny," she snapped. "Run for the doctor. Tell him your father has had another attack. Hurry!"

I ran.

7

Dr. Edwards was at our house within thirty minutes. By that time my mother and I and two neighborhood men who happened to be home had carried Pop upstairs and into the bed. He was unconscious. His lips and fingernails were blue.

"Kenny," mother said when the doctor arrived, "take your sister out in the backyard."

Mary started to bawl. "I don't want to go outside!"

I took her arm and marched her out, not wanting to leave any more than she did, but driven by my terror to obey without question.

"I don't know why I have to go outside!" she sniffled as we went into the yard. "Everyone always treats me like a *baby!*"

I led her past the apple tree toward the grape arbor, where flies and bees hummed in the afternoon heat. "The doctor needs quiet, sis. We have to cooperate, that's all."

"He's going to die," Mary said, tears streaking her face. "This time he's going to die, die, *die!*"

"Shut up your face! I don't want to hear any more talk like that!"

"That's all right for you to say! You're *big*. It wouldn't make any difference to you!"

I stared at her in shock. "I ought to wash your mouth out with soap for saying something like that."

Mary sobbed and crunched some dirt between her bare toes. "Gail is a man, practically. And you'll be finished at St. Aloysius this year, too. But Frank and me are just *little*, yet. What are *we* gonna do if Daddy dies and goes to heaven?"

"Now you just listen to me," I ordered, sweating. "In the first place, he isn't going to die. In the second place, whatever happens, we're a *family*. Don't you know that? We stay together." I held a hand out in front of her face, and to my astonishment I saw that it was clenched into a fist. "*Nothing* is ever going to tear us apart. So just stop blubbering!"

After a while Frank ran home and I had to watch and calm him, too. Then word got to Gail. But he went upstairs with the adults, leaving me in charge of the smaller ones. It was a very long time before Dr. Edwards came down, followed by the others.

It had, of course, been another heart attack. Dr. Edwards would be back after supper to look in again. Pop would not be taken to the hospital this time. The doctor said he thought everything would be all right.

Through the evening we took turns sitting at Pop's bedside. He seemed to sleep. His color was perhaps a little better. We kept ice in a pan and sponged his face and head. Fierce summer humidity made the house a furnace. At about midnight, exhausted, I staggered into the bedroom where Frank, innocent, already slept. I stared at the ceiling in the dimness.

After a while Gail crept in. "Ken?" His voice was very soft.

I sat up sharply.

Gail sat on the edge of my bed. "It's okay. I just thought . . . I'm going out on the porch for a while."

I got up and followed him soundlessly downstairs in my underwear. We went out onto the front porch and sat on the concrete steps. Gail produced a pack of Camels and offered me one. I took it. He cracked a match and we smoked together. I had never smoked more than a few puffs, and got dizzy. The light from the corner street lamp filtered through the growing maple trees, making the yard and the park in the street a silent, silvery wood. Not a breath of air stirred. I felt very grown-up, sitting there smoking.

"We've got to talk about what we're going to do," Gail said after a while.

"He's going to be all right, Gail, isn't he?"

"I heard Dr. Edwards say he'll never be able to do any work again."

"But he'll *live.*"

Gail breathed deeply. "I've got my job, Ken. I can . . . increase my hours."

"How? Until you finish school—"

"I'm *finished* school."

I looked at him, not comprehending.

"I'm finished school," he said. "Right now."

"You've got two years to go."

"No. I've got to have a full-time job now. And you've got to stay in school. But you've got to figure out how you're going to keep the radiator business going every afternoon. And all through the summer."

"Gail, you can't quit high school! Pop always said, if you get your education—"

"Quit dreaming!" Gail said with fierce intensity. "What are we gonna eat if I go back to school and just piddle in that store? How are we gonna keep the house? Grow up! That bank down there has just *failed.* Pop can't work. We've got nothing to fall back on. It's up to you and me now."

"Then I'll quit school too, then," I said.

"Don't be stupid. You've got to have at least a couple of years of high school. And you know how to fix those radiators. *I* don't. You can probably make more in the basement after school than you could any other way. And it will make Pop feel like we've still got the business."

"But what's Mom going to say?"

"What *can* she say?" Gail tossed his cigarette stub into the night, where it showered pink sparks on the pavement below us. "Listen. How many times has Pop told us? The world doesn't owe you a living. If you don't take care of yourself, nobody else will. Uncle Jack is practically broke. Uncle Jim is worse. Uncle Bob is worst of all, I think. We've got Gramaw to watch after. Frank and Mary are too little to do much. Mom can't go out and find a job. Where would she find a job when there are hobos walking every

street in the whole country right now, out of work? And Pop
. . . now this has happened . . . he can't do it for us anymore. I'll
find me a full-time job *some* way and you'll do the radiators. It's
that or starve, and Mom won't say anything because we've got
absolutely no choice."

I continued to stare into my older brother's face. I saw his
angry resolve, but I also saw how young his mouth and eyes were,
and the fear he was trying to hide. I felt sorry for him.

I asked, "You think we can do it?"

"Why, hell, yes," he snapped. "There's absolutely no question in my mind." He was not a very good liar.

Within a few days Pop was a little better. We watched his
progress with a desperate gaiety. By the time school began again,
Gail had two part-time jobs, one at the store on Broad Street and
another sweeping out at the *Dispatch* downtown at night, but he
had capitulated to Pop and was also back in school. In addition
to doing radiators I was repairing flat tires in the backyard. Frank
even found a couple of lawns to mow; with cool weather nearing,
piles of coal began to appear at curb sides and he worked many
of those with a fruit basket. Gramaw Prater sewed some party
dresses for people. My mother did washing for two other families,
rich ones who brought their laundry in cars. I returned to school
amazed at how young most of my classmates seemed. After
school there was always work to be done.

My nun that final year at St. Aloysius was named Sister
Frances. Early in the semester she told me one day at recess that
I would stay after school to clean erasers.

"No, sister," I told her.

"What?" she said, her eyes sharpening with anger.

"I said no, sister," I repeated calmly.

"I think, young man, you'll do as you are told, or we'll see the
principal."

"We have a business," I told her. "I fix radiators. I need to
go right home and work."

"And what if I say otherwise?" she demanded.

"Then I'll go home anyway," I said.

She studied my face, her fury dying. Finally she reached out and touched my hair with her fingertips, very lightly. "And never come back?" she asked almost inaudibly, in the voice of a girl.

"Yes, sister."

She took a deep breath and turned away. Later she told a boy named Webb to stay and do the erasers, and she never asked me again.

Uncle Jack came to our house almost every day. His fine truck, the last of what had once been a veritable fleet of vehicles for his roofing company, was gone too, as the Buick had gone earlier. He now came to the house in a rusty Tin Lizzie. Usually he was alone because Aunt Sal had a job in a five and dime. He would spend hours with Pop, sitting by his bedside or chair, the two of them talking about old times or about hunting and fishing. Sometimes Jack's big laugh would rumble through the house, but even when it did, I thought there was a different quality to it, a hint that it was forced and more a performance than an indication of his old zest. Sometimes when he drove up I caught a glimpse of him getting out of the old car, his big frame lankier and bent at the shoulders as if under a heavy load; if he caught me watching, the shoulders always came back and the big grin flashed, a carbon copy of Pop's act when he sensed observation. He was acting for all of us. I worried about him.

"There's no work," he told my father one afternoon in my hearing.

"Things will pick up," Pop said.

"I've got almost nothing left. If I get a chance to bid on a job, I've got no money for supplies, and if they don't promise to pay me by the week, I can't make promises to men. I've still got a sign. But I'm out of business."

"It's temporary," Pop said. "It's got to be."

"What if it isn't?"

"What?"

"What if it *isn't?* What if it's going to go on and on? What am I going to do?"

"Well," Pop said after a pause, "I guess you'll just do your best."

"I owe people money," Uncle Jack said. "A lot of money. I owe on the building, some of the trucks they've already taken back, supplies—even some back wages to some of my men. Good men, that didn't do anything to deserve being shortchanged by some deadbeat like me."

"Oh, now come on," Pop said. "You're no deadbeat and you know it."

"I said I would never owe anything. I said I would always be as good as my word. I always said any man could work if he wanted to. Now I'm sitting here as proof that everything I ever said I stood for was a damned lie."

"Well, things will pick up," Pop said softly.

There was another pause. Then Uncle Jack's voice sounded like he had braced himself up. "Sure. You're right. I mean, as long as I'm in business, I might get lucky again, right? I mean, it isn't like I had had to take bankruptcy or anything as bad as that!"

"And you've got your health," my father pointed out.

"Sure . . . Sure! And before long you'll have your health back, too! Then watch our smoke, eh?"

Sometimes when he left the house to head home, Uncle Jack would get me aside. "I think he's feeling a little low today, Kenny. Maybe you ought to go up after a while and talk about the box scores or something, eh?" Or: "He's feeling fine today, a lot better. Keep him grinning, Kenny, and I'll be back in the morning."

I guess I had always assumed that brothers were close only during childhood—that brotherhood, like growing pains, was something that faded almost to memory as one grew older and moved away. But my father's illness and Uncle Jack's business calamities drew them together again, perhaps closer than they had ever been as children. It was a beautiful thing to see, and I had to believe that as long as they had each other, they would come out fine.

Pop made a good recovery, more than we had hoped for.

He moved slowly, but he came downstairs each morning during that winter and on the less chilly days took slow walks as far as Broad Street. Some faucets started leaking and he replaced the washers, taking all morning to do so with his old plodding, systematic perfectionism. He did not work on the radiators with me but he talked to customers when they brought their cars and collected the money from them, and he always inspected my work closely. I learned to reverse-flush the cores more quickly, using a garden hose, and how to mix the caustic solutions needed to boil them out when they were badly plugged with rust and dirt. There was a full-fledged radiator shop farther west, near Hague Avenue, and when I occasionally ran into a job I could not handle, I put the radiator in our coaster wagon and pulled it down to Mr. Weil, the owner of that shop, who would do a pressure-boil for a quarter, a new bottom for fifty cents.

In the evenings sometimes we played hearts or checkers, or listened to Father Coughlin's radio show for children on WJR. "The radio priest" had not become political yet and my mother thought he was a saint.

One night Father Coughlin was talking about The Little Flower, and Gail got up abruptly and started out of the room.

"Gail—?" my mother said.

"I'll be back later," Gail said, his face dark with anger.

"What is it?" she asked.

"Nothing."

"No. Wait." Mom's voice was firm. "You're about to storm out of here right in the middle of this wonderful story. *Why?*"

"Because it's junk," Gail snapped.

"*Junk!* This wonderful man—"

"It doesn't have to do with anything," Gail said, his voice shaky. "Everybody is out of work. The banks are closed. People are losing their houses. Nothing *works* anymore. And we're supposed to sit here and listen to that fool spout off about The Little Flower, and how we're supposed to pray to her so she'll help America?"

"Gail Henry Riley," my mother said softly, shocked. "You should ask God to forgive you."

"The Little Flower isn't going to save this country," Gail told her heatedly. "And neither is Herbert Hoover. This country is *finished* unless the workers rise."

My father, who had been watching and listening silently, jerked his head back. "What was that, young man?"

"You heard me," Gail said, his eyes wavering slightly.

"Workers of the world, eh?" Pop said, his voice ringing. "Is that it?"

"What else? Do you think Hoover is going to do anything? Or Congress? They belong to the rich people. They don't *care*. The people are starving. Unless they take matters into their own hands, this country will die."

"That kind of talk is stupid," Pop told him.

"It's the truth!"

"No. Times are hard now. But we'll work out of it. We always have. If we have faith—"

"And you don't blow up a burning building to try to put out the fire," Gail said with dripping sarcasm. "I know."

It was the first time I had ever heard anyone address Pop in such a tone. His head shot back and his eyes narrowed. For an instant I thought he might rise from his chair and go after my older brother. In the deathly silence of the room, Father Coughlin intoned a prayer.

Pop, however, did not move. The moment dragged out. Then Gail, as if unable to stand the tension any longer, wheeled and fled from the parlor.

My parents looked at each other. She appeared stricken.

Pop took a deep breath and reached for a Chesterfield. "Could you turn it up just a little, Mrs. Riley?" His voice was almost inaudible. Then he seemed to shake himself mentally and he smiled. "Don't think a thing about it. The lad is overtired."

No more was said about it that night. But the next afternoon, in the basement, Pop brought it up again. "So what did you think of your big brother's speech?"

"Not a whole lot," I growled, soldering.

"He'll be all right."

"You should have punched him."

Pop surprised me by chuckling. "No. A man has to try ideas. Even crazy ones. He knows what's right. He'll get through."

I put the iron back on the hot plate to reheat. "He's got no right to talk to you like he did."

"Oh, that's all right, too, Kenny. No harm done."

I stared at him in amazement. "A few years ago you wouldn't have taken it."

He was sitting on the steps. He held out his arm, motioning for me to sit beside him. I obeyed and his arm rested on my shoulders. He smelled of coffee and tobacco and the medicine he took. "Things are different than they were a few years ago, son," he told me.

"They shouldn't be. You should have bopped him one!"

"Nah. That's one of the good things about getting sick."

"*What?*"

"I don't have to be all that tough now, Kenny. You see, it's all different now. Now I know I can die."

"You're not going to—"

"Knowing you can die. Really *knowing* it. That makes all the difference . . . you see? I don't have to make you walk the chalk anymore, the way I used to. I guess maybe a father can never love a son the way he should until he sees that he can die, and soon the son will be taking over everything."

"But you're not going to die!"

He hugged me briefly. "Well, I hope not . . . not anytime soon, anyway." Our hound Max came down the steps, tail wagging furiously, and Pop patted him with his other hand. "What I'm saying is that you don't have to worry about Gail. I'm not worried about any of you. You're honest. You keep your word. You work hard. You don't try to stand out by taking somebody else's space. You don't whine and complain. You stand on your own feet. You. Gail. Even Frank, as young as he is. I don't worry about you. I would have liked to have left you a lot more, but you'll be fine. I remember when we moved to Columbus, after my dad had lost everything. All we owned was in three big cartons. But we made it. You'll have some head start over that . . . you've got the house, good tools. Always be a man, Kenny. Don't lie or cheat; you don't have to shout at the top of your lungs trying to be a big shot; always give an honest day's work. You understand?"

"Yes, sir," I said.

"I know you do. And so does Gail. That's why I don't have to yell at him anymore when he does a little thing like get impatient with the world."

"Okay?" he asked finally, a little gruffly.

"Yessir," I said.

"Back to work?"

"Yep." I left the steps and walked back to the bench without looking at him. If I had had a cigarette to prove my independence further, I would probably have lit it.

Our hunting during that fall of 1930 was virtually nonexistent. Frank begged me to take him without our father, and the Rayburns always invited us on their expeditions. But it did not seem right to leave Pop at home. He would have waved cheerfully and watched us go. But I would have seen the sadness in his eyes.

He was trying to quit smoking. It made him fidgety and cross, and once in a while I caught him in the basement with a lighted cigarette, looking like a furtive kid caught behind the barn. I never mentioned the cigarette and tried to make a lot of noise whenever I went to the basement at an unusual time, to warn him. Sometimes I would hear his footsteps on the pavement as I lumbered down the stairs like a blind elephant, and there would be a little *phhhtt!* as the lighted butt hit the water in the open floor drain, and I would go on down to find him standing near the laundry tubs, a vacant expression on his face and pale gray smoke still visible in the air around him. For the record, I never saw any of that, either.

That Christmas we waited until Christmas eve to go out to buy a tree, rather than buy it early and hide it as we usually did. Gail said there were always a few trees left over that the merchants practically gave away at the last minute. He said there were a couple of dozen nice ones still standing on the sidewalk in front of the store where he worked. So after eight o'clock that night, with snow swirling in the air, he and I invented an excuse and left for Broad Street. While we were gone, Mary and even Frank—who was old enough to know better—would be required to go to bed and by some feat of will *actually go to sleep.* That was because at our house Santa Claus brought not only the presents, but the tree; and although Mary was eleven now, she had never definitely said she no longer believed in Santa Claus. So the formalities had to be observed, and mother had ruled that Frank, as closest to her age, had to go to bed, too, for the sake of appearances.

"I hope you got something for everyone," Gail told me as we hiked up Broad Street into the teeth of the snowy wind. There were few cars on the street, and the snow made halos around the streetlights. Most stores were closed and dark.

"I'm all set," I told him. "Except for you, of course. I didn't get you anything."

He looked sharply at me.

"You being grown-up, and all," I said innocently.

His eyes sagged but he set his jaw manfully. "Well, that's true. I don't need anything."

"Good gosh, Gail! I was kidding you!"

He puffed out his cheeks with relief, then grinned. "I thought you were serious."

"Would I kid a kidder?"

"I think you just did, you bunghole!"

We hiked nearer the store. I was feeling good. My presents were all ready, wrapped and hidden in the basement behind Pop's workbench: a wooden jewel box (62¢) ordered through school and worked on during art-class time for more than a month, drawing a design on the lid, burning it in with a wood-

burning tool, painting it three colors with oil paints, putting on
two coats of varnish, glueing inside both cotton padding and gold
silk cloth, for Mom; the plaster-of-paris form of a horse's head
(44¢) that you could hang on the wall, rubbed with oil-base stain
and then partly rubbed off with a soft cloth for antiqueing effects,
for Pop; a pair of work socks (28¢) for Gail; a yo-yo (15¢) for Frank; a
hankie with frilly stuff around the edges (19¢) for Mary; and a little
box of sachet (31¢) for Gramaw Prater. Everyone had been
scrimping and shopping and making things secretly and hiding
them for weeks. I knew it was going to be a great Christmas.

We reached the corner where Gail's store was. The lights
still shone inside through moisture-beaded windows. Gail
stopped and stared.

"Where are the trees?" I asked.

Gail walked closer and looked at the random piles of cut
branches and odds and ends on the snowy pavement.

"Where are the *trees?*" I demanded, louder.

Gail plunged into the store, leaving me on the sidewalk. I
held my hands cupped to the window and made out the blurry
scene inside. He accosted the owner, who seemed to be alone
behind the counter. He pointed. The owner shrugged and said
something. Gail stared like he had been poleaxed.

He came back out. "They sold them all."

"They did *what?*" I yelled.

"Don't get excited, don't get excited. We'll just go up the
street to Seilers'."

I could see he was upset, so I bit my tongue. I had to stretch
my legs out to keep up with his stride as we went the next block.
We reached the store. It was closed. In front, on the sidewalk,
were a few random needles.

Gail faced me with eyes like daggers. "That's all right. Let's
not hear any bitching. We'll just keep looking. There's no need
to panic."

"Right," I said before thinking. "Why should we worry? I
mean, if we don't have a tree on Christmas, it's not like it was a
special day or anything—"

"How would you like your block knocked off?" he yelled. I shut up. He wheeled and set off again.

Clearly Gail's thinking had been right. No one had ever heard of a Christmas Eve without Christmas trees. There was always a glut. Even I knew that. But as we trooped up and down Broad Street with increasing desperation over the next two hours, the awful truth began to dawn: *this* was the year when the merchants had *not* bought too many trees.

We ended up all the way out at Hague Avenue. There was little city left west of Hague, and no stores of significance. It was getting late. The snow swirled more heavily, driven by a rising, icy wind. A lone car, a massive Buick sedan, lumbered out of the snowy night, headlights yellow, and trundled off to the south. I saw a man hurry along the street on the far side, hat pulled down and collar up. I wondered if he, too, was looking for trees.

Gail lit a cigarette. His face looked cold and pinched in the brief flare of the match in his cupped hands. The wind gusted away the first breath of cigarette smoke.

"I don't know what we're going to do," he grated. "I don't know *what* we're going to do."

"We could walk down to Sullivant Avenue," I said, trying to be calm.

"It's miles down there! What's down there anyway? If there's no trees on Broad Street, what makes you think there are going to be any on Sullivant? Sullivant is a crappy street anyway! You're nuts!"

"Okay, then," I said, my teeth chattering. "You suggest something."

He heaved a massive sigh, shuddering. "We just won't have a tree. We'll just go home"—he was trying very hard to be calm —"and we'll say there weren't any trees. We'll just put our presents around the gateleg table with the manger scene on it."

Then, without making any further sound, he started to cry. I saw the big tears streak down his cheeks in the faint illumination from the snowy streetlight.

"Oh, God," I murmured despairingly.

"What? What?"

"Come on. Let's start back. Maybe there's something we missed."

We trudged east. After walking a few frigid blocks we met a young couple walking the other way, the man dragging a small but lovely Christmas tree. For just an instant, seeing the wild look in Gail's eyes, I was afraid he was going to attack them. The couple's laughter drifted back to us after we had passed.

We reached a grocery where trees had been sold in a vacant lot next door. There was a bulkily clad man out in the snowy lot, working with a broom under the illumination of a single bare light bulb. He was sweeping up broken bits and pieces of trees. Gail and I crossed to him.

"Little late," the man said cheerfully. "Sold out!"

"We were here before," Gail told him.

"Oh, so you was! Didn't find anything out farther west, huh?"

"No, sir."

"Well, you know, year after year, the merchants all overbuy. And ever' year we take a beatin'. Looks like this year we got smart, eh?"

Gail started to turn away with murder in his eye. He stepped on, then kicked viciously at, a long broken tree branch in the snow.

Which was when I got my idea.

"Mister," I said, "would you mind if we took a bunch of these leavings?"

"What're you gonna do?" the man asked, grinning. "Build you a tree out of spare parts?" He cackled and spat tobacco juice into the snow.

"That's *exactly* what we're going to do," I snapped.

The man stared. Gail stared.

"You're full of it," Gail said and started away.

"Wait a minute!" I yelled at him. I turned back to the man. "What do you say? Can we have some of these pieces?"

The man's smile faded. He looked crafty. "Twenty cents."

"You crook!" Gail cried.

"Take it or leave it!"

"We'll take it," I said, digging in my pants pocket.

Fuming and muttering that I was insane, Gail nevertheless helped me scour through the mound of rubbish for the best tree pieces. We even found a piece of a trunk with a couple of dead brown branches on it. We loaded our arms and staggered home with our burden.

"We'll go in the back way and in the basement," I said as we neared the house lights.

"If they come down and see this, I'm going to kill myself," Gail said.

"It'll be all right. You'll see."

We struggled around the house. There were lights on in every room downstairs. I got the back door open, propping it with my body for Gail. He started in. The door into the kitchen opened and there stood our mother.

"Finally!" she said cheerfully. "What took you so—? What are you—? Why, Gail Henry Riley, that isn't even a tree! That's just some pieces of a tree! Where's our tree?"

"We're going to fix it," Gail told her, strangled.

We staggered into the basement. By the time we had all our pieces piled on the floor, both Mom and Pop were down there, staring at us. Gail, coming back from the workbench with a tackhammer and jar of small nails, put them on the concrete floor and raised up with fire in his eye.

"Now just wait a minute," he said, his voice shaking. "This is the best we could do. Everybody sold out. Now, I know we're stupid idiots. But we *looked*. This is all we could find. Don't say anything. We're going to fix it."

Mom and Pop looked from him to me to the pile of branches and back again. Mom's mouth quirked. Pop scratched his head. The silence was deathly.

Mom said, "You're going to want some cocoa. You look like you're freezing."

Pop said, "It looks like we need to mix up some glue, too." He shuffled to the workbench.

Gail and I got out of our heavy coats, gloves, and hats. We set to work. I made a base out of some 1 by 3s and we nailed the long dead trunk to it. Trying not to think about how hideous the thing looked, we set about tacking some branches to it. Pop dabbed the ends with fragrant glue, Gail tacked the ends to the trunk, and I cut and tied lengths of black fishing line to the pieces and to the trunk higher up to hold them at the angle of a growing branch. I began to think it might work. Mom came down with hot cocoa that was sweet and delicious.

"Here," Pop told Gail, taking the tackhammer from him a little later. "I think the ends won't split if you nail in at a sharper angle. Let me try." He held a branch and whanged at it with the tackhammer. The tack went in cleanly, not splitting the branch, and the branch stood at a neater angle than any of ours had.

Pop reached for another branch and tacked it. Gail and I watched respectfully.

"It's all in the angle," Pop told us, hammering in another one. "By going in sharper, you don't penetrate the length of wood, and—" He stopped abruptly, taking in an audible breath.

I looked at him more sharply. His face had gone gray and he had that dreaded look in his eyes. He straightened up slowly.

"Pop?" I said.

"I think . . . you've got . . . the idea now," he said in a new tone, his voice tiny and pained. He turned and walked very slowly to the stairs.

"Pop," Gail said, "are you okay?"

"Yeah. Fine." He did not sound or look like it. "Go ahead, there." He started up the steps, taking each one as if it were a mountain.

Gail and I exchanged looks. Going to help him was simply not *done*. Gail grabbed a branch and started tacking it. I reached for the glue pot. Pop went up—we watched him with our peripheral vision, pretending we weren't—and reached the kitchen.

"He had a spell," Gail said softly.

"Yes," I said.

He tacked a branch and I tied. "Ken, you think you ought to go up and make sure he's all right?"

"What do I use as an excuse?"

"You got to pee?"

I nodded, put down the glue, and went upstairs. The kitchen was filled with light and the warm fragrances of the cookies and pies that were everywhere. But the room was deserted. I started across toward the hall door, but then heard Pop's voice, raised sharply, from the dining room. I turned to that door and peered through it cautiously.

Pop sat at the big dining room table, a glass of water and one of his pill jars in front of him. Mom stood beside him, wiping at his forehead with a damp cloth. Gramaw Prater stood beyond them, her hands clasped in the folds of her cooking apron and her face clouded with grief and dismay.

"No, I'm not!" Pop said sharply. "I'm not worth a damn—not a *damn!*"

"You just got a little out of breath—" Mom began.

He pushed her hand away. "What kind of a man am I when I can't drive a few *tacks* without having a spell? How much of a man am I when I can't hold a job, when I have to watch my fourteen-year-old son do my work for me?"

"You're getting better," Mom said huskily.

"I'm *not*. I'm never going to get any better. I'm going to die. And you'd all be better off if I'd just go ahead and *do* it instead of lingering, a cripple that's not worth—"

"Be quiet!" Mom cried, and hugged his head roughly against her body.

But he freed himself with a terrible convulsive effort, and now it was he who was weeping. "What good am I? How can any of you love me when I'm like this? I'm a drone—a parasite, living off my women, my kids—"

"Hush! You know none of this is true—"

"Oh, I try to keep a stiff upper lip," he said, his voice trembling. "I don't want to quit. I hate a quitter. But what am I, now, really? My boys have to go out on Christmas eve and buy pieces of a tree to try to make something out of them. Five years ago I was bringing home thirty-five dollars a week. We were going to have everything. Now—" He stopped, looked down at his own body, and shuddered. "God, I wish I would die! *God,* I wish I would die!"

"How is he?" Gail asked when I went back to the basement moments later.

"Fine," I lied. "He's doing better."

And indeed when we took our remnant tree up the stairs a half-hour later, he was back in the kitchen, sipping coffee, his color better, and grinning crookedly at us as if none of what I had secretly witnessed had taken place. The tree looked amazingly good if you did not examine it too closely, and our decorations further masked its defects. In the morning when we came back downstairs before dawn, Mary leading the way in her nightgown, the sheet was tacked over the door to the living room by Santa as it always was, with the glorious colored lights of Christmas shining through, and when Pop removed the tacks from the door frame and let the sheet fall, and we walked into our Christmas, we all agreed we had never had a more beautiful tree.

It was in February of 1931 that my father took me aside to talk about Frank, and my pride brought us new trouble as a consequence.

"You ought to take him hunting," Pop said. "He's moping around about it. A boy needs to get out."

"I've got work to do," I protested. "If he wants to go out hunting so bad, let him take himself."

Pop shook his head slowly and put a hand on my shoulder.

"Look. He needs to go. It's important to him. You'd enjoy it yourself. *I* can't go with him."

"He doesn't even have a gun."

"Let him use that blunderbuss of yours."

"Then what would *I* use?"

"You can use my gun."

"I couldn't use your gun!"

"Don't be silly. Of course you can. Now, look. You don't have a job Saturday. It looks like the weather will be decent. Take Frank and go. You can walk out south, that McBrayer farm where we had good luck a couple of times."

"The Rayburns are going Saturday," I said, dubious.

"Then you can go with them. They'll enjoy hunting with Max." Pop reached down and petted our dog's head, and Max's stubby tail thumped gladly on the floor. "You need a workout, don't you, Max?"

I hesitated. The truth was that I desperately wanted to get out and have some fun. "I guess we could sure use the meat."

"You bet your boots we could. So go!"

That Saturday the dawn came through broken clouds, and the temperature was above freezing, the ground flecked with old snow. Frank and I, with our guns and Max yelping along beside us, went to the Rayburn house. Mr. Rayburn was ready, bulky in his hunting jacket and pants, and his two younger boys, Jack and Hugh, were pacing the yard in their eagerness to be gone. We piled into their Nash and headed south.

"It ought to be a fine day for it, boys!" Mr. Rayburn told us. "Now—no carrying a gun with the hammers back. You keep that muzzle up to the sky or down at the ground unless you're wanting to fire. You make damned sure you know what you're shooting at, and where everybody else is. You come to a fence, you make sure the gun is put through first, muzzle first, and laid down where you can't do some fool thing and accidentally shoot yourself. We walk in a straight line—nobody gets ahead—and we'll just let old Max here do the hard work. Right?"

Max had seen the guns and probably smelled the scent of game on our hunting clothing. He was beside himself with excitement. As if to answer Mr. Rayburn, he lollygagged all over him, licking his face.

We found a farm where the owners cheerfully said we could hunt, parked our car well off their driveway, and got out and removed our guns from the trunk.

"Now, just remember," I told Frank quietly, handing him the big ten-gauge. *"Watch* it. This is no slingshot."

"I'm no kid anymore, Kenny," Frank growled, punching a big red shell into the chamber and snapping the gun closed.

I loaded two green shells, number six shot, into the chambers of my father's beautiful old weapon. I was aware of my responsibilities to it. I had to be very careful not to scratch the stock or damage it in even the slightest way. I had to shoot well. I was not at all sure this gun had ever missed in my father's hands, and it would seem sacrilege to go out there and blow holes in the air my first time out.

"Everybody ready?" Mr. Rayburn asked. Max was already through the fence and into the stubble cornfield, racing back and forth like a maniac.

"Let's go!" I said.

We went into the stubble field, working in a line abreast. Max, his tongue already hanging, looped back toward us and began zigzagging just ahead.

"He got one!" Frank yelled almost immediately. He was on my right and I saw him raise my old gun and blast away. "I got him! I got him!" He ran forward and came back, grinning from ear to ear, with a bloody rabbit in his grasp.

"Good shooting!" Mr. Rayburn said. "Looks like we're going to have a good day!"

Frank put his rabbit into the back of my hunting coat, since he didn't have one yet, and we proceeded. Jack Rayburn kicked out a rabbit and he and his brother both shot it. Then Max chased one across Mr. Rayburn and he missed it. The rabbit scampered briefly past my line of vision, out ahead in the stubble at about thirty yards. I threw down and blasted with one barrel, then the other. Missed both.

"Hard shot," Mr. Rayburn said as I reloaded, chagrined. "We'll get him."

In the next hour Frank got his second rabbit, Mr. Rayburn got one, and I missed another. I was getting upset. We finished working the stubble and moved into an adjacent woods. Frank jumped and shot another one.

"Good shooting," I said grimly as he loaded the latest into my heavy coat.

He grinned. "Is skunk in season?"

"Why?" I blurted.

"Well, I wouldn't want you to get arrested, Kenny. That's what you seem to be getting. Skunked."

"Very funny!"

I was seething by now. We moved into some heavy briars with Max out ahead of us some place. He got one out for Jack, who missed it. I plunged into the briars without regard for what the thorns were doing to my hide. I was going to show somebody something. I was not going to keep on disgracing Pop's gun.

A few minutes later something darted through the tangled briars just ahead of me—a flash of tan.

"There goes one!" I yelled, and brought the gun up level, blasting at the blurry movement.

Instantly Max began yelping and screaming in agony. He was down. Just ahead of us somewhere. I could see the dead leaves flying as he thrashed around in the briars. Gorge came up acid in my throat. I had shot our dog.

We all ran. Max was quiet by the time we reached him, lying on his side, eyes wild with pain, tongue lolling. His hind quarters were a glistening mass of blood.

I fell beside him. "Oh, Max! Oh, my God! I'm sorry! I didn't *look!*"

"Be careful!" Mr. Rayburn said sharply, kneeling beside me. "A hurt dog might attack."

"Not Max. He would never hurt me. But look what *I* did to him. How bad is it? Where is he hit?"

Mr. Rayburn gently examined Max while I held the dog's head, stroking him, my tears dropping on his face. "You really blasted him, Ken, I'm sorry to say. Left rear." Mr. Rayburn looked up at me, his face terrible. "I don't see that we have but one choice."

"What?"

"Put him out of his misery."

"*No!*"

"Look at this leg. That's muscle and bone sticking out, there. He's losing blood fast."

"We have to get him to a doctor!"

"A vet? What chance—"

"Ohio State!" I said, getting an inspiration. "I read in the paper—they work on small animals free sometimes, to give their students practice! We can take him up there!"

"He would never make it."

"Can't we try? How can we not try? Don't you see? If he dies, *I did it!*"

Mr. Rayburn looked at me. He bent over Max another few seconds. His jaw set and he heaved a great sigh. Then he stood and peeled off his heavy hunting coat. "Help me move poor Max into this. We'll wrap him up and carry him in it like a sling."

We carried Max back through the cornfield to the car and loaded up swiftly. I held him on my lap, only his head sticking out of the folds of the coat. He whined and struggled weakly. I held him tight and stroked his head, muttering meaningless endearments. The other boys were silent, stricken. Mr. Rayburn drove us straight to his house, where he told Frank to go home and report what had happened and where we were going. He told Jack and Hugh to go into their house and make telephone calls to Ohio State, trying to let anyone know who happened to be around the college of veterinary medicine that we were on the way with an emergency.

"Do you know where to go?" I asked as we drove away again.

"Oh, I know," Mr. Rayburn said. "It's on Neil Avenue. I just hope we've got a live patient for them by the time we get there."

"We've got to," I said. "I had to show off. I didn't even know what I was aiming at!"

"Well, now," Mr. Rayburn said softly, driving fast, "there's no use crying over spilt milk."

That was easy enough for him to say, I thought, looking down at Max's suffering expression. He wasn't an assassin . . . an idiot.

There was not much traffic. About forty minutes later we pulled up in front of a massive gray brick building on the south edge of the Ohio State campus. As we pulled into the driveway, a steel door opened in front of us and two students who didn't look much older than I and a gray-haired man who might be a professor hurried out to greet us.

One of the students climbed into the back with me. "This the shooting victim?" He unwrapped the coat. "Let's just have a look. Oh. Wow."

"You've got to save him," I pleaded.

"Jerry, give me a hand here. Let's carry this little guy inside where we can have a better look."

I let them take Max, using Mr. Rayburn's coat as a litter. The professor said a few words to Mr. Rayburn and hurried in after them. I climbed out of the car. There were bright drops of Max's blood forming a trail on the concrete. We followed it inside.

There was a cavernous brown waiting room, closed glass doors beyond. Mr. Rayburn sat down and started fiddling with his pipe. I paced the floor, berating myself. Five minutes passed, then ten, then a lot more.

"What's *taking* them so long?"

"They're thorough," Mr. Rayburn told me. He gave me a look. "Be glad they didn't come back out in a hurry."

Oh, God, I thought, *let Max be all right. Just let him be all right. I'll never cuss or smoke again and I'll say a novena every month. Just don't let him die because I'm such a fool.*

An eternity later the glass door opened. The man I knew was

a professor came out, looking grave. He faced Mr. Rayburn. "Are you the owner of the dog, sir?"

"This boy is."

"I see." The professor turned to me. "All right. Your dog has a chance."

"Thank you! Thank you! I knew—"

"Just a minute, son. Listen first. Now. His left hind leg is torn up beyond repair. The pellets destroyed everything in the upper area. We have him asleep on the table right now. We *think* we might be able to save his life . . . by amputation."

My breath caught. "You mean—*cut off his leg?*"

"It's the only chance. Then we guarantee nothing. Still, it's an interesting case. We're willing to give it a try."

"But how can he run or hunt or do *anything* without a leg?"

The ghost of a smile touched the professor's lips. "Oh, you might be surprised. I don't say he'll ever be as good as new, but if we can pull him through, he might get around a lot better than you would expect for a good long time."

I stared at him. I was crying again, and mortified that I would cry at my age. But I had caused all this.

"Do you want us to try it?" the professor asked me gently. "Or we can simply put him to sleep—"

"Try it."

"Now you have to understand. We might lose him anyway. There's a long-term danger of infection, a long convalescence at best. We'll want to keep him here at least two months, even if all goes well. Do you agree to all that?"

"How much will it all cost?"

"Oh, there's no charge except for his food. A few dollars, total. It's an interesting case. We ought to learn from it." The professor fixed me with his eyes again. "What do you say?"

I did not hesitate. "Do it."

He nodded. "You might as well go home. Do you have a telephone where we could report to you this evening?"

"I do," Mr. Rayburn said.

The professor took out a pencil.

"Can't we stay?" I pleaded.

"It will be hours before we know a thing."

"We'll go home," Mr. Rayburn said in a tone that brooked no opposition.

So we left Max and drove back to the Hilltop. My family was amazingly sympathetic in view of the fact that my stupidity had caused it all. Even Frank did not berate me. We cleaned the rabbits—his—and the guns, and went to supper. The only thing that was said directly came after the meal, when I was leaving the table.

Pop put his arm over my shoulder and squeezed lightly. "So, we all make mistakes," he said.

Later Mr. Rayburn walked over. Ohio State had called. Max had made it through the surgery, his left rear leg was gone, he was sleeping. As long as we heard nothing, we were to know that everything was all right. Visiting Max before a month was out of the question. We were to let them handle it.

It occurred to me to protest, but I had done enough for one day. I kept quiet.

For the next two or three weeks Max and his welfare were uppermost in my mind. At school the nuns were beginning to impress upon us how much improved our chances of getting to heaven would be if we attended a Catholic high school. We were also being indoctrinated in the finer points of sin. One day in particular stands out. Sister explained that taking one's own life was a mortal sin, but perhaps not quite always. Pressed by a girl named Carolyn Wareing to give an example, sister suggested that a woman being attacked by a rapist might be justified in killing herself to thwart the attack. There was always a danger, sister said, that the woman might, in the course of being raped, suddenly start enjoying it, and thus commit a sin worse than suicide. We all had to be constantly aware of the terrible dangers of impurity, sister said. Many of us boys in the classroom, for whom impure thoughts were beginning to become a daytime obsession and a nighttime torture, cringed and examined our bitten fingernails. Every Saturday night I trooped to confession, examined my conscience, stood in line, blurted out my three of this and two of that when the door slid back in the confessional, said the act of contrition, and went back out to my pew, sweat cold on my forehad, to say three Our Fathers and three Hail Marys. Most weeks I was in a state of grace for about fourteen hours, maximum, before sinning again. My chances of avoiding hell seemed remote.

Worrying about hell, however, was a problem relegated to the backwaters of my mind. On a more conscious level I worried about the radiator business and my future, if any, in school. My grades were about average, and except for literature and geography I had no consuming interest in classroom matters. But I very much looked forward to attending public high school. It would be a great new adventure. There would be hundreds in my class there, I was assured, and if half of what the Rayburn boys told me was true, a large percentage of that number would be glorious, beautiful girls with absolutely no sense of morality.

The radiator business, meanwhile, had slumped badly. There were many days when we had no customers at all, not even for help in fixing a flat. On those days I cleaned the tools and rearranged things in the basement and pretended we could use the slack time. Some days Pop pretended with me and was cheerful, telling me old stories or talking about the upturn that was clearly just around the corner. On other days his health was not as good, or his bitterness could not be controlled, and he sat on the front-porch glider, a pipe for which he had no tobacco clamped between his teeth, his eyes like old lead. If his heart was not killing him, then his inactivity—his loss of pride—was. I knew this, tried to ignore it, and never quite succeeded.

It was a terrible time in our neighborhood, in Columbus, in our country. At least once a week some hobo—sometimes a young man but more often a middle-aged one with eyes full of pain—came to our back door asking if we had any work. Whether my father or mother met the visitor, the reception was the same. We had no work, but the man was always invited in. Sometimes we could offer a dish of cornmeal mush and a cup of coffee. Sometimes it was bread and milk. Once I remember we had virtually nothing, and mother gave the man catsup and bread. He dumped the catsup on the bread and ate it ravenously. She gave him a little blob of our pear butter on the dish for desert, and he thanked us as if we had given him the world.

Fully a third of the men on our street were by now out of work or working only part-time. Conditions even hit the Rayburn house, and their car was sold for a fourth of what they had paid for it a year or two earlier. I watched Mr. Rayburn walk up the street each morning with his lunch pail, heading for the Union Fork & Hoe, where he now stood in line to see if there would be work that day, loading tools onto railroad cars. Some days when I was home I saw him return before noon, still carrying his lunch, his face and clothes clean. I asked Hugh Rayburn what his father did on those days when there had been no work. Hugh said he ate his lunch on the kitchen table "and sometimes he cries, but we act like we don't see it." For Sale signs speckled the street, foreclosures on loans. We did not buy a late load of coal as we always had in the past but ran the little grate in the fake fireplace. The weather turned bitter cold late in February and early in March, and in the mornings there was sheet ice on all the windows so that we could not see out. On those mornings, when I picked my toothbrush up in the bathroom, it was filled with little extra bristles of ice.

We no longer took the paper, but the radio said everyone agreed business had to take an upturn soon. I listened to political speeches on the radio and heard a new voice, a man who, it was said, was running for President. His voice sounded strong and confident, and it thrilled me. His name was Roosevelt.

Sometimes at the end of the week if business had been good, my mother counted the pennies in the kitchen cabinet jar. If we had enough, she went to the confectionery two blocks away on Broad Street and bought a Royal Crown Cola and five cents' worth of peanuts. Then she brought them home and divided the cola equally between herself, Gramaw Prater, Frank, Mary and

me, pouring it into cheese or jelly glasses. Then we sat at the
kitchen table and ate peanuts, one at a time, and sipped our
drinks. Pop never took any. He always said he didn't want it.

People today who did not live through those years have little
idea of how it was then. We knew that absolutely no one could
or would help us. Everyone else was in the same boat, at least
everyone we knew. We were broke, our friends were broke, the
government was broke, the nation was broke. If we came to a day
when we could not earn anything and had nothing left in the
pantry, then that would be the day we started starving. Something had gone terribly and fundamentally wrong somewhere,
but no one seemed to know what it was. More than half the stores
and businesses on Broad Street were boarded up now. Everyone
seemed to be getting the flu. Sometimes the day-old bread we
bought already had green moldy areas on the edges, which we
cut off before eating the rest. On the way to school most mornings I saw long lines of grayish men standing at the soup kitchen
run by the Lutheran Church. If rumor said some store or business
had a job opening, that line often was longer.

And yet, except for outbursts occasionally from Gail, there
was little outward sign of anger. The people waited patiently in
the lines, told each other things had to start looking up, sold off
their possessions if they could to help make ends meet, lost their
homes, sometimes died. Today there would be riots everywhere
because people would think that someone, somewhere, owed
them more. In those days it was quite the opposite. If you were
still alive and had your health, then you crossed yourself in
thanksgiving. And waited in line for whatever was to come next.

Early in March Uncle Jack was away for several days running. No one said anything about it in my presence. Then on
Sunday he and Aunt Sal and their girls came for dinner. There
were happy greetings at the door, but Aunt Sal was frightfully
pale and Uncle Jack seemed to have aged overnight, his complex-
ion pasty and carved with new lines of fatigue. Pop shook hands
with him in a quick, fervent way that was new. The girls ran
upstairs to play with Mary, and the rest of us—my mother and

father, Uncle Jack and Aunt Sal, Gail and me—sat in the parlor.
Gramaw had bustled back to the kitchen, and Frank was out
there helping her in hopes of getting some leftover dough with
cinnamon and sugar on it.

Uncle Jack, sitting in one of the big chairs, slapped his knee
and took a deep breath. "Well." Grimly.

"How did it go?" Pop asked.

"It went."

No one said anything.

"So now," Uncle Jack said after a long silence, "I'm officially
a failure."

"Jack . . ." Aunt Sal murmured, reaching across to squeeze
his hand.

He gave a ghastly imitation of his old grin. "Nothing to it,
really. You go into court with your lawyer and there's a lot of
mumbo jumbo, and all the people you owe money to are there,
and you admit you're a pauper and the judge signs a couple of
papers and whangs his gavel and that's it, you're officially bank-
rupt."

"Oh, Jack," my mother breathed.

"Not so bad, really," he said in that same brittle tone. "You
don't have to say much. It's all written out for you in the forms.
Everybody is doing it. They run you through pretty fast. I was in
between a crippled paperhanger from Kirkersville and this ratty-
looking crook from the east side that looked like he had never
done an honest day's work in his life."

"Now, you cut that out!" Pop said. "You couldn't help what
happened to your business. It's the Depression, it's doing it to a
lot of good people—"

"No, I had to be a big shot," Uncle Jack said. "I thought I was
so much smarter than everyone else. You told me, Joe. 'Don't
expand too fast,' you said. Sal was cautious, too. But I thought the
world was my oyster. I knew more than *everybody*. I had to build
that new building on short-term credit, take on more men, buy
more trucks. I was going to be a millionaire. *God!*" He looked at
the ceiling.

"It's not like you did anything wrong," Pop told him.

"I wasn't smart enough to read the signs. I just thought I was smart. And now I don't have anything. The company is gone. My men are out of work and I didn't even finish paying them off. Some of my creditors are even going to get our house. Even the *house*. And all because I thought I had to be big, keep expanding like I was a Rockefeller, drive a big, fancy car and impress people—"

"Jack, it wasn't your *fault*," Pop insisted. "There are people all over the country in the same shape! It's not the end of the world, man! You can start again—build again—"

"How can I?" Uncle Jack flared. "I've been through bankruptcy now. *Bankruptcy*. That disgrace will be on my name as long as I live. I'll never live it down. I've failed, my stupidity has cheated people out of what I owed them—honest debts I should have been man enough to pay—and now they're even taking the house. Sal and the kids will have to move into some duplex someplace, some cheap, trashy place with cheap, trashy people all around us, and it *is* my fault!"

Pop stared at him and then stood, hands on his hips. "So what are you going to do about it?" he demanded. "Cry over spilt milk?"

Uncle Jack looked up at him and *did* start to cry—without sound, the big tears coursing down his cheeks.

"Oh, hell," Pop muttered, and knelt and hugged him.

I sat transfixed, seeing the looks of shock and dismay on the faces of the women and on my own brother Gail. Uncle Jack made a few choking sounds, his shoulders quaking. Pop held him in a bear hug, kneeling.

"I don't know what I'm going to do," Uncle Jack said, muffled. "I don't think I can go on."

"Of course you can go on!" Pop told him gruffly. "That's what a man does, right? Everything is going to be fine. It's always darkest before the dawn. You've got to remember that."

"There's nothing left. Only the disgrace. I've shamed all of you." Without work, what good is a man?"

"The only thing that can finish a man is death," Pop said. "And you're not dead yet." He paused and blinked furiously, this man I so loved, himself on the verge of tears. So his voice toughened. "Just stop feeling so sorry for yourself. Every cloud has a silver lining. You fall down, you pick yourself up again!"

Uncle Jack slowly, in the agonizing silence that followed, tried to get himself together. After a while he blew his nose, a great, honking sound that for some reason made Aunt Sal laugh. Then we all laughed, but I didn't know why.

Pop got up stiffly and went back to his chair. He sat down and tapped a Chesterfield and lit it. "We're having dumplings for supper," he said through the smoke. "That sounds just right for a cold, blustery day like this, don't you think? Chicken and dumplings, and hot apple pie and coffee! Just what the doctor ordered for my diet!"

Uncle Jack wiped his tears on the sleeve of his sweater. He tried to smile. "You don't know what it's like, Joe, this disgrace. You don't know how it makes a man feel."

"Well," Pop said softly, "there's nothing either you or I can do about it anyway. So let's talk about something else."

Uncle Jack turned to me. "What do you hear about old Max?"

"He's doing fine," I replied. "I called Ohio State and they said he can come home, but not for another few weeks."

"Well, that's fine," Jack said, staring into some inner space. "That's just fine."

Gramaw and Frank came in.

"What's going on in here?" Gramaw asked brightly.

"We were just talking about those dumplings," Pop told her.

She sat down, her apron still on. "I'm afraid they're not going to be quite up to snuff. The dough didn't act quite right."

"Oh, sure," Pop grinned. "They're never quite up to your standard. How many times have we heard *that* one before?"

So it was all right. We sat there with smiles on our faces, talking nonsense. After a little while I had almost forgotten the things Uncle Jack had said, or the terrible intensity with which he had said them. Because on the surface we became normal again, I imagined things were again normal, as if by magic. I tried not to notice the haunted, haggard look of Uncle Jack. Things would be all right, I told myself, and tried to concentrate on outward appearances. Such is our boundless capacity for self-deception and wishful thinking.

In the next week or two Uncle Jack did not come around. They were preparing to move from their fine new house. My mother went there one morning and helped them pack some things, and came back to report that Uncle Jack had seemed even more depressed.

"It isn't like him," she told my father at the supper table.

"He'll pull out of it," Pop said.

"Don't you feel sorry for him?"

"Yes," Pop said, anger flaring in his eyes. "But what can I do? Go hold his hand? He's just got to be a man, that's all!"

On March 20 we received a registered letter. While the grown-ups were conferring in the kitchen, I managed to read it. Our mortgage company, Central Federal, had folded. This new company, Allied National, was liquidating old assets to pay creditors. Everyone who owed money to Central Federal would be contacted within ninety days.

"It *can't* mean they'll try to foreclose our mortgage," my mother said. "We've never been so much as a day late with a payment."

"What good would it do them to try to take our house anyway?" Pop asked. "The banks and mortgage companies don't want all the houses."

"Of course they do," Gail put in.

"Be serious," Pop said.

"I *am* serious. They *do* want all the houses. Then they can resell them and make a lot of money a second time. Boom and bust. The rich create a boom, get people to buy everything on credit, skim off the interest, then create a bust so they can take everything back and sell it all over again to a new bunch of suckers."

"People aren't like that," Pop said.

"Aren't they?" Gail demanded, angry.

"Of course not. And besides, even if they tried that sort of scheme, who would they resell things to? Everybody is as broke as we are, or worse."

"They'll figure something out," Gail told him.

"What?"

"If I was smart enough to figure that out, maybe I'd be rich, too!"

"Well, I'm not going to worry about it," Pop said. "I figure what they'll do is write us another letter in a week or two and give us some new address to mail our monthly payment to. And that will be that. I'm not going to worry about it," he repeated. And looked worried.

It may have been a coincidence, but we started our spring housecleaning a day later. Whenever she felt insecure, my mother cleaned a closet or washed the windows. I have been sent out to wash the windows on days when the water froze on the glass before I could dry it. The magnitude of the cleaning job seemed to be in direct proportion to how nervous my mother was. There was no response more massive than spring house-cleaning.

In those days the project meant practically taking the house apart board by board. The beds were stripped and everything laundered and aired. The rugs came up, the curtains came down, the floors were scrubbed and waxed, the pantry emptied and washed, the furniture vacuumed, the cupboards emptied and washed and new shelf paper installed, the closets emptied, the cedar chest gone through, the entire basement cleared and scrubbed and the walls whitewashed again, the structure from top to bottom saturated in the odors of soap, wax, and mothballs.

One of the last jobs was cleaning the wallpaper.

The coal furnace deposited a coating of oily grime on all the paper during the winter, and the solution was to purchase—even in our dire straits—many cans of green, putty like stuff that one formed into a ball and rubbed over the paper. The waxy material absorbed the black oil off the paper as it was rubbed along, shredding little greenish-black crumbs onto the floor. When the ball of wallpaper cleaner was so black and sticky you couldn't handle it anymore, you discarded it and started with a new piece.

Pop insisted on doing the ceilings himself, although it was the hardest work because you had to stand on the ladder with your neck craned back painfully as you worked over your head. He was on the ladder in the living room and Frank, Gail, and I were working on the walls that Saturday evening when someone drove up in front and there was a loud pounding on the door.

Gail, being nearest the door, went to open it. As he neared the door, it opened of its own accord and we were surprised to see Uncle Jim, his face shockingly white against the turned-up black collar of his coat, come in. There was a man with him that none of us knew.

"Jim!" Pop came stiffly down off the ladder. "What is it?"

Uncle Jim started to cry. "It's Jack. He's killed himself."

He had tried to be neat about it, make as little mess as possible; he had taken his twelve-gauge shotgun out into the backyard; there, sitting against a tree, he had tied a string to the trigger and his shoestring, cocked the hammer, reversed the weapon to put the muzzle in his mouth. . . . After the police and everyone had left and the body was taken away, Pop and Uncle Jim had gone into the yard and hosed things down, and when we were allowed to go out, there was only a dark stain on the tree trunk which might have been caused by anything.

"He didn't want to mess up the house," Pop said, standing there staring at the tree. Then he burst into tears again, awful sobs that shook him from head to foot. Gail and I tried to console him. Uncle Jim held him in his arms, crying also but not with the same bitterness.

"I let him down," Pop choked.

"No, no. You didn't."

"I didn't know he felt *that* bad. When he was at the house on Sunday and he said he didn't know if he could go on, I didn't *understand.* I told him to be a man. I had to talk tough. Then I didn't go see them. I thought he would be okay, he just had to be tough. *Tough!* He was getting ready to kill himself and I never lifted a finger!"

"You didn't know," Uncle Jim said. "How could anybody know?"

"*I* should have known. Ever since I got sick, he was at the house all the time. Doing for me. Supporting me. Then when *he* needed support, where was I?"

We had rushed across the city in a car driven by Uncle Jim's friend. There was an ambulance in front of the house, and some attendants were just carrying a metal stretcher around from the back, the form on it shrouded in a gray blanket. The police were there. Neighbors had taken the two girls somewhere. Aunt Sal was in the living room with Gramaw Riley and they were both in a bad way, despite the clumsy efforts of some neighbor women. Gramaw Prater had not come but had stayed home with Mary and Frank. But Gail and I were there, standing around. Pop and Uncle Jim conferred with the police.

"What did he *kill* himself for?" Gail asked me huskily, dazed.

"I don't know. They were broke—he took bankruptcy—"

"That's no reason to kill yourself!"

"He was ashamed. He didn't have any work—"

"That's no reason, either! *God!*"

Pop finished talking to the police, and they left. He came over to Gail and me, dazed, and hugged first Gail, then me.

The rest of that night is a blur. Neighbors and friends came and went. Someone made coffee. Men stood around smoking cigarettes. At some point very late someone handed me a cup of tea that had a funny odor of medicine. I drank it down and promptly fell asleep.

By morning everyone was there: Gramaw Prater and Frank and Mary; Uncle Jim and Aunt Gertrude, of course, and their kids; my mother and father and Gail and me and Gramaw Riley and Aunt Sal; and the two girls were back from the neighbors' house; and some cousins we hadn't seen for a long time; and then by afternoon Uncle Bob and Aunt Helen, in from Detroit on the train. Neighbors brought dishes of food, and sometime during that period the man came from the funeral home. For some reason I was ordered to go upstairs with him and Aunt Sal and Uncle Jim. To my horror, I realized they were picking out the burial clothing.

Aunt Sal, eyes swollen and red but under shaky control, pushed hangers of clothing around in Uncle Jack's little closet. She pulled out a dark suit, blue serge, with pale dust on the shoulders. "Isn't this the one you liked?" she asked, looking at me.

"*Me?*" I gasped.

"It's old, but he told me once, that you said you liked it. You have to help me pick one, Kenny. We can't let your father . . . the strain on his heart . . ." She brushed furiously at the dust on the shoulders. "Well?"

"It's real nice," I managed.

Handing the suit to the funeral director, she started whisking hangers of shirts this way and that with a terrible concentration. "You were always his favorite, Kenny. He talked about you all the time. He said you were really going to make something of yourself. That's why I want you to help."

I didn't reply. I had had no idea. *He never told me,* I wanted to say. I wished I had time to go talk to Tom Rayburn about this.

"This one," Aunt Sal said, taking down a white shirt that looked just like three or four others. She held it up in front of me. "Yes?"

"Yes," I managed, nodding.

She took down a blue tie and again I gave mumbled approval. Then she went to a chest of drawers and got out underwear . . . socks. The funeral director took them and stood waiting. We all looked at him. *Go!* I thought. *Get out! Leave with your pile of clothes because this is all crazy—*

"Now, about shoes," he said.

"Shoes," Aunt Sal repeated blankly.

"Of course, shoes aren't really necessary. With a closed casket—"

"No," Aunt Sal said sharply. "We can't—he's got to have shoes." She went to the closet and knelt, pushing things around. She came out with Uncle Jack's dress shoes, black. They too were dusty and a little scuffed. She looked at them, big and heavy, and the tears started to roll. Almost angrily she rummaged around and pulled out a little cardboard box and opened it on the floor. In it were Uncle Jack's cans of Shinola and a brush and some polish-stained rags. Opening a can, she dabbed polish on a rag and started rubbing it onto one of the shoes.

"Sal," Uncle Jim said, "I'll do that."

She pulled away from him. "No! *I'll* do it. I want to do it!" So we stood there and watched her cry and polish the shoes, her tears splashing on the hard waxed surface as she buffed them.

A few hours later we walked to the funeral home. There was a wake going on in the large front room to the right, people everywhere in their most uncomfortable clothes and syrupy organ music filtering through the flowers. The funeral director's son, a skinny boy, led us back a corridor to a much smaller rear room. There was subdued light and a spray of flowers beside a wood casket with the lid down. Clutching Frank's and Mary's hands, I went in after most of the adults. Everyone was crying. I stared at the closed box. He was in there, I thought, in that serge suit with the dusty shoulders. I thought about how close and airless and black it must be in there, and claustrophobia stabbed at my lungs.

My sense of loss was acute. I had been his favorite. But I had never known it. It was so like our family for something to be like that. I wondered if any of us ever said what was really on our mind about things we felt. I had loved him, too, a lot. Had I ever, *ever* told him?

And yet my own grief seemed remote, dammed up in some distant cavity of my being. What really made things unbearable was seeing all the adults weeping. Seeing the women was bad enough, but watching my father and Uncle Jim was infinitely worse. They were trying *not* to cry, of course. Men didn't do things like that.

In a little while the women left to go back to the house. Some of the men were supposed to stay. I found myself outside on the sidewalk, watching the sparse High Street traffic go by, while Pop and Uncle Jim smoked. It was late in the day, and a cold wind was blowing.

"Well," Pop said after a while with a tone of resignation. He looked at the traffic and then at me. "Well, son," he said.

"It's not right," I said.

He took a deep breath. His heart was bothering him; he had that gray look of pain. "What we've got to try to remember is that it's like the poem says. God took him because he was such a good man; God wanted him sooner because he was so good."

I said nothing. It rang completely false to me.

Uncle Jim added, "And he's in heaven. Right now. His worries are all over."

I looked at the two men. Did they really believe this? There was no way to tell. But, God help me, even at fifteen I *knew* what they were saying was absolute nonsense. God had not taken Uncle Jack. Uncle Jack, in total despair, had blown his own brains out. And now was I supposed to believe he was walking in some green field somewhere with a good bird dog beside him?

I desperately wanted to believe it. But all I knew was that someone I had loved was now a cold, mutilated corpse, wearing an old blue serge suit with dust on the shoulders, shut in a wood box, probably dusted with pink talcum powder, dead. Finished. Meaningless. You thought with your brain. Your self-awareness stemmed from your brain. Uncle Jack's brains had been blasted all over a tree. How could there be messages without a switchboard? Was I supposed to believe some silvery, invisible little *thing* wafted off into the clouds somewhere when all the rest of a person died? And was I supposed to believe in God when He let things like this happen? You had to have an infinite capacity for self-deception to believe in God under these circumstances. If such a One existed, He had to be a maniac. Better to have none at all.

But even as I thought all this, another part of me said, *This is sinful; you're going to have to confess these thoughts.* So there was only confusion.

Back at the house as night came on, the parish priest arrived. He was a nice man, about fifty, with a round face and bald head. He shook everyone's hand and then took us all into the living room. He gave Aunt Sal a scapular and produced a prayer book and read a scriptural passage about the lamb lying down with the lion. The book closed with a snap.

"Let us pray," he said, and the chandelier light gleamed on his bald head as he bowed. "Our Father, Who art in heaven, hallowed be Thy name, Thy kingdom come, Thy will be done on earth as it is in heaven."

We all chimed in, "Give us this day our daily bread and forgive us our trespasses as we forgive those who trespass against us, and lead us not into temptation but deliver us from evil, Amen."

He: "Hail Mary, full of grace, the Lord is with thee; blessed art thou amongst women and blessed is the fruit of thy womb, Jesus."

We: "Holy Mary, mother of God, pray for us sinners now and at the hour of our death, Amen."

"Eternal rest grant unto him, Oh Lord."

"And let perpetual light shine upon him."

"In the name of the Father, and of the Son, and of the Holy Ghost."

We all made the sign of the cross. "Amen."

The priest sighed and looked up at Aunt Sal. "I'm sure, Mrs. Riley, you know that everyone in the parish family shares your grief and offers sincerest condolences."

Aunt Sal dabbed at her eyes and nodded.

"Now. You understand that under the, ah, circumstances a

requiem mass in the church is out of the question. We have discussed that. But I will say a few prayers at the funeral home and will accompany the body to the cemetery. Your plot is selected?"

"Yes," Aunt Sal said. "It's . . . right beside the Catholic section."

The priest nodded. "Good." He patted her hand. "I hope you understand, Mrs. Riley, that burial in consecrated ground, like a mass, is impossible. Church law is clear. But you must hold to your faith. It's quite possible that, at the last instant, he changed his mind about taking his own life. He could have repented. God is merciful. I will remember your husband at private mass. The Rosary Altar Society plans a rosary this evening. Hold to your faith. At times like this, Jesus and the Blessed Mother are with us."

Aunt Sal nodded, crying without sound, her head down.

He looked around at all of us standing in the room. "Are there any questions?"

No one spoke. I wanted to cry out, *Yes, I have questions!* But I did not speak.

I remember little of the service either at the funeral home or at the cemetery. The funeral home was overheated, filled with the cloying scent of flowers. At the cemetery it was cold and windy, flapping the green canvas tent flaps. Later, back at Aunt Sal's house, there were mountains of food brought in and I ate ravenously, lacerated by guilt that I could be hungry at a time like this. Then someone drove us across town to our own home and it was supposed to be over. But it wasn't because the furnace had gone out and the house was frigid and everyone walked around in silence, and when my mother or Gramaw talked about something, their voices sounded loud and abnormal, echoing. Pop sat in a chair in the living room, ladders and dropcloths and the wreckage of our spring cleaning all around, and stared into space. I had never seen him like this. He was crushed.

Uncle Jack's death, combined with my father's continuing weakness, had worked changes in our lives that might, I feared, be permanent. Pop had changed, was still changing, and there was no predicting where we might end up. Did he still blame himself for Uncle Jack's despair and suicide? It seemed so. There were days when he said fewer than a dozen words, sitting on the porch and staring. At other times he seemed to try to rally, but his smile was faint and the good nature forced. A few times his bitterness had spilled out in anger, twice at me when I said or did something stupid. I no longer knew him. It was as if he had rejected me and everything else in life and now concentrated only on whatever thoughts filled his mind.

We all crept around the house. It was too quiet. At night I was plagued by dreams of earlier times, Pop's laughter and jokes. Sometimes I dreamed Pop, too, was dead, or Uncle Jack was alive again. I did not know what the dreams meant, if anything; I only wished they would stop.

The streetcar conductor looked sour. "Company regulations is against it."

"That's why I've got this blanket," I said, showing the bulky roll under my arm. "I'll wrap him up in it and hold him on my lap."

"He's still gonna be a mutt, isn't he?"

"Yes, but I've got to get him home. He's been up at Ohio State a long time. He's been sick. Nobody we know has a car anymore. I've got to get him home on the streetcar."

"I can't tell you anything, bub. Guess it'll be whatever the man running the Neil Avenue car says when you try to get on up there." He slammed the drive handle around, jerking the streetcar into motion that forced me to clutch frantically at a pipe for balance.

"You think it'll be all right, though?" I asked.

"As far as I'm concerned, regulations is regulations."

Yes, regulations were regulations, and we had learned in the last few weeks how many people were eager to enforce those regulations against anyone who happened to be poor or powerless. I bit back an angry reply and made my way to the rear of the streetcar, clutching the blanket against me. *I'm coming to get you, Max. They won't stop me.*

It was May, the Dutch elms were greening along Broad Street, and nothing in our lives would be quite the same again. Uncle Jack lay in his grave in Union Cemetery halfway across Columbus, no marker to commemmorate him.

I tried to think of other things on the ride to the campus.

Leaving the streetcar at the end of the Neil Avenue line, I walked north to the building where we had left Max a lifetime ago. Inside I found a receptionist who recognized my name when I gave it and escorted me into a small examining room with a high table and white tile walls. I waited a few minutes that seemed longer, and a door opened and the man I remembered as the professor came in. He had a leash in his hand and coming in behind him on the leash, hopping on one rear leg, was Max.

"Well, sir—" the professor began.

Max recognized me and rushed forward, tail wagging madly. I knelt and took the rush. Max frantically licked and slobbered all over my face, trying to hop up into my lap but falling back when his lone rear leg didn't balance him properly. I calmed him a little and gingerly examined him; the left leg had been removed all the way to the hip, so that it looked much as if a left rear leg had never been there. I could see the still-healing marks of many heavy stitches in his fur, which had been neatly sewn over the wound. Max was feeling no pain and hard to hold still long enough to examine.

"He still has balance problems," the professor told me. "He tends to forget he's missing something back there, and when he does that, it's curtains as far as his equilibrium is concerned. But he's healed nicely and he can go. We would appreciate it if in six months or so you bring him back by and just let us have a look at how he's doing."

"Yes, sir, I will," I said. "Can I take him now?"

"You owe us four dollars for his food. Here's the itemized bill."

I was prepared for this. I handed over the cash. The professor scrawled *Paid* across one copy and handed it back to me. "I guess that's about it," he said with a sigh. "Oh, one other thing: you ought to keep Max penned up at least for a while, and watch him very carefully with other dogs. He's a scrappy little devil, and if he picked a fight, he could get chewed up pretty badly until he's a lot more used to having a leg missing."

"I'll remember," I promised. "Thank you, sir. Very, very much." I got our old leash out of my pocket and clipped it around Max's neck and handed the professor's back to him. The professor walked with us through the outer office and to the sidewalk. He held out his hand. "Good luck!"

I shook hands, turned, and started up the street toward the streetcar line, the blanket under my left arm and Max's leash held in my right hand. Max was frantic with excitement, pulling hard at the leash and bounding all over the place. Struggling with his antics, I started to drop the blanket. I clutched for it and let go of the leash. Max was off like a shot, racing straight up the street with his lone back leg going like a piston.

"*Max!*"

Max reached the corner and swerved to turn right. Because he had no left rear leg, he lost his balance and simply rolled over and over like a ball. He was back on his feet, shaking himself and looking puzzled, by the time I reached him and got hold of the

leash again. He licked my face. I couldn't scold him. For some
reason I started crying.

"You'll be okay, Max," I told him, hugging him. "We all
will."

The conductor on the Neil Avenue streetcar gave me a dirty look
when I climbed on with Max's head sticking out of the blanket
under my arm, but he didn't say anything. I held Max tightly on
my lap all the way downtown, although he periodically wriggled
like crazy to be free. Using my transfer on the West Broad Street
car, I was in a crowd and I don't think the conductor even
noticed us.

When we got off at Terrace Avenue and I let Max down on his
leash, I swear he recognized where he was immediately. He
started going nuts, wrapping the leash around my legs, yipping,
and falling down repeatedly. I managed to get him across Broad
and partway down the block toward our house before he pulled
back, rolled over, slipped the leash, and took off tearing for home
on his own. I ran after him and just managed to be in sight as he
scrambled up the lawn but couldn't negotiate the steps to the
porch, falling over backward repeatedly. Mary rushed out and
scooped him into her arms and carried him into the house.

By the time I got there, he was in the kitchen and so was
almost everyone else. Frank was giving him a bowl of scraps,
Mary had his water pan filled, Mom was petting him, and Gramaw was standing back with a wide grin on her face. Max's tail
went a mile a minute. He was hysterical. He couldn't hold still.

He ran over and lunged at Mary, licking her face, and then yipped over to Frank and fell down trying to stand up to his leg, then ran back to me, sniffing and making little howling sounds. Then he ran over and started bolting the scraps.

"He's as crazy as ever," Mom said.

"Look at him eat!" Gramaw said. "Didn't they feed him up there?"

"Boy!" Frank exclaimed. "They really cut that leg off! It looks like there was never anything there."

It was true. Standing at his dish, walloping in the scraps with his tail wagging, Max looked almost like he had been born that way. When he was not in motion, he balanced perfectly well on his lone hind leg. The surgeons had made his skin and hair cover the amputation perfectly, so that there wasn't a visible scar unless you turned him practically upside down.

"I think he's glad to be home," Gramaw said.

As if in reply, Max gorged the last of the scraps, slavered into the water bowl for a moment, turned, and started barking at her, tail going all the time.

"You're as naughty as ever!" Gramaw told him, shaking a finger.

Max barked louder, shaking from end to end with his delight.

"Yes, you're a naughty dog!"

Max fell backward into the water dish, making water fly everywhere.

"Oh, brother!" Frank laughed and went for a towel.

"What's all the commotion?" a voice said from the doorway. Pop had come up from the basement. He stood there in his clean bib overalls.

"Max is home!" I told him.

We all watched, grinning, but my father's expression did not crack. He studied Max, being wiped off by Frank. Max eluded Frank's grasp and scurried over and sniffed Pop's shoes and legs. Pop did not bend down to pet him and he did not smile.

"Doesn't he look *great?*" I asked.

"He should have been put to sleep," Pop said.

"Joe!" Mom gasped, and the kitchen got as silent as a tomb.

Pop continued to look down at poor Max, pitifully slobbering on his shoes and rubbing against him almost like a cat. "He'll never be worth anything again."

"He's fine!" I protested.

Pop's lip curled down. "Sure. He can eat and make piles in the yard. He's supposed to be a hunting dog. He'll never hunt again. He's worthless. When a creature—or a person, for that matter—can't do useful work anymore, he's nothing but a waste."

Pushing Max aside with his foot, he walked past us and out of the kitchen.

No one said a word. Frank, still kneeling where he had been toweling Max, looked up at me with the most stricken expression. Max ran to the back door and clawed to get out.

"Let Max out, son," my mother told me.

"I've got to go with him," I said. "He might run off and get in a fight, and he can't fight too good anymore. The doctor warned me about that." I was on the verge of stupid tears. All the fun was gone again.

"Your father didn't mean anything," Mom said. "He's just tired."

"I know."

So I took Max out and he ran around the little yard, sniffing everything, and when he had finally picked the perfect spot for his royal contribution, he squatted and did his business. I whistled him back in and he followed me to the stairs. I started up. He fell over backward. So I carried him. Then he couldn't make it up onto my bed and I lifted him. He curled around and around about seventy-nine times and lay down contentedly in a ball. I sat and looked at him.

After a few minutes Pop came in. He sat on Frank's bed facing me, locking his hands together. His face twisted in a little grimace. "Well, I shouldn't have said that," he told me.

"He'll be all right, Pop. I'm going to take good care of him."

"I know you are, son. Sometimes . . . we all say things we

shouldn't." Bleakly he studied Max. "He's got as much right to live as any of us, I guess."

"Sure, and he'll get better, too."

Pop's chest heaved. "So you're about to graduate from St. Aloysius."

"Yes sir."

"Next fall, West Junior High."

"Yes sir." I wondered. Autumn seemed an eternity away. Maybe I could find a job. Maybe school would be a thing of the past.

"What are your plans for this summer?"

"Well, I thought I could look for a job."

"A job. That won't be easy."

"I know. But maybe I could find *something.*"

"What about the radiator business?"

The question surprised me. "That's *yours.*"

He looked off into space. I could tell this was very hard for him to say. "Gail has the grocery job . . . Frank is still too little to help me. But you're good help. Maybe, if you don't find anything else, we could work together some more."

"Sure! That would be great!"

"Sign in front needs repainting. We might put up a few notices in stores and such." He looked at me. "Might build the business up a little again."

"Oh, yes! I could help a whole lot! Together we could really—"

"Or maybe," he cut in, "I'm just kidding myself. Maybe I'll never do an honest day's work again."

"Of course you will! Listen! You're getting better all the time! I can *tell.* We'll get that sign repainted and some cards out around the neighborhood, and between us we'll really get the business going!"

He raised his eyebrows skeptically. "Well, we'll try it, anyway." He stood wearily. "You can't go back . . . live in the past. We've got to try to go on, no matter what mistakes we've made in the past."

"That's right," I said, not sure I understood.

He reached down, petted Max between the ears, and left the room.

The next day Pop seemed intent on continuing his rally from Uncle Jack's death. He helped me rig up a run for Max in the backyard, making loops of leash cord over the clotheslines. When Max started gnawing on the ropes, Pop even smiled and went off and found the wire we used as a substitute. Then he went down into the basement and cleaned up some of his tools, and walked to Broad Street for some more acid flux and solder. It was as if his explosion at Max had made him realize that he had to try to change his attitude. He even whistled a little, tunelessly. Mom seemed to brighten up, and Gramaw made a pie. I went to school and walked through the graduation-exercise practice with a lighter heart, sure things were going to straighten out.

An afternoon or two later when I reached home, however, I walked into a scene in the kitchen that complicated things.

Mom and Pop were sitting there with Gail and Uncle Jim. It was unusual enough for Gail not to be at the grocery at this time, but for Uncle Jim to visit was extraordinary. Gail and Uncle Jim looked upset, Mom was dabbing at her eyes, and my father was clearly angry, drumming his fingertips on the tabletop.

"It seems," he glared at me, "your big brother wants to throw his life away."

"Joe, be fair," Uncle Jim remonstrated.

"I am being fair! There's no other word for what the two of you have hatched up between you!"

"There's guaranteed oil-field work in Tulsa," Uncle Jim said.

"Tulsa!" I said.

Gail took a deep breath. His face was red. "Uncle Jim knows a guy. If we go to Tulsa, we can get oil-field work. It pays good."

"Leave *home?*" I said.

"Not go back to school in the fall," Pop said. *"Quit."*

"It's not quitting," Gail said. "It's a chance for a real job. I can send part of my paycheck back every week—"

"Who wants it?" Pop demanded. "Who asked for it? Are we in such dire straits that my children have to quit school and go halfway around the world to send us back their charity?"

"It's not halfway around the world! It's a thousand miles. That's all, just a thousand."

"You need to finish school. Without your education you'll never amount to anything!"

"You never finished high school!" Gail shot back.

"Right! And *look* at me!"

"Oh, gaw," Gail groaned.

"Joe," Uncle Jim intervened, "he can go back to school next year or the year after. As soon as there's an upturn around here—"

"He'll never go back once he's quit," Pop said. "You know that. He'll go off and never have a pot to bake his beans in." He turned back to Gail. "But you talk like your mind is made up."

The color had now gone from Gail's face, but he did not flinch. "Yes sir. It is."

"Then go. But don't send any of your paycheck back here. We don't need it!"

"Pop—"

"I won't let it be said that I was such a failure my oldest son had to quit school and go off and support me!"

"That's not what it's all about at all!"

My father stood. He was shaking. "Jim, I can understand why you want to go. You've got a family to support. But I want you to know I'll never forget that you went behind my back with my own son to get him to give up his education and chase a quick dollar."

"Oh, come on, Joe," Uncle Jim said, pale. "It—"

But my father stormed out of the kitchen, and we heard him going up the stairs out of hearing.

"I didn't think he would act like *that*," Gail said hoarsely.

"He'll . . . calm down," my mother said.

"I will finish school, Mom. I *will*. I just have to . . . postpone it."

She nodded and rose. "I'm going to go see about him." She left.

"Well, Kenny," Uncle Jim said, "I'm sorry you had to come in and witness any of that."

"Are you really going to Tulsa?" I asked.

"Yes. I talked to my pal on the telephone and he wants us there by the weekend."

"The weekend! Then you've got to leave—"

"The day after tomorrow."

I was stunned. I had always had the feeling somehow that our troubles could never get out of hand because we did, after all, have Gail with us, and Gail was almost grown. But now—

Uncle Jim seemed to read my mind. "Don't look like that, Kenny. I know it's going to be a little harder on you, being the oldest at home. But Gail is going to be sending money back, regardless of what your father says now. And it will take some of the pressure off."

"But Pop doesn't want you to *go,*" I told Gail.

He got to his feet and went to the sink for water, a skinny seventeen-year-old who looked scared. "I know that. But I've just got *to be a man.*"

"Your father is not a well man," Uncle Jim told me. "It's crazy, but he blames himself for Jack's death. Not being able to work anymore, that eats at him. Maybe if you can find something to do this summer and still give him a little support—"

"Oh, I'm going to, don't worry about that! We're going to get the radiator shop really going again, you'll see!"

"You think the two of you are going to get that going again?"

I had already so counted it in my plans that I was astonished he would ask. "Of course!"

"The sign is gone from the yard."

"I took it down. It's in the basement. We're going to repaint it. And I plan to put up cards at the Gulf station down at Oakley and there on Wheatland and some other places, too. Mr. Zimmer at the garage, I talked to him this morning and he says he might be able to send us some business, too. I've got that print set, the one with the rubber letters, and I'm going to print up a lot of cards. I'll be out of school real soon and I'll have more time to work on all of it. Frank is going to cut lawns if he can find any, but he can fix flats, too. We're going to have a terrific business!"

Uncle Jim studied my face. "Well, at least you've got big plans."

"You'll see how great we do."

He started to speak, thought about it, then went ahead. "There are just a couple of things."

"Yes?"

"For one thing . . . your father just isn't going to be able to do a lot of work."

"Oh, he'll probably do a lot more than you think, Uncle Jim. And I'm learning fast. I can do a lot of it."

"Well, maybe. But there's also a question as to how many people will bring their cars in for a boy your age to work on them."

"I'm fifteen!"

"I'm just talking about people and the way they are, sometimes."

"Pop will be here to talk to them. They know *his* work."

"Just don't expect too much, Kenny. Don't get your hopes up too high."

"You'll see," I told him again.

He got to his feet. "I think I'll go see if your old man will speak to me. I'll be back in a minute or two." He left the kitchen, and Gail and I were alone.

"This is going to mean more responsibility for you, like Uncle Jim said," Gail told me.

"I know."

"Mom and Pop are both going to be looking more to you now."

"I know."

"If something breaks around the house and you can fix it so Pop doesn't have to mess with it, you have to take care of it. And you've always had a lot of influence with Mary, so you've got to make sure she does her homework and all that. You've got to be cheerful, too. Keep Pop cheered up."

"I'll do my best," I told him.

"Mom will need cheering up too," he went on. "She'll probably miss me some and get depressed."

I saw how frightened he was. "Don't worry about any of us, Gail. Just take care of yourself. I'll write real often."

He blew his nose. "Now listen. I'm only going to be able to take one suitcase. So I'm going to be leaving a lot of my stuff here. I expect you to make sure Frank and Mary don't mess with any of my things. I've got rights, you know. I don't want anyone messing with my models or using my ball glove while I'm gone."

"Gail, I promise."

"All right, then. We'll do fine if you hold up your end here. I'll be making almost enough to send back the whole house payment every month. You and Pop will make some with the radiator business, and Frank will have some lawns. Mom can make a little doing washing and ironing, and Gramaw has her pension. Between us all we can keep food on the table and keep the house. We've got to keep the house, do you see?"

"Naturally," I said.

Gail pointed a finger at me. "Pop has lost his health. He's lost his job. Uncle Jack is gone. If we lose this house, it will *kill* Pop, don't you see?"

Ah. Then I did see.

This, I thought, was something Gail had seen earlier.

It was why he had to go to Tulsa.

"I'll do my part," I pledged to him.

We shook hands. It felt as if new, enormous responsibilities passed to me with that handshake.

Two days later Gail left the house early, carrying his suitcase. It was an old one of Gramaw's, and he had tied twine around it to hold it together. On the front porch he kissed Mary and shook my and Frank's hands and hugged Gramaw and Mom, both of whom were crying, and then he turned to Pop. Pop hesitated, then held out his arms and they embraced. Gail went down the steps quickly and started walking toward the streetcar stop, the heavy bag banging his leg with every stride. At the corner he turned and sent us a wave, and then went out of sight.

My father turned toward the door. "You'd better hurry," he told me. "You're already going to be late for school. Without an education, a man is nothing."

"If you paint that sign while I'm at school," I told him, "I'll get it put back up when I come home."

He stared at me a moment, then went into the house without another word.

We got to school only a few minutes late. There was another practice for the graduation ceremony, at which each of the graduates would receive a rolled scroll and a white missal we had paid twenty-one cents in advance for. After school I walked Mary home. Mom was doing somebody's washing and Gramaw was sewing. Pop was out in the backyard with Max, sitting. I knew without asking that he had had a bad day physically. I went to the basement, and he had not touched the sign.

I went back to the yard where he was sitting, staring into space. "Hi," I said. "I'm home."

"Hello, son." He did not look at me.

"Maybe you'd like me to repaint the sing?"

He raised the fingers of his right hand in a gesture that said he didn't care.

In the basement again I got out the paints and his small brush and set to work. Although I had only to retrace what he had already lettered, it was not as easy as it looked. My strokes wavered and ran a little. I worked on it very hard. When it was finally done, I dragged it back around to the front yard and tamped dirt around the stake again. If I walked back across the yard and looked at my work, it did not look too bad. Up close it was awful. Pop came out just before supper and looked at it. Up close. He went back in the house and did not mention it at supper. We ate with hardly a word spoken.

It was all right, I thought. Not many people would examine it up close, and at a distance they would not be able to see that my work was vastly inferior to his.

After the meal Frank and I were supposed to do the dishes. Mary helped us clear the table after my mother and father went to the front porch and Gramaw went in to the radio. I always liked to wash the dishes because you could wash twice as fast as you could dry, and I took some perverse pleasure in piling the dishes and silverware high on the drainboard, leaving Frank with half his work yet to do as I buzzed away from the kitchen. I started off with my usual gusto, getting several plates and glasses ahead of him while Mary was still bringing the last items from the table.

"Slow down a little," Frank complained.

"You go faster," I suggested, sloshing a handful of silverware in the sudsy water, rinsing it under the tap, and dumping it all on the drainboard.

"You're just going fast on purpose!"

"*You're* just going *slow* on purpose."

"I wish you two wouldn't fight," Mary said on a sigh as she brought over the last pan.

"I wish you'd mind your own beeswax," Frank muttered.

I swung over two more plates, a cup, two saucers, a sauce pan and another handful of silverware, burying the drainboard. "Maybe if you didn't talk so much, Frank, you could dry more than one dish an hour."

It was ritualistic. We fussed this way often and it meant nothing. I was scarcely thinking about what was going on. But Frank suddenly grabbed up a paring knife and held it out at arm's length, the point aimed right at my face.

"*Leave me alone!*" he whispered fiercely.

I stared in shock. His lips were pulled back from his teeth in a desperately angry grimace. The knife, still pointed at me, shook violently. He was on the brink of stabbing me.

"Stop it! Stop it!" Mary cried.

"Take it easy, Frank!" I gasped. "I was just teasing you!"

"You think with Gail gone you can just strut around here and boss me around! Well, you can't! Do you hear me?"

"I hear you," I told him. "Calm down. I won't tease you anymore."

He put the knife in the drawer. His eyes were wet. "Just because you're the biggest around here now, that doesn't mean I'm *nothing.*"

"No one said that, Frank." I was beginning to see that this was his way of reacting to Gail's departure.

"I know Gail is going to get a real job and send money home. I know you're going to help Pop with the radiator business. But *I* count, too. I'll get lawns this summer. I'll do my share. I'm not just some dummy."

"I know that, Frank." He was drying dishes furiously, catching up with me, but I didn't turn back to the soapy water. "We're all in this together, equals."

"They didn't want Gail to go. Since he left, Pop hasn't even *looked* at me. I'm just another mouth to feed around here, a drag."

"That's not true!"

"He used to play ball with us. He used to talk to us. At supper tonight he didn't even *look* at me."

"He didn't look at any of us."

"That's right, Frank," Mary chimed in. "He used to pick me up and call me his punkin. But he's just . . . funny these days. Mama says he still feels bad about Uncle Jack, and being sick and all."

Frank continued as if no one had said anything. "I know there are bills and the house payment and everything. The Slaters lost their house last week. They *moved.* I'm not big enough to do anything about it for our family. No wonder he hates me!"

"Gaw, Frank! Nobody can hate somebody because they're not *old* yet!"

"I just feel so helpless. I feel like a dope."

"We all feel that way sometimes."

"You don't."

"That's what you think!"

"You *do?*"

"Sure!"

He looked like that made him feel a little better. I resumed washing dishes, slowly.

"What do you think is going to happen?" he asked.

"To us, you mean?"

"Yes."

"Nothing. What I mean is, everything will be okay."

"I worry about it all the time. And now Gail has left. That makes it all seem a whole lot worse . . . like we're more in trouble, or something."

"What you need to do, Frank," Mary told him earnestly from the table, "is put your faith in God. That's what sister says. Remember the birds of the fields. She said that."

"We ain't no birds," Frank muttered.

"Don't *say* things like that! That's your bad angel talking! Don't you believe in God?"

"Of course I do!" Frank looked shocked. "Everybody believes in God." He looked at me. "Right?"

"Of course," I said.

"I pray a lot," Frank said. "It's just that I'm scared."

"Well," Mary told him, "pray *more.*"

Inwardly I sighed. *Oh, God,* I thought, *if You're there someplace, help me believe in You, too. Because I really, really want to!*

We finished the dishes in silence. Frank was still depressed. Mary, too, looked down.

"How are you on homework?" I asked them.

"I don't have any," Mary said.

"I did mine at school," Frank said.

"What do you say we go out and hit a few balls, then?"

Frank frowned. "It's dark already."

"We can see by the streetlight."

"We don't have enough players."

"Mary, do you want to play with us?"

"I don't play ball," she said. "I'm a *girl.*"

"Well, you can learn anyway. Come *on,* you guys! What do you say?"

They were reluctant at first, but I got the black-taped baseball and cracked bat and gloves out of the basement and we went out, past Mom and Pop sitting on the porch. All we had was a pitcher, a hitter and one outfielder, so if you swung and missed, you had to go chase the ball down in the absence of a catcher. We had to make it monkey move up because Mary couldn't catch a ball for beans, and she hit only about one in every ten we served up, throwing as slowly as we could. But she got into it and we had a little fun. I acted the fool, falling down, pretending the ball hit me on the head, batting lefty and doing a corkscrew when I struck out, and a couple of times going back and trying to make loping, graceful catches over the shoulder on long ones from Frank the way Pop always had. I got them laughing after a while. Every so often I would glance over at the two dim figures on our shaded porch, thinking maybe our father would come join us. But he didn't. When we finally quit, sweaty and itchy from falling in the grass, Frank and Mary both seemed a lot more cheerful, jabbering all the way through the house and upstairs, where they fussed about who got the bathroom first. I was the only one, it seemed, who had had the hope about Pop joining us, so I was the only one disappointed. But that didn't matter. My intent had been to cheer them up, and I had succeeded. I made a mental note that this was something I would have to try to do every day.

School closed for the summer soon thereafter and the weather warmed. There were real ball games in the park in front of our house again. Some days we had radiator work, but many others we did not. Broadsiding my rubber-printed business cards didn't seem to help. Frank got a few lawns, but not enough to keep him occupied. I got him to come to the basement when we had a radiator or tire work, and he watched.

Pop had good days and bad. He was very quiet almost all the time now, withdrawn from us into his own thoughts. There were days when I didn't hear him speak a word. I got in the habit of talking too much, always cheerfully, about current events or the ball game in the park or anything I could think of. He listened and sometimes smiled faintly, so I redoubled my efforts, probably making a fool of myself. He started taking long walks in the evening, saying they might help him build himself back up. Invariably he came back gray-faced, covered by cold sweat. But the next evening he grimly set out again.

"I'll go with you," I suggested one evening.

"No," he said, and that was that. So he went alone.

We had letters from Gail. They were short, pencil-written, and did not say much except that a lot of people were out of work in Oklahoma and it was very hot and there were dust storms. Each letter had some crumpled dollar bills in it. Pop's jaw set in anger when he opened the first letter and the money fell out, but later I saw him and my mother going over the bills on the dining room table, and Gail's dollars were in a pile beside that from the radiator-business jar and the washing and sewing money.

Early in June Frank and I spaded the garden plot, enlarging it to take in all the backyard except the space needed for radiator customers to pull in. Gramaw put little tomato and pepper plants in jars on the windowsills. After Frank and I thought we were done getting the garden place ready, Pop came out and inspected it, and his reaction was one of my first signs that maybe he was making a comeback.

"You don't think you're finished, do you?" he asked.

I knew better than to respond truthfully that we *knew* we were finished. The way Pop asked the question made it clear that we weren't. Poor Frank, however, never seemed to learn.

"Sure we are," he said jauntily. "Looks good, huh?"

"Look at those pieces of grass still sticking out, and those weeds. Isn't that a rock over there? And how are you ever going to get straight rows when you plant? It isn't square to start with."

"Oh," Frank said airily, "it's good enough for a backyard garden."

Pop went brick red. "It *isn't* good enough for a backyard garden," he snapped. "Don't *ever* let me hear you say something is 'good enough.'"

Frank stared, his eyes bulging.

"Do you hear me?" Pop demanded.

"Yes, sir," Frank murmured.

"Do you understand what I'm *saying?*"

"Yes, sir."

Pop went over to him and grabbed his head in a rough, affectionate hug. "*Damn* it, boys! That's what's wrong with this world—people saying a sloppy job is 'good enough.' If you don't give a job your very best, you're not even *alive;* you're a . . . a *slug.* Do you get me?"

"I guess so," Frank said grudgingly, embarrassed and strangely pleased at this attention, as I was. Because it was vintage Pop.

"Okay," Pop muttered. "See what you can do about fixing things up, then."

And we did, and it looked a hundred percent better. When we were finished, I cut some short stakes out of scrap wood with the hatchet and laid them out at both ends of the plot.

"What are those for?" Pop asked.

"I'll tie string from one to the other," I told him, "and lay the rows out along the strings. That way I know they'll be straight."

"Huh!" he grunted, staring. And walked away.

"*He* had never thought of *that,*" Frank said and grinned.

"I don't know about that," I replied. "But it must be okay. He didn't say anything."

A night or two later we had another encouraging sign. I was in the living room with Pop and Max, Pop reading the newspaper. He finished and looked around, and his eyes fell on his ukelele on the false hearth. He reached over and picked it up for the first time in months. I held my breath as he strummed it, frowned, and tuned the strings. Max seemed interested; he went over and sat in front of him. Pop strummed and returned, then hit a few soft chords.

"We'll build a little home,"

he sang,

"From which we'll never roam—"

Max raised his head and let out a long, mournful howl.

Pop stopped and looked down at him. "What did you say, Max?"

"Max, shut up!" I pleaded.

Pop strummed another chord. Max howled again.

"Max," Pop said, scratching his head, "one of us is going to have to change key." He strummed again and Max craned his neck. *"Aaaaoooe!"*

Mom and Gramaw came into the room. "What on earth—" Mom said.

"Duet," Pop said, and grinned as he resumed chording.

"Out there beneath the starry skies,"

he sang in his sweet, tenor voice.

"Life will grow more dear
As it passes year by year
Beneath a clear
And blue Ohio sky."

Max howled again. Mom laughed, and her eyes were wet. I almost bawled myself, I was so happy. I really thought things were going to be all right.

Then in the middle of June the two men came to talk about our mortgage.

11

Only my mother and I were at home when they appeared on our front porch: two men in business suits, each with a briefcase, their straw hats in hand. One man was perhaps forty, bald, with a slight paunch wrinkling his white shirt and unbuttoned coat; the other was quite young, pink from the unseasonal heat, with a little mustache and bright blue eyes.

"If they're selling something, Kenny, just tell them we don't want any," my mother told me after peeking at them down the hallway from the kitchen.

I went to the door. The house was quiet with Frank at the grocery and Gramaw with Mary at the confectionery. I opened the glass front door and peered out at the two strangers through the screen.

"Good afternoon, young man," the older man said. "Is the man of the house at home?"

"No," I said. "He's taking a walk right now."

"Is the lady of the house at home, then?" The man took a notebook from his inside coat pocket and flipped a page, frowning. "That would be Mrs. Joseph Riley, I believe."

"If you're selling something, I'm sorry, but we don't want any."

"We're not selling something, young man. My name is Caldwell and this is Mr. Emmer. We represent Allied National. Your parents would have received a letter from us two or three months ago."

I remembered the letter we had gotten back in the spring. I felt a little chill. "Will you wait just a minute, please?"

Swinging the door closed, I hurried back to the kitchen.

"Well, what did they want?" my mother asked, busy with bread dough.

"Mom, they're from Allied National. Remember that company that wrote about Central Federal going out of business?"

She stopped kneading the dough, her eyes blank. Then she hurriedly washed her hands, drying them on her apron as she preceded me up the hall and to the front door. She swung it open with the stiffness of someone braced for something. "Yes, gentlemen?"

"Mrs. Riley?"

"Yes?"

"Allow me to present myself. I am John Caldwell and this is Frank Emmer. We are representatives of Allied National, the firm liquidating the assets of Central Federal, your mortgage holder. May we come in?"

My mother hesitated, then opened the screen door. She led the men into the parlor. They sat on the couch side by side while she took her usual chair facing them at an angle. They paid no attention to me. I took Pop's old chair and kept quiet.

"Mrs. Riley," Caldwell began briskly, opening his briefcase on his knees and beginning to take papers out to spread all over the coffee table, "as you know, Central Federal declared bankruptcy this spring. Our firm, Allied National, has been appointed by the court to collect all debts outstanding to Central Federal and negotiate payments to its many creditors." He extended a thick sheaf of legal papers for my mother to examine. "You recognize this, of course?"

"It's our mortgage on this house." Mom's voice was very soft.

Caldwell nodded, put down that sheaf, and took out a set of legal pages covered with columns of figures. "Yes. Now, this is the current amortization schedule on the property. To review, the price of the house and lot . . . we'll skip the legal description for the moment . . . totaled four thousand one hundred dollars. You purchased said property from Casey Merriman Construction Company in October of 1927, paying one thousand one hundred dollars down and signing a mortgage agreement with Central Federal for the balance of three thousand dollars, to be repaid on a fixed schedule of thirty-three dollars and forty-one cents. The current loan balance—"

"The first year, we made some extra payments against principal," my mother said huskily. Her hands were twisted in her apron and she looked pale.

"Yes," Caldwell said, nodding at another sheet of figures. "We have that record. The current loan balance, after the June first payment, stands at two thousand two hundred and thirty-four dollars and eight cents." He looked up expectantly at my mother. "That figure jibes with yours?"

"I don't have a—it sounds about right, yes."

"Mrs. Riley, you *do* have a copy of the amortization schedule?"

"I'm sure we do. My husband has been ill—we're disorganized—"

"I'm sorry," Caldwell said with every evidence of sincerity. "I can assure you, however, Mrs. Riley, that these figures on all accounts have been checked and rechecked. The courts require that. Your current loan balance is, as I said, exactly two thousand two hundred and thirty-four dollars and eight cents."

"What is it you want?"

Caldwell stifled a sigh. "Mrs. Riley, this is never pleasant. But in these times, when a firm such as Central Federal folds up, it leaves a great many other businesses, including corporations and insurance companies, with considerable debts owed to them. In 1929 and 1930, Central Federal overextended itself with new loans to home buyers and small businesses. To fund many of these loans, it in turn borrowed from the larger firms I mentioned. When Central Federal finally collapsed, it left massive debts to legitimate creditors. That's where the courts step in, you see. Our firm has been appointed by the court to collect as many debts outstanding to Central Federal as possible, in order for us, as receivers, to pay as high a proportion as possible on all of Central Federal's old debts. That, you see, is why we're here."

"I don't understand," my mother said. "We've never missed a payment. We've never been so much as a day late. We paid extra on the principal when my husband was in good health. What can you want from me?"

Caldwell's smile was forced. "Mrs. Riley, this is unpleasant. But let me be clear with you. We are here to find out how you intend to pay the sum total of your indebtedness."

My mother's hand went to her throat. "The total! You mean—"

Caldwell glanced at his pad. "Two thousand, two hundred—"

"You're demanding we pay it *all? Now?*"

"Actually you will have until September 15. On that date, if we have been unable to work out some suitable arrangement for discharge of your obligation, a request will be entered for a court judgment against you."

"You think we can pay you twenty-two hundred dollars by September?" My mother stared, incredulous. "We're as poor as church mice!"

Caldwell looked at his younger companion. Emmer leaned forward, his face strained and earnest. "Mrs. Riley, I'm an attorney. Let me assure you that the court is determined to collect the maximum possible on all this firm's outstanding debts. If you don't reach a satisfactory cash agreement with Allied National by the deadline in September, the court will order your property sold at auction to the highest bidder—"

"*No!*"

"—to the highest bidder, and whatever cash money is paid will be applied as closing your outstanding mortgage account, and that total will be applied to Central Federal's debt structure, after court costs and legal fees and Allied's percentage, have been deducted, of course."

"You can't *do* that!" my mother choked. "Our contract says you can't touch us as long as we stick to our part of the bargain. We've never missed—never been late—"

"Mrs. Riley," Emmer said, his lips turning down. "That contract is meaningless now. There is no more Central Federal. You're dealing with Allied National as an instrumentality of the court."

Pink spots of shocked anger appeared in my mother's cheeks. "It's a new ball game now? You're changing all the rules? You can do whatever you want, and there's nothing we can do about it?"

"Mrs. Riley, in effect that's precisely the situation. Now, everyone wants to be fair—"

"Fair! Fair? When you come in here and say you're going to put us in the street?"

"Certainly no one wants to put anyone in the street, Mrs. Riley—" Emmer was silenced in the middle of his statement by his partner's hand on his arm.

"Mr. Emmer is here to explain the legal aspects of the situation," Caldwell said. Sweat glistened on his face. "As to any auction of the property or any other legal action of that magnitude, let me assure you that Allied National views that as strictly a last resort. We are not here to make threats, madam, or plan any such extreme remedies for our mutual problem. Allied is willing to consider each case individually and make adjustments insofar as our own legal obligations make it possible. The total of your indebtedness is clear. In cases of this kind, however, a certain flexibility for negotiation is always possible."

"Negotiation?" my mother repeated, clutching at the straw.

Caldwell smiled and spread his hands, palm up. "We're reasonable. If a debtor is unable to make full restitution, then we are willing to consider any reasonable counterproposal."

"You mean if we can't pay all of it, you might settle for part of what we owe?"

"Yes. That's a possibility. Within reason, of course."

Emmer added, "Such compromises must be approved by the court, of course."

My mother's eyes glistened. Her breathing was heavy, and

she was struggling terribly to maintain control. "Then what happens now?"

"Well, first, is the family prepared to pay in full?"

"Of course not!" Mom's eyes flashed with teary anger.

"Within the period from now until September 15—"

"No! No! I told you! We don't have anything! My husband is very sick! This little boy here is the closest thing we have to a man in the house right now—someone who might earn a full-time wage!"

Emmer's chest heaved. "Well, then, Mrs. Riley, I suggest that you determine as soon as possible what amount you and your family can offer as a reasonable settlement." He proffered a card. "We can be contacted at any of these numbers."

My mother took the card, stared at it a moment, then raised her eyes. "And if we can't pay? If we just make our regular monthly payments—as we agreed to do? What then?"

Caldwell looked grim. "Then, Mrs. Riley, I'm afraid the sort of legal action mentioned by my colleague would eventually have to be taken."

"You would put us out?"

"We don't like to speak in those terms—"

"*You would put us out?*" Mom's voice rose sharply.

"Yes. If it came to that, yes. Of course—"

"And sell our home at an auction?"

"Yes."

She stood abruptly. "Thank you."

Caldwell looked up at her, startled. "Are there any questions?"

"No." Her face was glacial, composed.

Both men began hurriedly putting papers away. Caldwell said, "I hope we will hear from you soon?"

My mother said nothing. The tumult in her breast was evident even to me, as shocked as I was at the moment.

They gathered their last papers, snapped briefcases closed, fastened straps, stood. Caldwell appeared uncertain and nervous.

He extended his hand. "Thank you for your courtesy. If there are any questions—"

"Good day, gentlemen," my mother said, ignoring his hand.

They went to the door. She closed it behind them, watched through the curtain as they went down the steps to a car at curbside and drove away. Her shoulders began to shake.

"Mom," I said, "we'll raise the money!"

"*How?*"

"We've got all summer!"

"Where are we going to get more than two thousand dollars?"

"There are other banks—other places to borrow. And we've got our radiator business."

"This is just going to kill your father," she said.

I chilled. "No it isn't! He'll figure out what we should do!"

"All the months and years we saved. The way he paced the floor at night, figuring ways to save another few dollars, taking extra jobs. And then they come in and do something like *this.*"

"Maybe we could not tell him," I said.

She looked at me like I must be crazy. "And how do we hide something like this from him? Are you that good a liar? I'm not. What do we tell him when they come and post the eviction notice? That it's a *joke?*"

The front door opened behind us. We both turned to see Pop enter, mopping his face with a bandana and grinning wearily.

"Really hot today," he told us. "It's sure a lot cooler inside here, closed up. Good thick walls, that's what does it." He tossed his cap at the coat tree, scoring a ringer as usual. "Say, who were those two gents I saw driving away just now? Trying to sell us a new Electrolux or something?"

My mother had gone terribly pale. Her hand stole to her throat.

Pop sat in his favorite chair. "Made it over a mile today." He cocked his head at her. "Who *were* they, anyway?"

In a voice like tissue paper, she told him who they were and what they had said. I watched my father as the news sank in. He seemed to shrink in his chair, the smile fading, his face becoming gaunt.

"They can't do that," he said finally, his face splotching with anger. "There have got to be laws against things like that!"

"How can we stop them? If they say the court is on their side—"

Pop stood abruptly. "We'll see about that. I'll go see our lawyer. What's the name of the man who wrote our will for us? The one down there at Eldon and Broad? Washington?"

"Washburn," my mother said.

"Washburn. Yes. Washburn. Where's our copy of our house contract? Is it in the cedar chest in our room? I'm going down there and see that lawyer right now."

"Take it easy, now, Joseph," Mom cautioned. "Don't get yourself all worked up."

"If I don't get worked up about someone trying to take our house, what *should* I get worked up over?" He started for the stairs. "Come on. Help me find those papers."

Still scared but feeling a little better, I waited until they came downstairs in short order, Pop carrying a large brown envelope. He jammed his cap on again and steamed out of the house, walking much too fast up the street toward Broad. My mother watched, her concern stark in her expression.

"It'll be all right, Mom," I told her.

She looked around abstractedly. "I've just got to do some cleaning. Everything is in a mess. Look at those windows!"

I went down to the basement and stared at the tools on the workbench awhile, wishing some business would come, then went up to my room. It was much hotter upstairs even with the windows open. The air was very still, the humidity high, dark clouds gathering for possible rain. Out in the park, three or four of the neighborhood boys were playing marbles: David Vincent, his brother George, and Hugh Rayburn were scrunched around a circle drawn with a stick in the dust beneath a tree. Sylvester Smith stood watching. I didn't feel like playing, but the room suffocated me. I stole down the steps and past the dining room, where Mom was scrubbing furiously at windows, and went outside.

As I walked up to the group at the marble ring, Hugh Rayburn shot a steelie from the rim and hit two other glassies but did not knock them out of the circle. With a muffled groan of anguish, he sank back on his haunches.

"Boy, oh boy," George Vincent said with a chuckle and knelt at the circle. He aimed carefully.

"Knuckles down!" Hugh protested.

George shoved his dirty knuckles into the dust and fired. His solid blue marble crashed into Hugh's steelie and knocked it clean out of the ring and into the grass. The blueie spun and stayed put. George scooped up Hugh's steelie and took aim again, knocking two more marbles out of the ring. His shooter marble spun well out of the ring, however, and his shot back missed. He sat back, putting his newly won marbles into his sock bag, while his older brother lined up.

"Good-bye, marbles," Sylvester muttered.

"Bet your boots," David said, taking aim with his shooter marble poised viciously between thumb and index finger.

No one in the neighborhood could shoot marbles in the same league with David Vincent. He had a killer instinct. He could hit a teensie in a divot at twenty-five feet and probably knock it across the yard in the process. The size of the marble sack beside him attested to his skill. He was the only one in the area with a genuine leather marble bag, and it was three times as big as any of the socks the rest of us used. And it was always bulging. He had to have two hundred marbles won from me alone in there. I was glad I had decided to outgrow playing marbles. I had gotten pretty sick of saving up to go back to the dime store and buy more marbles all the time. I sometimes thought I was the only person in Columbus who didn't win his marbles.

David fired his green cat's eye. It slammed into two others, knocking them out of the circle. His next shot glittered into the pile of marbles in the middle, knocking out six. There were three left. He blasted out two on his next shot, knocked out the last one, picked up his shooter, and started putting his new winnings in his bag.

"Anybody for more?" he asked.

"I'll *never* play with you again!" his younger brother George said bitterly. "You cheat!"

David looked at Hugh Rayburn. Hugh grimaced and nodded.

"Lag?" David said.

So they walked a few paces away from the dusty circle and turned to face it. Hugh, frowning with concentration, tossed a marble underhand toward the circle. It bounced outside it and rolled in, winding up almost in the exact center, perhaps four inches off. It was a great lag, almost sure to give him first shot in the new game.

David, however, lagged casually. His marble bounced twice and seemed to sit down like a golf ball with backspin *precisely* in the center of the circle.

"Gaw!" Hugh groaned.

"Foursies," David said and dropped four marbles in the middle of the circle. Hugh matched his four so that there were ten marbles altogether, counting the ones they had lagged with.

David took out his glassie with a crimson spot in it—one I had never seen in jeopardy—and blasted all the marbles out in three shots.

"Anybody else?" he asked grandly, bagging his winnings.

His younger brother glared at him as if he had been a loser again, instead of Hugh Rayburn. "One of these days somebody will come along that just *destroys* you at marbles, you big can of lard!"

"Not likely," David told him. "When you're great, you're great."

"If you had any decency, you'd give back some of them marbles!"

David grinned. "Never." He hefted his heavy bag. "I'm going home. Are you coming, half-pint?"

We watched the two of them walk away from us across the parkway.

"Boy," I mused, "he bragged more than usual today."

"Sure," Sylvester Smith said. "He has to. His old man got laid off from work yesterday. If David doesn't brag about his marbles, what's he *got?*"

The news startled me. Breaking off the conversation, I hurried home. I had come out to the game in hopes of getting my mind off our problems. I had found only a new reminder. Perhaps there was no place a person could run anymore.

Pop came home a long time later and slumped in the chair. "It's legal."

"I don't know how it can be," Mom said, bringing him a glass of water.

"Our only real chance," he added grimly, "is to have some cash on hand and good enough employment that they'll extend us new credit." He slapped his palm on the arm of the chair. "So in the morning I go look for a job."

"You can't! Your health—"

"Damn my health! I'll look for a clerical job I can do! *Something.* You can't tell me there aren't jobs out there somewhere if a man is willing to look hard enough."

"What about the radiator business?" I asked.

He grunted mirthlessly. "That's a good one! My aching back. How much have we made this week? Fifty cents?"

"It'll pick up, though. We've got all those cards out—"

"We can't *wait*, boy," he snapped. Cords stood out on his neck. "Haven't you been paying attention? They want our *home!*"

"Don't take it out on him," Mom said.

Pop got up and left the room. We heard the basement stair door slam.

No one spoke for a moment in the living room.

"I'll find a job, too," I said.

"What about the radiator business?" Frank asked, repeating my own earlier question.

"If there's work, we do it at night," I told him.

Mom sighed. "Where is it going to end?"

Frank said, "What makes you think you can find a job somewhere?"

"You heard what Pop said! If you look hard enough, you're bound to find something."

"Then you have to quit in a couple of months to go back to school, and so what?"

"I won't go back to school," I said.

"Kenneth!" Mom gasped.

"Gail quit. I can too."

"No!"

"Are you all tetched in the head?" I asked. "We're talking about saving our house here!"

"It's only a house, Kenny. If worse comes to worst—"

"Only a house?" I repeated incredulously. "How can you say that?"

"He's right," Frank said. "We've all got to do more. I'm going to hunt for more work, too."

"You've got the deliveries at the store," I told him. "You've got your lawns."

"I'll go to the sewer department."

"The sewer department!"

"Yeah. I heard they like to hire little guys."

"What for?"

"To crawl through some of the small pipes and inspect them."

I stared at him. The situation made it impossible to laugh. Were *all* our ideas as crazy as his idea about crawling through pipes?

Outside, thunder rolled and it began to rain.

In the morning my father was gone from the house when I appeared in the kitchen a little before eight. Mary, sleepy-eyed, sat at the table picking at her cereal. Gramaw was starting bread dough and Mom stood at the sink, washing a few dishes.

"Where is everybody?" I asked.

"Thank you very much," Gramaw said. "I guess that tells us how *we* rate."

"I mean, where's Frank?"

"He said he had a lawn."

"And Pop?"

Gramaw mixed her dough in silence. My mother did not turn. Her tone showed an effort at being casual. "He went looking for a job."

"Where?"

"I don't know."

I could tell she was worried, and so was Gramaw Prater. The worry stemmed not just from the visit yesterday by the men who would take away our house, although that was certainly bad enough. They were worried about Pop.

I tried to be reassuring: "The rain cooled things off some, anyway. It won't be too hot, walking around."

No one replied. Mary made spoon valleys in her cereal.

I added, "Maybe he'll find something right off."

"Oh, Kenneth," my mother said crossly.

"Well, he might!"

"Do you think he's going to walk down there on Broad Street and find a job that half the men in Columbus can't find?"

"It's better to be looking than sitting around playing dominoes the way Mr. Rayburn does."

"In *his* condition?"

"Maybe he's better than you think!"

"If he had been here a little while ago," my mother said, "he would at least have been able to fix the radiator on that man's car."

"*What* man's car?" I demanded.

"The man who drove in a half-hour ago. In a Ford. He wanted the radiator repaired. I had to tell him your father—"

"Why didn't you wake me up?"

"What could *you* have done?"

"I could have fixed it!"

"Without your father? Oh, Kenneth, don't be silly!"

I stared at her in dismay. The one justification I had for my existence, I had imagined, was that at least I could stand by and watch after the radiator business. But while I had been asleep, she had turned someone away.

My face was hot as I got up from the table. "I'll see you."

"Where are you going? You haven't eaten."

"I'm going out and look for a job, like Pop!"

"What chance do *you* have? Come back here!"

"And sit around all day?" I stormed up the stairs and into the bathroom. I scrubbed my face and wet my hair and combed it, and went back to my room to change clothes. I put on my best pants and summer shirt, went back downstairs. Mary met me in the hall. I could tell she was upset because she had her thumb in her mouth until she spied me.

"Kenny, where are you going?" she asked.

"Out to look for a job," I said.

"Why?"

"Because nobody around here thinks I can do radiators," I told her.

"I think you can."

I sighed and hugged her. "I'm glad somebody does. But I guess if Pop is out looking, I'd better go look, too."

"Kenny," she said soberly, "are we going to *starve?*"

"No! Of course not, sis."

"Maybe we're just going to not have anything at all to eat and we'll starve to death and then we won't have anyplace to live and we'll be out in the dark and it'll rain or even snow. And we'll freeze to death."

"No. Listen, don't talk like that. We might be a little poor right now, but look at this nice house. Look at Gramaw making bread, and that nice dress you've got on. Don't you worry any. There are a whole lot of people in this world worse off than we are."

"But then why are you and Daddy going out all of a sudden to look for jobs?"

I thought about it. "Well, I guess for the same reason Mom washes windows."

Mary tilted her head. *"What?"*

"Never mind. You be a good girl and I'll see you later."

I went back into the kitchen. "I'll be back this afternoon sometime."

Gramaw glanced at me, thought about saying something, and tightened her lips.

"Oh, Kenny," my mother said. It mixed regret with disapproval.

I had thirty-nine cents in my pocket. Nine streetcar rides. I set out for Broad Street. If Pop was looking on the Hilltop, I thought, I would look in the Bottoms. There were a lot of stores and shops down there. Rehearsing my speech, I lengthened my strides.

12

It was past five o'clock in the afternoon when I dragged back up Terrace Avenue, my stomach knocking a hole in my ribs. Most of my brave plans were in shambles, along with much of my self-esteem.

I had never looked seriously for a job before. I had not known how hard it was to stand outside a store or a shop, trying to screw up my courage to go in and *ask*. Each place I went into only made the next one seem harder. My God, here I was *alone* in the whole of Columbus, for all practical purposes, pounding the pavements for a job that probably didn't even exist.

"A *what?*" one of the first storekeepers said, looking at me like I was a microbe. "A *job?* I'll tell you what, kiddo. If you find one, let me know and *I'll* take it!"

"Congratulations," sneered a mechanic in a welding shop. "You're the ten thousandth person to ask. You win a lollipop."

"What are your qualifications?" a jolly-looking grocer asked, grinning at me from behind thick glasses that made his eyes look like onions.

"Well, I'm an eighth-grade graduate—"

"Are you, now! Do you know cost accounting?"

"No, but I could learn fast."

"How about the calculus?"

"I guess not—"

"What's two and two? Quick, now!" He snapped his fingers at me.

"Four," I said, face burning.

"Good! Son, if you're smart enough to know two and two are four, you ought to be smart enough to know there aren't any jobs. Nowhere. Go home and shoot marbles or something."

I tried a print shop, several more groceries, an automobile dealer, a tavern, two drugstores, three dime stores, a candy shop, a variety store, a butcher shop, a furniture store and a wallpaper store, two paint stores and a spooky Chinese restaurant where a grinning Oriental escorted me back through a darkened eating area to a kitchen where two others were chopping vegetables and pieces of raw meat. They carried on a long conversation in their own tongue and laughed shrilly and put me out the back door in the dingy, sun-drenched alley. Next I tried a dry cleaner and then a movie theater.

At a feed store somewhere near Sandusky Street I went in and made my usual pitch. The man facing me among the barrels and huge feed sacks looked like he weighed three hundred pounds. He heard me out unblinkingly.

"Well, I'll tell you what," he said. "Can you lift that there sack?"

The burlap bag looked as big as I was. I bent to it, grabbed hold of its squishy sides, and heaved. It did not budge. The back

seam of my pants let go. The man started to laugh. His bellowing
roar filled the dusty storeroom. I fled, his laughter following me
out onto the sidewalk.

There was nothing to do after that but head home. I
managed to stand against a pole at the streetcar stop to hide the
rip in my trousers, got on last, and backed into the nearest front
side seat. Not many passengers remained when I got off and I
could only hope they did not observe me as I swung around fast
into the exit well and got off the moment the door opened.

So here I was, I thought, coming home after busting my
britches. Literally. I felt like the world's biggest dummy.

And tomorrow I had to go out and do it *again.* The prospect
made my insides shrivel. There was *nothing* as bad as going in
somewhere and asking for a job. You felt like a beggar, a fool. You
placed yourself so totally at someone else's mercy. I felt like my
insides had been spread out on a table under hot, bright lights
and strangers had sifted through them with forks and spoons.

A few of the gang had a ball game going in the park. I waved
to them and climbed the steps to our house. Entering, I smelled
the last vapors of the freshly baked bread mixed with the fine
aroma of vegetable soup simmering. The house was quiet; too
quiet. No radio in the parlor, no racket from Mary or Frank. The
living room was vacant.

I went into the kitchen. My mother was at the stove.

"What's going on?" I asked.

She held a finger to her lips. "Be very quiet."

"Why?"

"Your father is not feeling well."

"Where is he?"

"In bed."

"What *happened?*"

"Nothing happened, Kenneth. He came home in the middle
of the afternoon. He had overdone. He's resting now."

"Did he find a job?"

"No. Did you?"

"No ma'am," I admitted. "Can I go see him?"

"Peek in. He might be asleep."

I climbed the stairs carefully, not allowing them to creak. My parents' bedroom door was ajar. I looked in. Gramaw sat in the rocker by the bed, gently rocking. Pop lay in the bed with a sheet over his torso. The blinds were pulled and it was hot and shady in the bedroom. Gramaw saw me and nodded.

"Is he asleep?" I whispered.

Pop's eyes opened. "No, he isn't asleep."

I crept in. He was very pale, with bluish tinges around his lips. His hands atop the sheet looked waxen. "Are you *okay?*" I asked.

"I'm fine," he said hoarsely. "But I would be a lot better if you had been home tending to business today instead of skylarking around Columbus."

"Home?" The attack was so unexpected, the anger in his eyes so bright, I was at a loss for words. "Skylarking around?"

"Do you know we had a customer at seven thirty this morning?" he demanded.

"Yes, sir, I hadn't gotten up yet—"

"Do you think this is some kind of a resort? Maybe we should install a swimming pool and some tennis courts."

"I—"

"We had another customer this afternoon, I'm told. You weren't here for him, either."

"I was out looking for a job."

"Who told *you* to go look for a job?" he demanded, voice rising.

"Joseph," Gramaw said softly, reprovingly.

"You be quiet," Pop snapped. "He's my son." His eyes swiveled back to me. He was irrationally angry. "Well?"

"I—I thought I could help," I said. I was crushed. This attack was the last thing in the world I had expected. "I missed the first customer, and I didn't think—"

"You didn't think," he snapped disgustedly. "That's right. You didn't *think*. Two customers missed. Ten dollars gone. All because you didn't *think.*"

"*You* went off looking for a job," I said. "I thought I should, too."

"What made you think that?" he asked. "Who told you to think that?"

"Nobody told me to think that! People don't have to tell me everything to think!"

"Don't they? Is that because you think you're some kind of a law unto yourself?"

"*No!* I was trying to help!"

"If you had a head on your shoulders to use for more than a hat rack, you'd know a kid won't find a job when men are going begging."

I stared at him. He waited, eyes fiercely bright. After the day I had put in, I was suddenly very close to tears. I bit my lip and said nothing. I didn't trust myself.

"Go on," he said weakly, looking away. "Get out of here."

I fled to my own room, wanting only to be alone. But there sat Frank, the picture of dejection.

"I guess he bawled you out, too," he said.

I didn't reply. My ball glove was on the bed. I kicked it into the corner and threw myself down on the covers, staring at the ceiling.

"I hate him," Frank said softly. "I came home and went out to play ball and he came over and bawled me out in front of Frank Schroeder and *everyone*. I wish—I wish he was dead!"

"Don't *ever* say something like that!" I snapped, newly shocked.

"*We* can't help it he's sick," Frank retorted bitterly. "*We* can't help it there's a depression and some guys want our house."

"No," I said. "And neither can he."

"He doesn't have to take it out on us!"

"Frank, you're not big enough to understand."

"And I suppose you are?" he flared. "I suppose you're the big shot that understands everything?"

I got off the bed and left the room. In the hall, I realized there was really no place to go. I crept down the stairs and went around the back way, through the dining room, and to the basement stairs. I went down to the workbench. The basement smelled wet and clean from Mom's washing, which hung on ropes everywhere. I sat at the workbench and looked at the tools. One of them looked like it might need oiling. I wiped it carefully and then oiled it very lightly, as I had been taught, and replaced it on the rack. Then I got into Pop's secret cache of Chesterfields and lit one and tried to inhale it. I could not make the smoke go down right.

Max came flopping down the steps to join me. He nuzzled my foot.

"Stop it," I told him crossly.

He made a sneezing sound and curled up at my feet, tail thumping.

If the world were *right,* I thought, people like Uncle Jack would not kill themselves, there would not be depressions, brothers would not have to go clear to Tulsa for work, fathers would not become invalids. If the world had a God, there would not be feed-store owners who laughed at you when you could not lift thousand-pound sacks. And you would not love people so much that you hurt from it, and then have them turn on you for no reason.

I tried to rally myself. I knew I was feeling sorry for myself, and if there was one thing in the world I could not abide, it was self-pity. I was just tired and hungry, I told myself.

And Pop had plenty of reasons to be angry at the world, and to lash out at me when he probably didn't really mean it.

But I was *sick* of being sweetly reasonable, sick and tired of trying to understand everyone else's problems. *I hate him,* Frank had said. I hated him, too, if I was honest enough to admit it. I hated him for getting sick and putting us in this pickle, and I hated him for making me love him so much and then turning on me for no reason. I had always *believed* in him. But he was no more or less than any other man. He could be as unreasonable as the next person, and as weak. He was no God.

No gods—no God—of any kind.

No heaven or hell, no guardian angel, no Holy Roman Apostolic Church, no communion of saints, no *nothing*.

Just this—just living, until you were dead and they threw dirt in your face, and that was *it*, end of the last chapter, finished, done, *over*. What else was new?

I sat at the bench, staring at the tools, feeling more devastated than ever before. *Is this what it means to grow up? If so, I didn't ask for it.*

There was another sound on the steps. Turning abruptly, I saw Mary coming down, her doll under her arm. She was getting too big for dolls. It occurred to me to tell her. *They hit you, you hit somebody else.* I kept my mouth shut.

She came over, very serious. "Kenny?"

"Uh-huh?"

"Why are you crying?"

"I ain't crying. My eyes are just watering."

She reached up and threw her arms around my neck. She smelled of candy and soap and little girl. "I *love* you, Kenny!"

I held her close. "I love you too, Mary."

"If you feel bad, I'll read *you* a story!"

I chuckled and wiped my eyes. "That's a deal."

"Only first you're supposed to come for supper, Mama said."

"Okay. I'll be right up."

She hesitated. "Did you find a job today?"

"No, not today."

"Neither did Daddy, and he came home sick."

"I know."

"Are you going to look again tomorrow?"

"Yes," I said. "And the day after that, and the day after that. I'm going to show some people a thing or two. You just watch."

She beamed. "Goodie. Then you'll buy me an ice cream!"

"Six ice creams."

"Six might make me sick."

"Five, then."

"Goodie!" She started up the steps. "You come eat now, like Mama said."

"I'll be right there."

She went on up and I heard her reporting in the kitchen. I slipped off the stool, petted Max, and wiped my eyes again. They would *not* know I had been crying. And tomorrow or the next day I would find a job if it killed me.

I started for the stairs. How I wished everything . . . were different.

As I started up to the kitchen, the faint sound of yelling and whistling penetrated the basement all the way from the park out front. Someone had hit a long ball. I envied them.

13

Andrew Finnegan, who hired me, was one of the stingiest, meanest men I have ever known. Or at least it seemed so at first.

Finnegan operated a garage and machine shop on West Mound Street just across the river from Columbus's downtown. His plant consisted of a mammoth old barn with a dirt floor and two smaller metal buildings on either side, all of it surrounded by an acre or two of rusting wrecked cars, disembodied bumpers and fenders and engines, stovepipe, pieces of a radio tower, rotting lumber, chunks of scattered concrete, piles of empty paint cans, broken ladders and scaffolding, and the front half of a bright blue, open-cockpit racing car with number *87* emblazoned on the side in garish yellow. The sign on the side of the barn main building, painted over a Mail Pouch advertisement that still vaguely shone through, said FINNEGAN'S—AUTO— WE FIX.

When I walked into the dusty yard, a mechanic in the main

building was hammering industriously under a Ford, two others were working at metal lathes in one of the steel sheds, two were lowering an engine back into a Buick with an outdoor block and tackle, one was patching a tire, and one crouched beside an ancient touring car, his face obscured by his welder's mask, while he welded a bumper brace. I stopped near the welder and waited.

He was tall and lanky, all bones inside his bib overalls and gray undershirt. He had a railroad cap on backward. He seemed to notice me, or at least his mask tipped my way. Then he resumed work. I continued to wait and watch. It was afternoon and I was tired.

The welder stopped abruptly, cutting off his torch. He hung it on the tank with a clatter and raised his mask to reveal a long, lantern-jawed face covered by a week's stubble beard, a beak nose, and close-set bloodshot eyes. His beard and the hair sticking out from under his filthy cap were the color of carrots.

"What do ye want, besides to go blind?" he croaked.

"What?" I said, startled.

"What do ye want, besides to go blind? Ye must wanna go blind, ye blamed idjit, er ye wouldna stand there like an oaf staring direct into the light of the torch."

My eyes, I realized, were a little dazzled by the brightness. I could still see it in the middle of my vision even though it was gone. "I'm looking for Mr. Finnegan," I said.

"And what would ye be wantin' with that old coyote?"

"I'm looking for a job."

He stood, arching his back as if it hurt wonderfully. Taking a pouch of plug tobacco out of his pocket, he bit off a chunk and began chewing. He looked me up and down. "What makes ye think the old bag would be hirin' midgets today?"

"I'm not a midget," I said stiffly.

"Oh, yer not, are ye. What are ye, then?"

"Where's Finnegan?" I countered hotly. It had been a long day.

The man spat a brown stream and turned his railroad cap

around. On the front over the bill he had sewn red letters that said BOSS. "I'm Finnegan, ye little dumb butt. Now git off my property before somebody falls over ye and hurts hisself."

I contained my surprise. Knowing it was hopeless, I tried again anyway. "Mr. Finnegan, I heard you might need a good radiator man and general mechanic."

"Radiator man, maybe," Finnegan grunted. "Radiator dwarf, never. Git on with ye."

"I can fix radiators," I snapped. "I've been running my own radiator business on the Hilltop for quite some time now."

"What's yer name?"

"Riley. Ken Riley."

Finnegan bent slightly at the waist, fixing me with his narrow eyes. "Kin to old Joe Riley, used to work for Craner's?"

"That's my father, sir."

"How come yer not working with him?"

"He's not too well right now. Business is off."

"Humpf." Finnegan spat again, hitting a stray tin can six feet distant. "Well . . . I can't be hiring no kids."

"I'm sixteen," I lied.

"Yer lyin'."

"No, sir."

Finnegan jammed his hands in his pockets and walked slowly around me. "Ye wouldna last a day around here."

"Try me!"

He stopped pacing. "And what would ye think I'd pay ye? I pay that boy over there fifteen a week. Top hand. Been everywhere. Don't drink . . . much."

"I'll work for twelve," I said.

"Yer overpricin' yerself. I might pay ye ten."

He was really thinking about it! I started to sweat.

"Eleven?" I tried to act casual.

"Boy, would ye like to be throwed clean into the river, an' yer nose give a good bleed to boot?"

"I'd be glad to start at ten," I said quickly.

"Ye'll start at ten an' ye'll stay at ten. I'm no millionaire. I don't tolerate dillydallyin' around, neither. But ye better be good. They's no sense wastin' yer time er mine if ye ain't."

"I am," I told him.

"Ye report at seven. Ye work till seven. Bring yer lunch. Ye git thirty minutes at noon, an' there ain't time to go no place else."

"Yes, sir!"

"Ye work tomorrow fer free. On trial. If I like yer work, I'll put ye on. I pay ever' Friday, cash. First time yer late, first time yer absent, first time ye git drunk, first time ye talk back, first time ye mess up a job, first time ye fail to do what I tell ye, first time anything else I don't like, yer fired. Understand?"

"Yes, sir."

"Okay. Yer hired. Subjeck to approval." Finnegan moved slightly and his welder's mask slammed back down over his face. He squatted, fired his torch again, and returned to work.

I started toward the gate, resisting the impulse to leap and yell for joy. One of the men who had been lowering the engine was staggering across the yard with half a transmission in his arms. He was black and sweating profusely. Our eyes met.

"Hi there!" I grinned. "My name's Ken and I just got a job here. I start in the morning."

The black man's chest heaved. "God help you," he muttered, and staggered on with his burden.

I didn't know what he meant. My concern lasted only a moment. As I walked on toward the distant streetcar line, I could hardly contain myself. I had a job! *I had a job!* After more than a week of being laughed at, turned down, made a joke of, and facing outright hostility for even asking, I had found a *job*.

Now all I had to do was become a journeyman mechanic overnight.

When I walked up our street, my father was sitting in the front porch swing. His setback the day he sought work had lingered and he looked thinner . . . weaker, grim. I went onto the porch bursting with pride.

"I found one!" I told him.

He looked at me without expression. "You found one what?"

"Job! I found a job! I start tomorrow morning, working at a garage, and I'm going to be paid ten dollars a week!"

He mustered a smile. "Son, that's fine. I know you looked hard."

"Tomorrow I'm on trial," I added, "but after that I'll be on the regular payroll."

"That's amazing," he said. "A summer job. I didn't know there was one anywhere in Columbus."

Nothing had been said with Finnegan about summer employment only. I had assumed from the start that a job, if I found one, was permanent. I did not reply, and Pop must have seen a change in my expression.

He said, "It *is* just for the summer. Until school starts again."

"Well," I hedged, "I guess we just have to wait and see."

"You're going back to school in September," he snapped.

"If we still need more money," I said, "maybe I could postpone going back a year or two—"

"So you're planning your own future now?" he flared. "The old man is a worthless invalid now, out of work, so you don't have to do what he tells you anymore?"

"Pop, I didn't mean that at all! But gaw, if we need money to get credit and save the house—"

"You're going back to school in the fall! You may think you're a big shot and I'm nothing, but until you're twenty-one, or big enough to whip me, you do what I say. Do you hear me?"

"Yes, sir," I said, shocked by his anger.

"And if you took a man's job on false promises of working there after school starts, you'll just have to go back in tomorrow morning and admit the truth."

I said nothing. My pride was gone, the pleasure out of my achievement.

"Do you hear me?" Pop demanded.

"Yes, sir."

"You don't take a job under false pretenses. That's not honorable."

"Yes, sir." I already knew I had no intention of telling Finnegan anything about school. Bringing in money and saving the house came first.

"So what's the name of this place?" Pop asked, calming a bit.

"I don't know what its right name is, but the man who runs it is named Finnegan."

"Finnegan! Down there on Mound Street?"

"You know him?"

"He the biggest crook on the west side. Oh, my aching back! How did you get tied up with *him*?"

"I beat the pavement for two weeks and he was the first person who said he would hire me," I fired back hotly.

"Nobody with an ounce of pride works for Finnegan," Pop said. "He cheats his customers and he cheats his help out of honest wages. Couldn't you *tell* he was a crook, just talking to him?"

"He didn't seem like any more of a crook than half the people who laughed at me," I said.

"Finnegan!" Pop said, swinging the glider. "A son of mine, going to work for Finnegan!"

"*I* won't cheat anybody," I told him. "And the money I bring home will help a lot, won't it? When you go down to some of the banks and ask for a loan to pay off those mortgage guys and keep the house, won't it be good for you to say I'm bringing in forty dollars a month, regular?"

"Is that what I'm going to do?" Pop demanded. "Go ask a bank for a loan?"

I stared at him. Could I say *nothing* right? "Well, I thought—"

"So you've got it all figured out for me," he said. "How to save the house. I can't work and now I can't think. My sons have to do all of it for me."

"Why are you twisting everything around?" I pleaded. "I'm just trying to *help!*"

He stared at me, facial muscles working. He thought about
it. His chest heaved. "Okay," he said finally. "Sorry. Congratulations on the job. The *summer* job. I hope it works out. Who
knows? Maybe Finnegan has changed his ways."

I waited, heart thudding. He did not say anything else. We
watched each other, some kind of ageless antagonism sharp between us.

"I'm going to go tell Mom and Gramaw," I said.

He nodded and resumed swinging. I was dismissed.

I went inside. Mom was in the kitchen alone.

"I got a job!" I told her.

She turned, beaming. "Kenneth! That's wonderful!" She
came over and hugged me. "Sit down here at the table and tell
me everything! Where? When do you start? What will you be
doing?"

This was more like it. I told her about my interview with
Finnegan, the hours, the pay, tomorrow being a day of trial.

"I know they'll love your work," she told me enthusiastically.
"That's just the grandest news! It just shows what perseverance
will do for you. Have you told your father yet?"

"I told him on the way in."

"This is wonderful," she said. "This may be just what he
needed, after today."

"Something happened today?"

Her face clouded. "He started down to Broad Street to
. . . do some more looking of his own. I guess he almost fainted.
The next thing I knew, two men I had never seen before were
helping him up the steps. He was terribly upset about it."

I could imagine. What a blow that had been to his pride,
being aided by two strangers—brought back home. For him it
was disgrace.

"Was he cheered up when you told him?" Mom asked.

"Oh, yes," I said. "He thinks it's wonderful. He's real proud
of me."

She hugged me again. "We all are, Kenneth! God bless that
man who hired you! What did you say his name is?"

"Finnegan."

"And is he a nice man?"

"He's fine," I lied. "Tough, but okay. I know we'll get along real well."

At supper everyone was in an almost festive mood, thanks to my news. Gramaw teased me about things she would put in my lunch bucket. Frank was practically awed. Mary asked me a hundred questions about the work place and Finnegan and how I got paid and things I would do on the job. Even Pop cheered up a little, it seemed, and said he knew I would do well.

It was hot that night, not a breath of air moving, and I could not sleep. I lay awake with my head near the useless window, listening to Frank breathe and the house make little noises as it cooled from the sun. A rafter creaked somewhere, a board shifted slightly, a pipe in a wall contracted slightly, making a series of tiny popping noises. *They'll never get this house,* I told myself. *We'll live in it forever.*

A new sound in the room startled me. I turned to see Pop's shadowy figure in the doorway. For some reason I pretended to be asleep.

He came to the bed and sat down on its edge, his weight making the springs groan. His hand touched my hair, moving it off my forehead. His fingers, very gentle, traced my eyebrow. Then I felt his breath on my face and his lips touched my cheek. He sat still, unmoving beside me, for what seemed a very long time. Then the springs creaked again as he got up, and when I opened my eyes he was gone.

"No, *no* NO!" Finnegan yelled at me the next morning. "Nobody told ye to repair the core! Drain an' flush! Read the ticket!"

"It's leaking!" I protested.

"I don't care if it's gushin' like Old Faithful, dummy! The man said to drain an' flush. That's the estimate I give him. Now ye've give him a core job, free. Ye think this is a charity ward I'm operatin'? Have ye had damage to yer brain?"

"I thought—"

"Don't think! Do me a favor, dumb boy! *Never think!* Jest read the ticket an' do what's ordered! I make all the decisions! Have ye got that?"

"Yes, sir," I said, wondering if I would ever understand him.

"Ye'll be docked fifty cents off next week's salary fer the wasted time—*assumin'*, that is, I hire ye at all."

I looked down at the radiator on the bench, newly soldered, my best work. I felt mortified and foolish. Nobody had ever talked to me like this before.

"*Well?*" Finnegan screamed. "What're ye *settin'* there fer? Put it back in the car! Put it back in the car! Git a move on! Ye got that Studebaker to fix the bumper on an' yet got to sweep up an' I want ye to try to fix the toilet back there an' paint that fence out back if nobody else brings work in. Time is money, dumb boy! I'm no millionaire! *Move!* If I'd wanted me a statue, I'd of stole one from the cemetery!"

The only thing that got me through that interminable day of trial was the fact that Finnegan treated everyone alike. Just as miserably as he treated me. Stein, the beetle-browed body man, was ready to start smoothing a hammered-out fender about noon when Finnegan went to inspect his work. One look and Finnegan went crazy. He grabbed a ballpeen hammer and started attacking Stein's work, knocking the fender back in again worse than it had been in the first place. "Don't call thet good enough! Don't try to tell me thet's good enough! That's slop work, ye dadblamed idjit! If ye can't fix it right, don't fix it at all! If ye can't smooth it out, then find another fender an' put it on!" And all the time he was yelling, Finnegan was smashing the fender to bits with the hammer.

Davis, the black man, fared no better. He tuned a Chevie engine and Finnegan walked by just as he was about to close the hood.

"Wait a minute," Finnegan snapped and propped the hood up again. Then he took a nickel out of his pocket and stood it on the rocker arm cover on edge. The engine at idle shook ever so slightly. The nickel fell over. "Reset the idle," Finnegan said stonily and pocketed his test nickel and strode away.

One of the machinists named McGiver, however, had the worst of it that day. It was just a little past lunch when Finnegan rolled out from under a truck, spied McGiver hurrying across the yard toward the main building, and lurched to his feet to intercept him.

"Where are ye going *this* time?" he demanded shrilly.

McGiver, a plump man with bad facial color, said something low.

"The toilet!" Finnegan yelled. "The toilet, is it! How many times do ye plan to go to the toilet in one day? This is yer fifth trip to the toilet today thet I know of, an' I didna even start counting till past nine o'clock!"

McGiver shook his head and said something. Several of us watched covertly from our nearby jobs. McGiver seemed to be in some discomfort.

"Well," Finnegan told him just as loudly as before, "If yer sick, ye should of stayed home, man! It's bad enough, stealin' all my time I'm payin' ye fer, settin' on the toilet. But not only that, yer usin' my water. Water costs money, an' money don't grow on trees, ye know. I'd be better off if ye'd stayed at home. I wouldna have to pay ye, an' I'd be savin' all that water!"

McGiver said something else low and earnest.

Finnegan threw up his hands. "All right! All right! Go ahead! Go a hunnert times! I guess when I see the river over there go dry, I'll know they're comin' in the police car fer me because I let ye flush it dry. A dollar, McGiver!" This he bawled after the man was already well into the main building. "I'm dockin' ye a dollar fer this! Ye don't like it, ye can lump it! The next time yer this sick, jest stay at home an' I'll hire me a healthy man. . . . *Ye hear me?*"

McGiver slumped out of sight. Finnegan whirled and caught me and Davis watching and listening.

"What is it ye want?" he screamed at us. "A free ticket to the poorhouse? Stand around like thet an' impersonate politicians, an' ye'll be getting worse'n McGiver!"

By the end of the day I was exhausted, covered with dirt, rust and paint from the fence. But I had been bawled out only one other time, when I found a new brush to paint with rather than cleaning up an old one that looked like it had been on the floor of the toolshed, filled with red, crusted paint and stiff as a plank, for years. *"Do ye think we're made of money around here? The old brush is fine for a fence. What did ye think ye was gonna be paintin', dumb boy? A new Packard?"* So I faced Finnegan in the slanting evening light with a sense of wary accomplishment.

Finnegan sighed, removed his filthy cap, and wiped his sleeve across his face. "Well, sir. I wish I could hire ye."

"What did I do wrong?" I asked, astonished.

"Ye did all right. I'll give ye thet. Yer stupid, but ye did fine fer a stupid person. The truth of the matter is, though, I've given it a lot of thought. I can't hire ye. I got no more money. I can't afford ye."

"But you said this was a trial today!"

Finnegan scratched his head and spat. He looked honestly embarrassed. "I jest can't afford ye, boy."

"Then what am *I* supposed to do?" I demanded, the bitter disappointment almost overwhelming me. "You said if I did good, I had a job! I've told my family and everything! I was *counting* on this job!"

"Lad, there's nothin' I can do about it. Sorry." He started to turn away.

It has occurred to me only in later years that Finnegan might have given every boy who walked into the yard a one-day "tryout," gratis, and gotten hundreds if not thousands of hours of free labor that way. At the time he turned from me, however, I thought no such thing. I only knew I was very near the end of my rope.

"Wait a minute," I said.

He looked at me. "They's no use beggin'."

"I'll do it for nothing," I blurted.

He squinted and bent forward from the waist. *"Eh?"*

"I don't have anything else," I told him. "At least this way

I can learn. I can have work to do. I'm sick of sitting around waiting." I might have been close to tears.

"Yer crazier an' dumber than I thought, boy . . . ye'll work fer *nothing?*"

"If I have to . . . yes."

Finnegan looked truly stunned. The idea of anyone doing anything without a profit motive was as alien to him, it seemed, as a meteorite from outer space. It was the only time I ever saw him speechless.

"Please," I added, driven by motives I did not fully understand. "I *have to* work. Don't you see that?"

"Don't think ye'll take advantage of me," he grunted. "Ye won't get no special favors. I'll boss ye just the same, an' expect jest as much outta ye."

"That's all right! I understand, sir!"

"Ye'll report at seven an' leave at seven. Like I said."

"Yessir!"

He rubbed dirty hands over his face, creating an ocean of wrinkles. "Ye'll work fer *nothing.*"

"Yessir."

"Well . . . ye'll haf to work a half-day on Saturdays, too."

It seemed almost a blessing. I had assumed a full day. I said nothing.

He ejected a stream of brown tobacco juice, hitting a pop bottle seven feet distant. "All right. We'll try ye out on thet basis."

I hitchhiked a ride home that night. Once away from the garage, I pondered the enormity of what I had done. What good did I think it would do to work without pay? How did that help us any in trying to maintain our household? Worse, how was I going to tell the family?

As it turned out, the matter was taken out of my hands.

Darkness was stealing across Terrace Avenue by the time I walked up the street, swinging my lunch bucket. I was so tired my bones ached, and terribly discouraged. Mary was sitting on the front porch, and Gramaw was in the porch glider. Seeing them, I made my step jaunty and gave them a big grin as I sauntered up the steps.

"There's the working man," Gramaw said fondly.

"We're waiting supper!" Mary told me unhappily.

"I'll hurry," I promised, and went in and hurried to bathe. Then I worked hard on my fingernails, using a small pocketknife and brush. It was devilishly difficult to get all signs of grease out from the nails and around the cuticle, but finally my hands looked as clean and nice as Pop's always did. I went to the table to find them waiting for me.

"Whew!" I said, sitting down. "What a day!"

Pop passed the mush. "Tell us about it," he said, the smallest smile quirking the corner of his mouth.

"It was real interesting," I said. So then I told them about the shop and how much business it did, and about Mr. McGiver being ill (trying to make it funny without being rude), and about Mr. Davis and how I painted the fence and all, leaving out Finnegan's insults. I made quite a yarn of it, trying to be amusing the way Pop always had been when he came home from the shop downtown.

"Did you get terribly tired?" Mom asked finally.

"Not really," I said, cleaning my plate. "We get a half-hour for lunch, and everybody gets two five-minute breaks, and to go to the bathroom, so it's not like you're working *all* the time."

"What did you do when they asked you to pull that gas tank?" Pop asked. "You've never done that before."

"I just managed to get over near Mr. Stein and asked him where I should start, and he told me. After that, I figured it out."

He nodded in approval. "That's the best way to learn: by doing it."

"Oh, I learned a lot."

"And what did Finnegan say when you told him you're going back to school in September?"

My heart missed a beat, but it didn't show. I had worried about this moment all day but now amazed myself with my brazen coolness. "Oh, he didn't like it very well, but he said if I was good help, he would keep me on anyway."

Pop watched me closely. "Finnegan said that, did he."

"Yes, sir."

"Hmmm." Pop sipped his coffee.

For a minute or two, no one spoke. Sweat trickled down my back. I knew I had done many reprehensible things in my life, but this was probably by far the worst.

You lied to your father! my guardian angel said.

It was necessary! my bad angel fired back.

I wondered how many of the things people said to one another every day were lies like this. It dawned on me in the instant that I had gone blithely through my life so far believing almost everything anyone told me. What if everybody lied as easily as I just had? I felt a sharp twinge of disillusionment in human nature.

Perhaps I was so preoccupied with this that I was not ready for what came next.

"So what day do you get paid?" Frank asked.

"Well, the experience is the main thing," I said.

"Okay, okay. But when do you get *paid?*"

"Frank, you can't always think of nothing but money, you know."

Suddenly everyone was watching me.

Frank, oblivious, said, "I just asked when you get your money."

"And I said money isn't everything!"

Pop put down his coffee cup. "Son, has Finnegan pulled something on you already?"

"No, not really," I said, knowing I could not lie my way out of this one. "It's just that . . . things being tight . . . well, for the time being . . . I won't be getting paid."

"*What?*" Frank yelped.

"It's just temporary," I said. "Probably."

"Kenneth?" Mom said. "What on earth . . . ?"

"Let us get this straight," Pop said. "You'll get *nothing?*"

"It's temporary," I insisted, my face heating.

"I knew it! I knew Finnegan would find some way to take advantage of you!"

"He didn't take advantage of me. I volunteered to do it for nothing."

"You volunteered? You—! Oh, my aching back!"

Mom had brought some sugar cookies to the table and still stood with the plate. Frank had already taken one and dunked it in his milk. He was so enthralled that he didn't see the end of the cookie break off and float in his glass. "What kind of a job is it when you don't get anything?" he asked blankly. "Gaw!"

Mom said, "I thought you were going to get ten dollars a week."

Gramaw intervened, "Let the child speak!"

"Mr. Finnegan checked things out," I said, "and I did real good work, but he said he just couldn't afford me right now. So he was going to let me go."

"I wonder how many free days of work he's gotten like that!" Pop said indignantly.

"So I told him," I went on, "I would do it for nothing . . . right now, anyway."

"My aching back," Pop repeated.

"That's the dumbest thing I ever heard of," Frank said, and his piece of cookie sank out of sight.

"A man has got to have work," I shot back at him. "What's better? To do an honest day's work or go out in the park and shoot marbles or play dominoes?"

"What good is it going to do us for you to work for nothing?" Frank countered.

"It'll help. It'll help. At least I'm doing *something*. I'm going to be the best worker Mr. Finnegan has down there. After a while I'll be so good he *has* to pay me something."

"What if he doesn't?" Frank pressed.

I felt about *this* big. But Pop said quietly, "Get off him, Frank. Maybe you don't understand. But I do."

I turned to him. "You *do*?"

"Any job is better than no job," he said. "I wish, son, you were working for somebody besides Finnegan. But by golly, as long as you're working for him, I expect you to give him everything you've got. Maybe he will embarrass himself and start paying you."

I could have burst with pride. I had done something right, even if it was stupid! Turning to Frank in triumph, I saw him discover the wreckage of his cookie in the milk. That made me feel revenged. There are few things in life worse than having to drink milk filled with cookie crumbs.

After supper a car pulled into the backyard. It was a Pearce-Arrow with a steaming radiator. Pop went out to talk to the man, and I left the living room to join him. Pop was bent over the open engine when I got there with the flashlight.

"Thanks, son," he said, spraying the light inside. "Well, it's a bad leak, all right. Can be fixed, though."

The customer was a large man who looked rich. "Any chance you can do it tomorrow?"

Pop hesitated. I knew what he was thinking. The car had a big radiator assembly. He was wondering if he could get it down to the basement by himself.

"We could do it tonight," I suggested.

"Tonight?" the customer said. "Say, that would be grand!"

Pop studied me. "You've had a big day."

"I'm fresh as a daisy," I lied.

Pop turned back to the man. "Well, then, you heard what my partner said. We'll do it tonight and you can come by for it first thing in the morning, if that meets with your approval."

"Absolutely!" The man turned wary. "How much?"

"Four dollars."

"You've got a deal. Can I cut around your house to the street? I just live over here a couple of streets."

Pop shook hands with him. "Around that way."

The man left, whistling.

"Okay," Pop breathed, rolling up his sleeves. "Let's see what we've got here." I ran for some wrenches.

An hour later we had the radiator out on the grass. Pop had done most of the heavy work and was sweating profusely. His face looked pale in the flashlight. "All right, son. You think together we can heft this monster down the steps?"

"Easy!" I told him, grabbing one end.

It was not really that heavy. I got inside the door first so I would be the one to back down and take the slanted weight. We got the radiator to the bench and put it up on it, rusty water trickling from the fittings on either end. Pop hustled to the hot plate and lit the gas and put his three big soldering irons in the flame. Climbing up on his stool, he started examining the core.

"Not too bad," he murmured. "Fix this seam here, and touch up this area here near the bottom." His hands shook badly.

"Do you want me to look in the closet for new hoses?"

"Yes, a new bottom hose. The top one came off all right."

I went to the closet he had built and inspected the row of new hose material neatly lined up on his perfectly fitting shelves. I heard the soldering iron hiss in the flux and knew he was starting to work. Finding the hose, I went back to the bench.

Pop was bent over the radiator. His left hand held the solder bar, his right the iron. He was shaking so badly he could not get both of them anywhere near the break at the same time. Sweat dripped off his nose and chin and he looked ghastly.

"Maybe you'd like to have a try," he said.

"That would be great," I said.

Breathing deeply, he slid off the stool. Walking bent, betraying his pain, he walked to the steps and sat down. Out came his bandana and he mopped his face.

I climbed up on the stool and started doing the seam.

Frank came down after a while, trailed by Max. "How's it going?"

"Fine," I told him. "Stick around. I need you to help me carry this back up to the yard in a few minutes."

"I was going down to—"

"I said stick around!"

Wide-eyed, Frank obeyed.

Pop sat on the steps, watching us. He said nothing. The silence in the basement was punctuated only by the hiss of the iron when I dipped it into the can of acid flux. I could only imagine what it was costing him in his pride to watch me do his work. He had had many spells before, of course, but this one seemed the cruelest of all, just when he had been feeling better.

"There we are!" I said finally, admiring my handiwork.

"All ready to put back in?" Pop asked, getting slowly to his feet.

"I think so. But why don't we let Frank help me? After all, he needs to start learning some of this stuff."

Pop hesitated, staring at me. We both knew the lie.

"Fine," he said. "That's right. You're never too young to start learning, right, Frank?"

"Right," Frank said, catching on for once. He grabbed one end of the radiator and lifted. His knees buckled a little.

"Too much for you?" Pop asked.

"No! Easy!"

We staggered up the steps with the radiator and manhandled it back into position in the car. Pop did not even come out to hold the flashlight.

"Kenny, what in blazes are we going to do?" Frank asked softly.

"Put this thing back in and fill it with water," I said, struggling with the bottom clamps.

"I mean about the *house*. About *living*. Pop can't work. You're working for nothing. Gail doesn't send that much. We've only got a couple of months, and they'll come throw us out!"

"We'll get a new loan," I said, barking my knuckles as the wrench slipped. "We'll get an extension. How do *I* know what we'll do? Shut up about it, will you! Hold that fitting, there. Higher!"

14

During my first full week on the job at Finnegan's, I learned a lot more about him. It was not that he was dishonest, exactly. He liked to call it being shrewd.

Berg, Stein, and Davis, the mechanics who did most of the engine work, were under standing instructions to set the valves extra tight whenever they did a major tuneup. "Make 'em quiet, boys!" Finnegan liked to order, often in front of the unsuspecting customer. "I don't wanna hear no valve noise in this machine!" I was impressed with his concern for noise under the hood until Berg explained to me that setting the valves tighter than tolerances usually resulted in burned valves in about four thousand miles.

"We grind a hell of a lot of valves," Berg added thoughtfully.

Another thing Finnegan always tried to sell was brake fluid. He explained to customers that fresh brake fluid kept the lines in good shape and prevented accidents. Unless the old brake fluid was very dirty, it was drained into Container A. The "new" fluid was pumped in from Container B. That was on Monday. On Tuesday, the containers were reversed, and so on.

Carburetors were, however, Finnegan's specialty. A car came in running rough, let's say, like most of them did. Finnegan himself would open the hood, poke around, meddle with the idle adjustment, and then deliver his standard pitch.

"Well, sir, we can probably take this old carburetor apart an' try to clean it. *Maybe* we can make it work right again. Might take a kit . . . that would be three dollars, labor fifty cents, gaskets a quarter . . . three seventy-five, an' ye've still got the same old carburetor. I can't guarantee that, but we can *try* it." Then he would remove his cap and mop his forehead with his sleeve and look worried.

Invariably the customer asked what *should* be done.

"Well," Finnegan would say, replacing his cap, "I could tell ye what I'd do if it was *my* car."

"Yes? Yes? What?"

"What ye need is a different carburetor. Not a new one, ye understand . . . that would be too expensive, an' I want to save ye all I can, while guaranteein' results. We get a different carburetor, ye see, one that's been cleaned an' fixed to factory specifications, an' we install thet. Actual, we can do thet fer four dollars, an' it's a *lot* better deal."

Most customers looked vastly relieved and pleased by Finnegan's concern and expertise. They would order the changeover to a "different" carburetor and leave.

"Kenny, what're ye doing right now, dumb boy? Take this here carb off this DeSoto an' steam all the varnish off it. Put it in thet Plymouth over yonder. Take the carb off the Plymouth an' clean it up real nice an' put it in the DeSoto. Ye understand, boy?"

It was all a benign sort of skullduggery. Finnegan was a genius for knowing what parts were interchangeable and which weren't. The customers went away happy . . . most of the time. If they came back with burned valves, he always gave them "a very special deal, bein' yer a regular here." And paradoxically he insisted on good work. I saw him make Davis work almost all one afternoon on some Buick brake shoes that were too noisy. They tried three sets of shoes and turned the drums without charge. Finnegan was obsessed with milking the last dime out of every customer, and I couldn't understand why he sometimes so insisted on perfect work.

"Why not just let them squeak and keep charging the man?" I asked.

"Lad," Finnegan said, scowling, "ye understand nothing.

Thet's a poor, honest man. We never do extry work fer a man thet comes in here who's honest an' hardworkin'. The ones we give the extrys to are bad people—bankers, real estate salesmen, like that."

"How do you always know what they are?"

"Ye can take one look an' know! They drive in with thet crafty look in their eye, wantin' to skin ye."

"So the man with the brake shoes—"

"A good man. An honest man. We'd never skin him."

Of course, as I learned later, he docked Davis an hour's time as if the defective shoes were somehow his fault.

On the Thursday of my first full week, I got home late to find the house in an electric mood. Max met me on the steps and ran around and around my legs, nipping at my feet. Mary burst out before I could open the screen.

"Daddy's got a job and it starts right away and he's going *tonight* and we don't have anything ready for supper yet!" she told me.

I went inside to meet my mother and father heading toward the door. Pop was wearing neat gray trousers and a white shirt, and he was carrying his lunch bucket.

"Like ships in the night," he said, smiling.

"You got a job? Really?"

"Night watchman. For the city. It isn't permanent, but maybe it will work into something else."

"What do you do?" I asked. "Are you sure you can—I mean—"

"I go down to city hall and sit at a desk, and once an hour I walk around and punch a clock," he told me. "Don't start talking like your mother. I can do this just fine."

"You're going now?" It was past seven o'clock.

"Yep. Hours are eight till eight. And I'd better hurry." He pulled my mother close for a brief kiss, tousled my hair, and went out the door.

My mother followed to the screen and stood watching him

until he was out of sight. She turned, then, eyes bright with excitement and worry. "I just hope he isn't taking on too much."

"Gosh, Mom, I'm sure he isn't. He looks better already, just having something!"

She sighed. "I hope so. We've been in turmoil around here ever since he got home with the news. I had to wash and iron his good work clothes. We don't have a thing in the house for supper."

"I'll go. Let me clean up first."

She nodded. "Frank can go with you. You can stop at the White Castle on the way back and get some hamburgers."

"White Castles? Wow! We haven't had any White Castles *forever!*"

She smiled. "I guess we can splurge . . . this once."

I hurried upstairs and rushed through my bath and fingernail cleaning. Even so, the shadows were long by the time I got the short list from my mother and Gramaw, and Frank and I set out for Broad Street. At the store we bought stew meat, cornmeal, potatoes, crackers, catsup, beans, and several other items. The grocer put them in two small brown bags. Frank and I each carried a bag as far as White Castle, where we bought six hamburgers for a dollar. I took both grocery sacks and Frank carried the hamburgers in the white bag and we started home. It had gotten dark.

"Pop was really excited," Frank told me. "He went right down and talked to our lawyer again, and the lawyer said what we have to do now is save every cent we can, and then we go down and tell that mortgage company how much we've got, and we've been making all our payments on time, and how much we can pay them right now, and ask them to draw up a new contract. He said with Pop working and you and Gail having jobs, the company will probably want to work with us."

"I don't guess Pop told the lawyer that I'm working for nothing," I said.

"Well . . . I dunno."

We neared Terrace Avenue. On this stretch of Broad Street, several businesses had closed. A streetlight was out at the intersection of the alley just ahead of us, and in front of the boarded-up buildings it was very dark. No traffic was going by.

"It's spooky along here, boy," Frank said.

"Don't be a scaredy-cat," I told him.

Which was when the man stepped out of the mouth of the alley.

With a gun in his hand.

Frank dropped the white sack. One of the White Castles rolled out onto the pavement.

"Don't move!" the man said. He was tall and black, wearing frayed work clothes, and he looked as scared as I felt.

"What do you want?" I asked hoarsely.

He waved the revolver, which looked as big as a howitzer. "Them groceries. Hand them over."

I thought about how much we had spent. *"No!"*

The gun hand shook more violently. "What you say, boy? You hand over them groceries or I'll blow your head clean off!"

"Give 'em to him!" Frank said.

"They're for our family," I protested.

"Boy, you gonna get hurt real bad!"

"We don't have anything to eat at our house!" I told him. *Was I out of my mind?* All I knew was that the idea of going home empty-handed was a horror to me. "You got no right to take the food out of our mouths!"

"Kenny," Frank groaned.

"I got a family too," the man told me. "They're hungry too." He pronounced it *hongry.* "A man's got to give his kids food."

Suddenly I felt sorry for him, and I did not think he was going to shoot us. "I'll tell you what," I said. "I'll give you half our groceries. I'll share with you. One sack. What do you say?"

"You wanna die, boy?"

"Do you want half the groceries?"

He hesitated, then shot out his free hand. I held out one of the grocery bags. He snatched it, turned, and ran into the blackness of the alley.

For a moment Frank and I stood there. My heart was crashing in my throat.

"*Gaw!*" Frank burst out at last. "You almost got us *killed!*"

"Pick up that hamburger," I told him, and began shaking from head to foot.

"I can't believe it!" Frank enthused as we hot-footed it for home. "Did you see the size of that guy? He must have been seven feet tall! I bet he weighed four hundred pounds! I never saw a meaner-looking guy in my whole life! That gun he had must have been a forty-five. It would have blown a hole in you the size of a watermelon."

"Shut up about it, Frank," I suggested.

"Yeah, but what you did was heroic! You stood right up to him! I couldn't believe it! Wow! Wait till I tell everybody about *this!*"

Which of course he did. By the time we got home, our robber had become ten feet tall and weighed a ton and a half. To hear Frank tell it, I had scared the ogre half to death with my brilliant repartee. Mom and Gramaw went pale and made sure we hadn't been hurt, then took inventory of our one sack to see what the robber had gotten. He had taken mostly vegetables.

"Do we call the police?" Frank asked excitedly.

Mom thought about it. "No."

"*No!*" It was a protest.

"We'll wait and see what your father says in the morning. You weren't hurt, and I have an idea that poor man was telling the truth when he said his children were hungry. There are even more Negroes out of work than white people, I hear. I see no reason to have policemen swarming all over us. At least not until I speak with your father."

"I'm going to tell the guys!" Frank said.

"Frank," I groaned.

"They won't believe it!"

There was no holding him back. We ate our White Castles and drank some milk, and he was off into the dark, heading for the Rayburn house.

"I wish he wouldn't spread it around," I told Mom.

"He was scared half to death. He has to talk about it. And why should you be ashamed?" She hugged me. "I think you did just the right thing. I think that man *needed* the groceries."

"We did too."

"So you shared them. Isn't that the Christian thing to do?"

It had not previously occurred to me that I might have actually done something decent. I looked up at my mother uncomprehendingly. She hugged me.

But what will Pop think? I wondered.

I had to leave the next morning before he was home. When I got home that night, he was gone again. My mother said he had been angry about the robbery but relieved that we were not hurt. He had agreed with her that no good would be done now by calling the police. We had nothing to do with police in those days. We seldom saw an officer. They patrolled neighborhoods where there was crime, where trash lived. We didn't need them. The less contact with them, the better.

Frank, however, had done a wonderful job of spreading the tale around the neighborhood. A couple of the Rayburns came over and looked at me like I was Buck Jones or something. Gramaw gave me an extra helping of rice pudding for dessert. Mary asked about six hundred questions, trying to learn just how big and mean the robber really had been and how I had felt when he pointed that machine gun at me.

About nine o'clock things settled down. Mary was sent to bed and Gramaw started listening to her radio. I went to the basement to practice smoking. Max followed me. I was sitting on the steps, scratching his ears, when Gramaw opened the door at the head of the stairs. "Kenny?"

I rushed to the floor drain and dropped the butt in it. "Yessum?"

"Come up here, please."

I went up. Gramaw looked sober. "There are some men on the front porch. Your mother and brother are talking to them."

"Who are they?"

"They're asking about the robbery."

"Cops?"

"Boy, just *go.*"

I went at once. Mom and Frank stood inside the screen door. The porch light had been turned on. I saw three men, one portly and past middle age, the other two considerably younger. All three wore clean work clothing. They looked agitated.

"Here he is now," my mother said as I approached.

"What's going on?" I asked nervously.

"These men are asking some questions about your, ah, little problem last night."

"Lady," the older man said, "we don't consider it a 'little problem' when children in this neighborhood are robbed at gunpoint by niggers." He studied me grimly. "We were just asking your bud, here, what happened."

I already knew I disliked these men with their grim expressions and rough manners. "Who are you?" I asked.

"Neighbors," he said. "We want to keep this area safe for decent people, law-abiding people. You just tell us what happened up there and what the shine looked like."

"We had some groceries," I said. "He said his family was hungry and I gave him half our groceries. That's all."

"That's *all?"* the older man muttered.

Frank piped up, "He had a gun. It was as big as a cannon, boy! And—"

"Shut up, Frank!" I said.

"No! He said he'd blow our heads off if we didn't give him the groceries. Then he grabbed one sack and ran for it."

"What did he look like?"

"He was tall. He was wearing old clothes. He was real black."

"Shut *up,* Frank!"

The men ignored me, concentrating on Frank, who seemed in the height of his glory with all the excitement he had caused. "Would you recognize this spade if you saw him again, son?"

"Sure!" Frank said.

"Are you sure? They all look alike, you know."

I managed to slip around my mother and get beside Frank. He started to reply just as I got a good handful of his back muscle. "I'd know him anywhere! He scared me, boy! I—*ow!*"

"If you don't shut up, Frank, you're going to get a lot worse."

The tallest man looked at me. "You want to talk, is that it?"

"I'd like to know who you guys are," I said.

"We told you."

They were KKK, I thought. I had read enough about them in the papers. I was scared but I didn't want to help them.

"Well, I'll tell you what," I said. "It was real dark and we didn't see anything very clear. And nobody got hurt. I talked to the guy and we made a deal—half our groceries."

"A deal at the point of a gun? You call that a deal?"

"His family was hungry, he said."

"Maybe if a lot more of those jigs went hungry, this country would be a better place." The man addressed my mother. "We're looking into this matter. If we run onto anything, we'll be back to let you know."

"We don't want any trouble," my mother said huskily.

"Lady, there won't *be* any trouble."

"If I can help—*aiee!* Quit, Kenny, that *hurts!*" Frank writhed.

"Why don't you want your bud to talk, boy?" the tallest man ask me.

"Because I want to," I lied.

"You got something against the Klan?"

"No," I lied again. "I've got a picture of the Grand Dragon in my bedroom. Do you wanna see it?"

The men looked at each other, not sure if I was making fun of them or not. "We'll be back if something comes up," the spokesman said. He raised his fingertips to his brow in a salute to my mother, and they left the porch.

"Boy!" Frank gasped after we were back in the house. "The *Klan* is after that nigger! I bet *he* never robs anybody again!"

My mother moved with shocking and uncharacteristic swiftness. Her hand caught in Frank's curly dark hair, twisting him painfully to face her. "Don't *ever* let me hear you use that word in this house again!"

"Ouch! Ouch! All right, Mom!"

She released him. She was very pale, filled with rage and fear. "And if they come back here, you don't talk to them, Frank, not under any circumstances. Is that clear?"

"Aw—"

"Is that clear?"

"Yes!"

"And there will be no more discussion of what happened to the two of you on Broad Street. Not in the house and certainly not outside it. Is *that* clear?"

Frank was angry, too, but there were tears in his eyes. "Yes."

"Yes what?"

"Yes *ma'am.*"

"Go to your room."

Frank slumped up the stairs.

My mother turned to me. "There are enough dreadful things happening in this world today without our adding to them. I think you understand that."

"I think I know what they'd do to that guy if they caught him," I said.

She shuddered. "I think I do, too."

"I won't tell 'em anything, Mom. That's why I tried to shut Frank up."

She took a deep breath. "Well, it's over now, anyway. And if those men come back—"

"I wouldn't give them the time of day if I had six wristwatches," I said.

She smiled wanly. "Good. Neither will I."

We studied each other. I felt shaken but good about what had just happened. My mother and I had far more in common than I had realized. Since Pop's sickness, she had become infinitely more precious to me. I was glad we stood together on this.

She went back to the kitchen. Instead of going to the basement again, I went up to the bedroom. In the dark, Frank lay
across the bed. He had been crying.

I sat on the edge of his bed. "Frank," I said softly, "I know
you meant well. But those guys are KKK. That man that robbed
us—"

"Shut up!" Frank whispered bitterly. "Just shut up and leave
me alone!"

"I'm only trying to—"

"Well, don't!" Frank sat up, eyes blazing with shocking hate.
"You think you're such a big shot! Well, I think you stink! Get off
my bed! Leave me alone! I hate you!"

"Frank—!"

He swung ineffectually at me. "Get off! *Get off!*"

I retreated in confusion. I had never reacted this way when
Pop had tried to talk sense to me. Where had I gone wrong?

I went back to the basement and rearranged some of the
tools. When I went back upsairs much later, my brother was
asleep, his back to my side of the room. I undressed and lay in
the dark, wondering if those frightening men had any chance of
finding "our" robber . . . wondering, too, if I had lost my younger
brother for good. Sometimes it seemed the weight on me was
almost more than I could bear.

On Saturday, shortly before noon, I was sweeping out the
machine shop when Finnegan came in. "Who told ye to do thet?"
he demanded.

"Nobody," I said. "It needs doing."

"I suppose ye figger ye'll curry some favor?"

"I suppose," I said, "I thought I would clean up the floor."

He strode to the nearest workbench where I had cleaned
and oiled the hand tools. "What's this?" he croaked, picking up
a wrench. "Who did all this?"

"I did," I told him.

"Why?" He bent his body at the waist, leering at me in his
most malevolent way.

"They were dirty and they were starting to get some rust," I said.

"I suppose ye used about a dollar's worth of *my* oil?"

"I dipped a rag in that waste oil that's out back to be dumped."

Finnegan glared at me another instant, then stomped out. I finished sweeping, turned out the lights, and pushed the sliding doors closed. He was outside in the yard, watching.

"Do you want the padlock locked?" I called.

"Yes, an' then git yerself over here!"

I locked the shop and walked over to him. We were the last to leave. Mr. Davis was just walking out through the front gate, his great shoulders slumped and tired.

Finnegan looked me up and down with a stare that made my flesh crawl. "I guess ye think yer purty smart, don't ye?"

"No, sir," I said. *Now* what?

"A man can't have somebody else workin' fer him fer nothin'. Not even a dumb boy like ye. It ain't fittin'. I got my pride." He took a ragged breath. "All right. I'll pay ye eight dollars a week. Not a cent more."

"Before you said ten," I reminded him.

"That was *way* before, ye little mongoose! The *last* before, I said *nothin'!*"

I realized I was on thin ice. "I'll take it."

"All right, then. Just remember, dumb boy: one mistake an' ye've got yer walkin' papers; waste my material an' yer docked; get in my road an' I'll knock yer block off. Do we understand each other?"

"Yessir," I said. "I think we do."

To my utter amazement, he got out a scummy old billfold and removed a five-dollar bill. He handed it to me, the look on his face like the money was being amputated along with part of his arm.

"What's this?" I asked.

"Yer pay for this week."

"But—"

"Don't say it ain't enough, ye rascal, er I'll take it back an' box yer ears good fer ye! Yer lucky to be gettin' anything! Our agreement was thet ye'd work fer nothin'!"

"Yessir! Thank you, sir! I'll be the best worker you ever—"

"Git outta my sight, dumb boy, before ye make me throw up! Monday!" he yelled after me as I scurried out the gate with the five dollars clutched in my hand. "If yer late, don't come at all! Remember! Git outta line an' yer finished with Finnegan! If ye tell anybody else how much yer makin', yer fired! Don't think ye can take advantage of me!"

He was still yelling when I ran out of earshot. I felt I could run all the way home.

Pop grinned from ear to ear when I told him what had happened. He said we had done just right with the vigilantes on our porch, too.

"When the day comes that we need somebody like a Klansman to take care of us, that'll be the day we're really in trouble," he told us at the supper table. "The Klan. Oh, my aching back!"

15

In the next few weeks, before our friends from the Klan came back, we did everything we could think of to save our house.

The summer turned very hot and dry, and each day the clotheslines in our backyard were filled with washing as word of my mother's excellent laundry and ironing work evidently spread among people without our financial worries. Gramaw, with summer weddings, had a heavy sewing load. Frank, still harboring his grudge against me, picked up three or four more lawns. Finnegan paid me like clockwork, handing over the money each week with threats about my stupidity and declining business that might make him let me go. Gail's letters came every week, and each time he enclosed a few dollars; he said Oklahoma summers were like nothing we would believe, and he could not understand how he kept his job because everyone else seemed to be out of work. Pop's fill-in job as a night watchman continued and he seemed able to handle it, although I seldom saw him, with our hours overlapping.

We did not talk much about the approaching deadline for some sort of settlement on the house. But we did have what Pop called a war chest now, the painted jewel box I had made for my mother at school. Into it went whatever cash we had. Including some money Gramaw had gotten for some beautiful old dresses, we soon had almost two hundred dollars. I knew it was impossibly meager against our loan balance, but I told myself that every dollar meant additional credit . . . additional hope.

On the fourth of July our block had an impromptu party. First the Smiths, then the Andersons brought picnic blankets and food out into the narrow park. The Rayburns followed, and then came the Schroeders and the McCalls, strolling and visiting. A ball game started, and some of the smaller children played tag. Boys chased each other, popping cap pistols, and the older boys had a few firecrackers although Frank and I didn't have any. Some of the alphabetical Vincents had a tiny pot-metal cannon that shot a hard red rubber ball high into the air every time a firecracker was popped in its base, and every time you looked around, someone was getting hit on top of the head by the ball. Except for the many For Sale signs up and down the street, it might have been any year.

We dragged our deck chairs down off the porch and parked them on the sidewalk facing the park. Gramaw made lemonade and we had some sugar cookies. Pop got up at three and joined us. He was pale and had lost some weight, but he tapped a Chesterfield on his hand and leaned back with a look of relaxation on his face.

"Well, this is a fine day," he told us.

"It seems a little funny, celebrating," I said.

"Why?" He looked sharply at me.

"With the hard times and everything."

"This doesn't have anything to do with the Depression, son. This is the birthday of our country and what it stands for."

Frank stirred. "Like people trying to take our house?"

"Like freedom of speech," Pop replied, nettled. "Freedom of worship. Like our sitting here, free to criticize if we feel like it. Think of the people across the ocean. They don't have anything like this."

I thought of what Gail might say. I didn't want to spoil the moment, so I said nothing. Frank, however, in his usual headlong way, said it for me:

"Maybe some people are a little *too* free. Like that mortgage company."

"I don't want to hear that kind of talk," Pop said.

"It's true, isn't it?"

"This country is founded on the free enterprise system. Those people downtown have a right to try to make a dollar, just the same as you and I do. We may not like it, but that's the way this country works."

"Well, if you ask me," Frank said, "it stinks."

"What would you have?" Pop demanded. "The government coming in and telling people how to run their business?"

"If it helps me, why not?" Frank asked.

"That's a selfish attitude. Don't let worrying about this house deal warp your appreciation for all the freedom we have in this country. We'll work it out. If you work hard enough and keep your nose clean, you'll be all right in this country. That's the way the system works. It's the people who mope around all day and don't try, and then go down to Bank Night at the Rivoli expecting a free ride out of sheer luck, who get themselves in trouble."

Frank sighed and said nothing more. Somebody popped a firecracker in the park, and children squealed.

"Take me, for example," Pop went on. "With any luck, this

part-time night job looks like it's going to turn into something
more permanent. It's something I can do. Sure, I got lucky,
finding it. But I've done the job well and they've noticed. They
tell me they're putting me in for a regular slot. You pull yourself
up by your own bootstraps. This is the only country in the world
where you can do that."

"You're going to get it permanent?" I said. "That's great!"

"Well, it isn't certain yet," Pop said, smiling. "But it looks
good." He pulled out his pocket watch. "If I don't start being late,
or something. So I'd better go get ready right now." He got up
and walked stiffly up the steps and into the house.

I looked at my mother and Gramaw Prater, who had been
listening. "That's great news!"

"I just hope it works out," Mom said.

"That *really* makes it look like we won't have to move."

"Well, you know what the lawyer said. We made the payment on the first, and in August we'll go offer them everything
we've saved and show how we can continue paying regularly."

Mary looked up from her jacks. "And I won't have to change
schools again after all!"

"Oh, you wouldn't have to change schools at any rate," Mom
told her. "There are a lot of nice doubles for rent between here
and St. Aloysius. Gramaw and I looked at one just the other day
that was very nice, down on Clarendon. It was very reasonable
and it had three nice big bedrooms. If we move, it won't be very
far."

No one responded. I could not. It dawned on me that they
were *already looking* for a new place to live. While I had been
living in a fool's paradise of hope, they were getting ready for
disaster. What did *that* say about our real chances?

I felt like screaming. Here we all sat, watching the Fourth
of July celebration, as if everything were normal. And my family
was getting ready to leave this house in which father had in-
vested all his strength.

Gramaw fanned herself with a funeral-parlor fan. "Land, it's
hot!"

I scanned the sky, half-filled with plush, puffy white clouds.
"Maybe it will rain and cool things off."

It didn't rain. Some people went in and others came out, and
the holiday mood endured through the afternoon. The first spar-
kler blazed not ten minutes after sunset, while there was still
more than an hour of twilight remaining. Some of the boys
popped remaining firecrackers, and now you could see their flash
as they exploded in the grass. A massive game of hide and seek
got under way, and every once in a while a girl's voice would cry
out, *"Ollie, ollie, in-free!"* and there would be a mad scramble.
As darkness gathered, Mr. Rayburn came out with an automotive
flare he had picked up somewhere and stuck it in the ground of
the parkway, and lit it. The flare smoked bright pink, making
plumes of pink smoke and lighting the faces of the dozens of
people who ringed the area, watching it burn. A few more firecrackers popped. Frank Schroeder, grown now, came out with
two roman candles. We all oohed and aahed as the red, green,
and yellow balls arced into the darkness. Then each family decided it must be time to light the sparklers for the littler ones, and
the dazzling small scintillations sprang up across the parkway
and through yards until it was amazing and very lovely, all the
sparklers silver and gold. When the sparklers threatened to burn
low, accepted procedure was to spin around with them, or do an
arm-spinning motion, or run.

Watching and listening to the laughter and voices, I could
not help wondering whether it was our last July Fourth on South
Terrace.

Only a few nights later, our visitors from the Klan came back
again. I happened to be in the living room when they walked up
the steps, and I saw them before they sounded the doorbell. It
was the same three, and they had someone with them—a black
man, his arms evidently pinioned behind his back. I saw them
shove him roughly onto the porch. One of them pressed the
doorbell button. I ran for the kitchen.

My mother and Frank and Mary were there just finishing

the dishes. Frank had started toward the hall to answer the bell.

"Frank," I said, "you stay in here."

"What's happening?" he demanded.

I turned to my mother. "Mom, it's those guys from the Klan. Frank has to stay out here and not meddle in it!"

"I'm going," Frank said determinedly, starting past me.

I grabbed his arm. "Frank—"

"Leggo!"

"Frank," my mother said sternly, "sit at the table!"

"Mom!"

"Sit. At. The. Table."

Frank groaned and threw himself onto the nearest chair.

"You and Mary stay here. Under *no* circumstances are you to leave this room. Understood?"

"I wanna see what they say! I—"

"Frank!"

"Aw . . . !"

"I mean it!" Mom's face was ashen and her eyes brooked no opposition.

"Yes ma'am," Frank grumbled.

She pushed past me. "Come on, Kenny."

The doorbell sounded a second time, impatiently, as we went past the parlor to the door. My mother opened it, switching on the porch light. Her little intake of breath warned me before I stood beside her and saw for myself.

The black man—and there was no question but that he was *our* black man, the one who had tried to rob us at gunpoint—stood between the two younger Klansmen, his arms tied behind his back. Blood streamed from his nose and mouth, staining the front of his shirt and pants. Other blows had brought bright blood from his left ear or his skull in that area. His clothing was filthy and half-torn from his body. He was breathing hard, sobbing with the effort, his eyes darting. When they saw me, the glint of recognition mixed with an awful new terror.

The older man did the talking this time. Removing his

straw skimmer, he bowed slightly. "Mrs. Riley? Do you remember us?"

"Yes," my mother said almost inaudibly. "What is this?"

"Ah!" the man said, spying me. "There's the boy himself. Youngster, we think we have the nigger that threatened you and your bud."

"Is that so?" I said, almost stammering.

"Get him up here closer to the light," the older man ordered, and his companions roughly shoved my black man forward. "There he is. Is he the one?"

For a second all time stood still. Only the ragged sound of breathing broke the silence. I looked at the man—saw the terror and despair in him. I could smell the sour odor of his fear in his sweat. He did not seem as big here on the porch, tied and bleeding, without his gun or his desperate bravado.

"Well?" the older white man grunted.

"Him?" I said, trying to make my decision, torn at this last moment by fear of *them.*

"Is he the one?"

"Gosh, no!" I said. "The guy who robbed us was quite a bit bigger. And he had a lot more hair. His teeth stuck out," I added, ad libbing desperately.

The black man's eyes widened slightly in shock, and then another look—realization that I did know him but was lying to save him—changed his eyes entirely. I had never seen fear vanish so swiftly, to be replaced first by shock, then a dawning realization of something else.

The older white man bent slightly at the waist to peer at me from my level. "Are you sure about that? This spade has a lot of kids. We searched his shack and found a gun."

"Gosh, no!" I said. "He doesn't look *anything* like the guy who stopped me and Frank!"

Suspicion narrowed the older man's eyes. "Your bud here?"

"Frank? No."

"Where is he?"

"Gone to the show. Downtown."

He looked at my mother for corroboration. "That true?"

"My son doesn't lie," she told him. "Besides, I've questioned both boys. Even I could have told you that this couldn't possibly be the man. They were clear about how tall he was, and this man is only average height. And—Kenny—didn't you say the man had a scar?"

"A scar?" I echoed blankly.

"Yes. On his face?"

"Yes! Right!" I described a curl with my finger on my cheek. "He was a lot taller, and had a lot more hair, and his teeth stuck out and he was real ugly, and he had this scar on his left cheek, kind of like a question mark!"

The three white men looked at each other. It was clear they did not entirely believe us and were bitterly disappointed.

"I'd still like to talk to the other boy," the older man said after a long pause.

"He won't be home until quite late," my mother said. "And I think you can trust Kenny's word. This is *not* the man. Obviously."

The older man took a deep breath. "All right, boys."

"What now?" one of them, loutish, asked.

"Turn him loose."

"Fletch—" the man started to protest.

"I said turn him loose! Now!" The older man's anger boiled at his own companions.

They untied the rough rope circling the black man's torso and fixing his hands. His shoulders slumped with pained relief as his arms came free and he rubbed raw flesh on his wrists.

"Nigger," the older man told him, "you got lucky this time. If we come back down there and find any other weapons in your shack—ever—you'll decorate a lamp post. Don't *ever* let us see you in this neighborhood again. You understand?"

"*Yes*, sir!"

"Okay, then. Run. Before we change our mind."

With the briefest glance at me, the man turned and hurried off the porch. He cut across our lawn and broke into a shambling, dizzy run. One of the white men walked to the end of the porch and took something—a revolver—from his pants pocket.

"Hey, nigger!" he yelled, and raised the gun to the sky. It exploded with a deafening report. The black man, half a block distant, flinched violently and ran much faster. Chuckling, the man put his gun back in his pocket and sauntered into the light. "He won't be back."

The older man put his hat on with deliberate insolence, his eyes never leaving my mother's face. "That nigger was the one," he said flatly.

"No," my mother said.

He looked at me. "He *was* the one."

"No," I said.

He turned back to Mom. "He was the one that robbed your boys, and you both lied to protect him."

"No," my mother said again.

"What are you people, anyway? Catholics?"

"Yes," my mother shot back, a world of defiance in the word.

"I should have known it was something like that. Come on, boys, before I puke."

They left the porch and went down to their car. We stood in the doorway and watched them drive away. Then we went in and shut the door.

Mom looked at me. "It was the man?"

"Yessum."

"I knew it."

"Mom, they would have killed him."

"You don't have to explain to me." She locked the front door. "I'm going to go talk to Frank."

"Mom, he mustn't blab any more about it! He—"

"He won't. That's what I'm going to make clear to him. Now, you stay in here while I talk to him."

"Yessum."

She studied my face, and then with a little maternal sound she hugged me tight. "I love you very much."

"I love *you*, Mom. And everything is going to be fine!"

"Of course it is." She released me, her eyes brighter than normal, then headed for the kitchen. I went into the living room and sat alone, feeling enormously pleased with myself and with her. We had not had many victories lately, and this one felt good. I could remember what Pop had said about the Klan during their shirttail parade down Broad Street, and even if I had not had that for guidance, I think I would have known that vigilantes were more dangerous by any standard I knew than a half-starved black man desperate to feed his children.

Pop, I thought, would be proud of us.

He was, too. "You did just right," he told us the next day. "That poor guy they had caught! Damn, it makes my blood boil sometimes!"

"I just hope they don't retaliate in some way," my mother said. "They were furious. I think they were almost sure we weren't telling them the truth."

"Don't give it a thought," Pop said. "What could they do?"

Less than a week later we found out.

16

"What are you doing home?" I asked with surprise when I got home from work that night.

Pop, in his favorite chair, looked up from the magazine. He was slightly pink, a sign of anger. "Where am I supposed to be? China?"

I didn't reply to the sarcasm. He was more upset than I had first realized, and I did not want to make things worse. Gramaw was in the rocker with her sewing ignored on her lap. Frank sat

on the couch, popping the taped baseball into his battered glove.
Mary was on the floor with a storybook but was not reading it.
Everyone looked solemn.

I started past the living room, thinking Mom might be in the
kitchen to provide some answers.

"What happened," Pop called after me, "was that I didn't
get the regular job after all." His voice was hollow, with that note
it sometimes got when he was swallowing bitterness.

"I thought it was all set!" I said, walking back into the room.

He shrugged. "There's many a slip, et cetera."

"But you said you'd done good work, and the supervisor had
your name in for a permanent placement. All it had to do was go
by the mayor's desk—"

"It didn't," Pop said.

"It didn't what?"

"It didn't get by the mayor's desk."

"*Why?*"

Frank looked up at me. "You're so smart, you ought to know
that. When those guys came to the door with that nig—with that
colored man, you *knew* they were mad about your lying to
them."

"You mean the Klan blocked your appointment?" I demanded of Pop.

"We don't know that," he said, lips set grimly.

"Of course we do," Gramaw put in, rocking vigorously.

"Those guys couldn't have gotten all the way into the
mayor's office!"

"Couldn't they?" Frank shot back. He was angry at me all
over again, blaming me because our father had not gotten the
permanent job.

I didn't know what to think. "I never imagined—"

"Right!" Frank told me. "You were too busy being a big
shot."

"Frank," Pop said sharply, "that's enough."

My mother came in from the kitchen. "Supper will be ready
in just a minute, Kenny. You'd better wash up."

I looked at her. "He didn't get the job."

"I know. Everyone is tired right now. Let's talk about it later."

I fled upstairs, rushed through my ablutions. My mind was a welter of contradictions: outrage, surprise, anger, guilt. *Had* the Klan wielded such influence that the mayor of Columbus would go out of his way to block a routine job appointment in revenge against us? I had never foreseen such a development and it still seemed farfetched. But the explanation fit the facts. If this was the explanation, how was I supposed to react to Frank's outrage? Mom and I had done the right thing; but Pop had been the one to suffer for it, and in the long run all of us might. I told myself it was impossible, but knew better. I told myself I had no reason to feel guilty, but did.

Supper was eaten with scarcely a word spoken. Max scurried around our feet, looking for handouts. He was ignored. Mary watched me with big, soulful eyes, searching for a clue as to how she should react. I pretended I didn't notice her.

After supper she and Frank were supposed to do the dishes. Pop and Gramaw went to the front porch and Mom followed. I started out after them, but heard their voices in the tone used by grown-ups when they were talking seriously out of hearing of kids. Ordinarily I might have barged in on them, but I felt like a pariah. I skulked back through the house and out the back door, going down the alley and cutting through the vacant lot a few houses south to get to the Rayburn house.

Standing out in front of the terraced lawn, I called, *"Tah ... um! Hey ... Tah ... um!"* And waited. In those days you didn't call a pal on the telephone because you had no telephone, and you did not walk up to the door and ring the bell or knock. I don't know why. The door was ... an *adult* thing, and to knock on it was to place yourself in the category of the grown-up. When you wanted a friend, you walked to the front of his house and "called him out," summer or winter. If he did not come out in answer to your call, you went away.

Right now I had to talk to someone, and Tom Rayburn was

one of my best friends even though my job had not let us see a lot of each other lately.

"*Tah . . . um!*" I called again, and waited.

My method of calling was never distinctive, a fact that troubled me at odd moments. Frank Schroeder's was the best, a soft, melodious call, almost a yodel, that could be recognized anywhere. Jack Rayburn's call was a gutteral bark. Gail had had a good call that sort of broke and changed note in the middle. Frank had a fine whistle, four-noted, like a wild bird's, which he followed by the callee's name in a sweet tenor that sounded like Pop's voice when he sang. I had never been able to develop anything worthwhile; I was reduced to standing out there like a dummy, just . . . *calling.* All names were broken into more syllables than they really had, but that was standard procedure and everyone did it.

After a moment, Tom Rayburn opened his front door and came out to curbside. "You wanna play a little catch or something?" he asked. He had grown, was a head taller than I now.

"I just thought maybe we could mess around," I told him.

"You sick?" he asked as we strolled into the parkway.

"Nah."

"So what's going on?"

I squatted under an elm tree. "You know that job my Pop had lined up?"

"Yeah." Tom watched me closely in the dying summer light.

"He didn't get it."

"Huh!" Tom picked up a twig and traced a pattern in the dust. "How come? Do you know?"

"I think," I admitted miserably, "I made somebody mad and he got back at us by making Pop not get the job."

"Down at where you work, you mean?"

I did not know where the Rayburns stood on the Klan. I hedged. "Well, sort of."

"I guess your old man is really mad, huh?"

"I can't tell how he feels about it."

"If my old man had almost had a job and then didn't get it, I don't know *what* he'd do."

"I feel like it's my fault. And I don't know what to do about it."

"Well, if you know who this guy is you made mad, maybe you could go say you're sorry."

"No!"

Tom sighed. "My dad was talking the other night. He said he heard of a couple guys that got jobs by going down and talking to the Dragon."

"If you have to get a job that way, maybe you shouldn't have a job!"

"I dunno. My dad went down and talked to him."

"He did?" I was dismayed.

"Why not?" Tom demanded. "They're not such bad people. It's just a sort of social club, sort of like the Knights of Columbus."

"Did your father think they'd help a *Catholic?*"

"Well, he didn't tell them *that.*"

"And is the Dragon going to get him a job?"

"Well, my dad thinks he might."

"What sort of a country have we got," I demanded, "when you've got to kowtow to people like that? They're not the government. They're not a business. They're not anything."

"They're patriotic," Tom said. "That's what my dad says. In times of trouble like this, a lot of people are trying to tear down our country. A lot of *big* businesses are going under. Radicals—"

"Am I supposed to worry about big businesses?" I asked. "Did they ever worry about us?"

"This country runs because of business. Without business, none of us would have anything."

"That's just about what we've got now! I suppose if that mortgage company that's trying to take our house went out of business, we should be sorry for *them,* too."

"You're skating on thin ice," Tom told me darkly. "That's radical talk. There's nothing wrong with this country that supply and demand won't cure eventually. It's always worked. That's what my dad says. It's just a question of riding things out."

"Or starving to death," I suggested.

"Who do you know that's starving?"

"A lot of Negroes are probably starving."

"How many Negroes do you know?"

I looked at him. He had me there. I thought of the man with the gun. Once, two or three years earlier, I had stood at the candy counter of the confectionery with a black youth my own age, and we had nodded to each other without speaking a word. In truth, I had *never* known a black person. Blacks were the ones who lived on over there a few blocks, and you didn't walk down their streets, I don't know why. Blacks were always *getting closer*, moving into new blocks . . . creeping nearer so that if they ever lived on your street, you would have to move. But I didn't know the why of that, either. It occurred to me that I talked a good game about blacks possibly starving, but Tom was absolutely right: I didn't know any blacks.

"Do you know any?" I asked him.

"Of course not," he said.

"Well, they're probably just like us."

"I doubt it. And I don't care, as long as they stay where they belong. That's all the KKK wants, incidentally: just for the colored to stay where they belong and not get uppity."

It was a kind of talk I never heard at my house. My dismay was growing. "Well, I can't go see a Dragon or a Wizard or whatever the hell he might be called. I'm sorry. I may be wrong, but I just can't."

"Well, then," Tom said, "all you can do is pray."

"Pray?"

"Pray."

"At church?"

"That's the best place. God does listen, you know, especially if you pray through the Blessed Virgin. She's got all kinds of suction with Jesus, and *He's* God."

I didn't say anything. Could I still believe any of this? What kind of an outcast rebel was I?

"I'd go to church if I were you," Tom went on. "If you've got a dime, light a vigil candle."

"A dime?"

"That's what they cost. Haven't you ever lit one?"

"I didn't even know I could. Nobody in our family ever lit one."

"What do you think they're up there for?"

"How should I know?"

"Didn't it ever occur to you to ask?"

"Listen! There are a lot of things in our church you're not supposed to ask about!"

"Every one of those vigil candles was brought by somebody just like you and me. They burn twenty-four hours, and every minute that thing is burning, it's reminding God of your petition. We light one every Saturday night after confession, and it *helps.*"

I sighed, wishing for a cigarette. To my great delight, I was actually beginning to get the habit now that I had finally learned how to inhale properly. Some people said you would never get TB if you smoked properly.

"I don't know what I'll do," I said finally.

"Well," Tom said, and stood.

"I'll see you," I said, and started home.

"If you need to talk more, come on over," Tom called after me. "After all, that's what friends are for, right?"

"Right," I called back over my shoulder.

At home, my parents and Gramaw Prater were still on the porch with their heads together. They stopped talking as I crossed by them and went inside. I went upstairs and got a dime from my drawer and went back down again, using the back door as before. I cut through the yard to the alley and headed north toward Broad Street. A few minutes later I was tugging open the massive oaken door of St. Aloysius church.

The place was just enormous. Night made the slender stained glass windows ranked along the sides mysterious and black. Only two dim lights illuminated the endless rows of dark wood pews and the gleaming tile floor from the altar area, far to the other end of the building, where the sacristy light—crimson glass suspended from golden chain—flickered its ruby color to remind all that Jesus was present in the Holy Sacrament. There were two women kneeling together partway up the St. Joseph side, and an old man and a young woman, not together, seated on the Blessed Virgin side. My heels echoed on the tile as I went up toward the enormous gold-white altar, looming beyond the silvery marble communion railing.

Silence lay deep in the vast air beneath the Gothic ceiling as I genuflected and slid into the front pew. My dime was hot and slippery in my hand. I said an Our Father and a Hail Mary and then got my nerve up to leave the pew and walk to the shimmering banks of red and blue glass candles in their tiered bronze holders along the railing beneath the statue of the Virgin. I knelt there, looking into the candle holders. About half of them were lit, some very recently so that the wick stood above the rim of the glass, others long ago, with only a little puddle of melted wax far down, golden, inside the glass. I tried to get into the proper frame of mind, then stood and dropped my dime down the slot in the front of the nearest tiered rack. The coin slid and tinkled and finally chunked down the slide, falling into other coins way down there, making a hell of a racket. I knew I had disturbed everybody in here. I struck a match and quickly lit the nearest fresh candle and went back to the pew.

Dear God, I thought, *I know You've got a lot on Your mind and I probably shouldn't be bothering You, but I haven't asked You for a whole lot lately, so here it is. If You could just see Your way clear to get Pop a job and fix it so we don't lose the house and make Pop's health get better, and make Frank not hate my guts so much . . . and possibly Gail could get to come home. And if Finnegan would raise my pay it would be good, and bless Mom and everybody, keep Gramaw healthy, bless all our family, let me not be such a dodo bird all the time, and anything else You think would be good for us, we'll appreciate it, and please help the coloreds if any of them need it. I've got my candle burning, You can see it there. So if you'll do all that, I'll never sin again. Amen.*

My knees ached from kneeling. I started to say some more Hail Marys, but my mind wandered.

Why does He need a candle to remind him? I thought. *If He's that stupid—*

Then I thought, *I didn't think that, God, please forgive me.*

But my damned brain would not shut off. I knelt there sweating, one part of my mind doing the Hail Marys while a deeper part of me raced through speculations.

Who was I to think I could pull the wool over *God's* eyes? I had only thrown in that part about the blacks to make it sound like I wasn't selfish, and I had about as much chance of not sinning again as I had of being President.

Worse, what if I was sending these messages out *and there was no one there?* What if, as I had thought so often in secret before, it was all just kidding ourselves because we couldn't stand to face the prospect of death?

Or what if He was there, but didn't give a flip?

—blessed art thou amongst women and blessed is the fruit of—

I was doing just what I had done a few times at the Rivoli theater, I thought suddenly, before my father had made fun of people who did that. Coming here was just like going to the Rivoli for bank night, sitting there with my ticket stub clutched in my sweaty palm, watching the manager rotate the big drum onstage and pull out a number of the lucky person who won the dishes . . . or the money.

Except that you could see the manager. At least you knew he was *there.*

There was no way I could make this work. Everybody in the world knew God except me. Somehow, somewhere, despite all the help from good people who cared about me and had tried to teach me correctly, I had lost my way. Coming here had only shown me that I had no faith left—not a shred. I could not turn off my mind and simply believe.

I stopped the rote prayers in the middle of an Our Father and got up abruptly to leave. In a depth of depression I genuflected and turned to walk back down the long, long aisle toward the rear doors. I saw to my surprise that the others who had been here with me were now gone. I was, as far as I could see, absolutely alone in this enormous place.

I turned and looked back at the altar. Something came over me.

"God?" I called aloud, and then again, much louder, *"God?"* My voice echoed shockingly off the altar, the floors, the walls, the stained glass, coming back with the sharpness of a thunderbolt. I cringed in embarrassment.

From one of the side entries to the sacristy came a quick movement. A nun, black-clad, with a flash of white at her breast and forehead, looked out at me. Her face was furious. She held a finger to her lips. *"Shhhhh!"*

I rushed out of the place to the night sidewalk with cars going by and a gloomy half-moon looking down out of a cloud-shaggy sky.

When I got home, Pop was alone on the front porch, his glowing cigarette tip announcing his shadowy presence. I started by him without a word.

"Tired?" he asked softly.

"A little."

"Sit down a minute, okay?"

I sat on the steps. *What now?*

"Look," he said. "Maybe what your mother and you said to those men had something to do with the situation downtown. Maybe it didn't. It's done with. No use crying over spilt milk."

"I got smart with them. I said I had a picture of the Grand Dragon on the wall and they *knew* I was lying to them."

"You said that to them, did you?"

"Yes, sir."

To my infinite surprise, he chuckled. "You're quite a guy."

"I was *stupid.*"

"Look, son. Don't worry about it. I'll go see the lawyer again. We'll write those people at the mortgage company a letter, outlining what we can do and what we can't do. They're reasonable. We'll work something out. You wait and see."

"What if they're not?" I demanded.

"What?"

"What if they're *not* reasonable?"

There was silence before he spoke. "Well, then, we'll just do . . . next best."

"It's all my fault."

"You're not responsible if a few people are bullies. You're not responsible for my getting sick, or what's going on in this country or anything else. You're only responsible for yourself."

"Maybe," I suggested, "not just a few people are bullies. Maybe people are just no good—selfish, *dumb.*"

"A man can't allow himself to think like that," he said more firmly.

"But what if it's *true?*"

"You've got to believe in people. If you don't have faith in the common man, you can't even believe in our country. Man is made in God's image."

"Do you believe in God?" I asked.

"Of course." His voice was quietly shocked.

"And heaven . . . and all that?"

"I believe what it says in the Bible. In His house are many mansions. Son, this big world of ours couldn't work right unless there was an Almighty Father, looking over all of us. I may not go to church. But I *know* there's a God, and I know things turn out for the best in the long run, even if we can't always understand His will."

"And Jesus?" I asked, driven.

"I believe Jesus was a holy man. Was He the Son of God? I don't know. I think He was. I think we're all children of God, and maybe Jesus was more than that, or maybe He just saw it more clearly than most of the rest of us. But I know . . . Uncle Jack . . . is in one of those many mansions now. We'll all be there with him one day. So some of this that happens . . . it doesn't matter a whole lot. We do our best. What happens . . . happens."

I did not reply. He finished his cigarette and tossed it out onto the lawn where it glowed and then went out. Fireflies winked on and off, and somewhere a car horn honked. The moon was gone beneath the clouds.

"All right?" he said finally.

"All right," I said.

"Good."

I got up and went into the house. Gramaw was in the parlor, sewing. It was a grand wedding dress that cascaded off her lap onto the rug all around her, and her thin hands worked with machinelike precision.

"Night," I said to her.

"Kenny?"

"Yessum?"

She smiled. "Things will be all right, child."

"Yessum."

In the kitchen, my mother was scrubbing canning jars, Mary at the table with the ever-present storybook.

"Where did you get off to?" Mom asked.

"I just took a walk."

"I've told Mary and Frank. We're going to see our lawyer and write another letter to—"

"Pop just told me."

"Good. I want everyone to know, because there's no sense anyone moping around. We have some money saved and we'll have some more by the end of the summer. I'm sure we're going to work things out."

I stood silent, reading her expression. *She was being cheerful for our benefit.* I felt a rush of love for her, accompanied by an equal sense of my own unworthiness. *I* could not even believe in God, much less a mortgage company.

"You didn't have a cookie after supper. Would you like one now?"

"I think I'm just going on to bed. I've got a big day at the shop tomorrow."

She left the sink, came over, hugged me, and brushed her lips across my cheek. "Good night, dear. We love you."

I went upstairs and to the bathroom. After brushing my

teeth, I started down the hall to the bedroom. A movement on the steps caught my attention. It was my little sister, sitting there on the top step in the dark.

"Hey," I said softly.

"Kenny," Mary said in her little voice, "do you think this winter we could make an igloo outside like the Eskimos do?"

"Why, sure," I said, puzzled. "That ought to be a lot of fun."

"We could make it right out in back," she told me. "Beside the grape arbor."

"That's right."

"We could roll up snow from the front, and roll the balls around, and get out the hose and put water on them to make them real icy. And then after we're through we could come in and clean up in the basement, and wash Max off, and go in the kitchen and have some cocoa."

I tumbled to how her mind was working. "That's right," I told her. "And then we can go in the front room and sit on the davenport and I'll read you some of your book."

"And me read some of it to you." She tilted her head. "Kenny, do you think we'll have the Christmas tree in the front room, there in the corner, like last year?"

"Why, I'm sure we will. I think *everything* will be like last year. Only even better."

"And Gail will come home."

"Sure!"

She stood. "I have to go to bed, too, now."

I kissed her. "Good night, sis."

"Good night, Kenny. I sure love you!"

I went into the front bedroom. Frank was pretending to be asleep. Max was curled at the foot of my bed, his tail thumping to greet me. As I undressed, I thought about Mary.

The grape arbor. The kitchen. The living room. The corner for the tree. Everything had to be the same. And I had done a good job of reassuring her even without any hope of my own.

But there *was* hope, I told myself. I had my job. Gail knew what trouble we were in, but his letters were always hopeful. As long as any of us was employed, it could sway the mortgage company. There might be very little I could believe in anymore, but I could believe in my job. That was real. That meant something.

I slipped into bed. Max crawled up the length of the sheet and licked my face. I petted him. He cuddled down, warm and itchily hairy against me. The moon peered down at me through the open window, flooding the bed with silver. I thought about what Pop had said about many mansions and God. This, I thought, was our mansion. It protected us from everything. We needed no other.

17

The summer fled before our attempts to save or raise money.

At work I lost the days in Finnegan's constant complaints and harassment. Once, early in August, we went fishing along the Olentangy River with the Rayburns and it was fun although no one caught anything. We had a few radiator jobs at night, but they did not shake Pop out of the moody withdrawal that typified him most of that time. One weekend a couple came to the front door and Gramaw sold them her radio, and we no longer had Vic & Sade or the other shows we had come to love. We sold our old and outgrown clothes out of the attic, including dresses from a chest that my mother cried over. The milkman no longer stopped his recalcitrant old mare at our doorstep because we could save a penny or two by walking to the store. Gail's notes arrived regularly, usually with a little money. We now had over three hundred dollars in our war chest, but our lawyer's letter to the mortgage company seeking a delay in settlement had gone unanswered.

Some nights I dreamed I was rich, and that I walked into that company office with Pop at my side, and together we dumped a colossal basket of paper money onto a desk and saved our home. Other dreams had us walking endlessly down a strange street, carrying our possessions, with nowhere to go. Our deadline was almost at hand; time had nearly run out. In the still, hot nights of late August we sometimes sat on our front porch, seeing faint movements on the porches of our neighbors and hearing their faint voices now and then. It was all familiar, reassuring . . . *right.*

"What's the matter with ye, dumb boy?" Finnegan demanded late one Thursday afternoon. "I've told ye two times already to try an' straighten' thet bumper over yonder!"

"I'll get right on it," I promised.

He squinted down at me out of the blast-furnace sunlight. "Git right on it, git right on it! Ye should've *did* it already!"

"I'm sorry."

"What's the matter? Ye sick er somepin?"

"No. I was thinking about something else."

Finnegan spat derisively. "Thinkin' about somepin else, was it? What? Some girl? Whether yer gonna git to the matinee on time? The price of tea in China?"

"No," I replied, stung. "Whether we're going to lose our house!"

"Eh?" Finnegan cocked his ear. "What's that?"

I told him in a few bitter words.

"Huh!" He removed his oily cap and scratched his head. "They might put ye out, eh?"

"Yes. No. I don't know. Our time is almost up."

"What's yer daddy say?"

"He says to keep hoping. He's working as hard as he can."

"Huh! Which ain't very, from what I've heard."

"Don't you say anything against my father, or—"

Finnegan caught my upraised fist. "Hold on, hold on! I only meant, he's sick, ain't he?"

"Yes, but that's no reason for you—"

"I didn't mean anything by it, boy! Calm down! Yer a fury on some subjecks now, ain't you!"

I didn't answer him.

"Ye say yer deadline is just next month? September?"

"Yes."

Finnegan thought about it. He spat his chew of tobacco into his palm and threw it over the fence into the yard of the paint company next door. "I guess ye do have somepin on yer mind, at that." He turned and limped away, his expression thoughtful.

The next day he remained quiet. When I did a bad job on a fender, he corrected me gently. Several times I caught him watching me from a distance across the yard as I did this or that job of work, but he did not approach me except when necessary, and then politely.

On Saturday morning we had a light load and most of the crew went home early. I was sweeping the machine shop when Finnegan came up to me with a card in his hand. "Would this be yer correct address, boy?"

I looked at it. "Yes, sir."

"Do ye know if yer parents have special plans fer this afternoon, say, about three?"

"I don't know. Why?"

"Well, I was thinkin' I might drop by fer a brief visit, if ye think yer parents would allow it."

"Why?" I demanded again.

"Thet's fer me to tell them, dumb boy! I'll tell ye what: I'll come by about three. If it's all right, yer mama an' daddy an' me will have a visit. If they don't wanna talk to the likes of me, why, thet's fine 'n' dandy, I'll drive right on. Will ye tell 'em thet?"

"Yes, sir, but I don't understand—"

"Ye don't have to understand, dumb boy! Jes' deliver my message. Understood?"

"Yessir."

"Aw right. Git back to yer sweepin'. At the rate ye work, we'll be here till next Tuesday."

"What does that old pirate want?" Pop asked when I told him and Mom.

"I don't know," I replied honestly.

He sighed. "Nail down the silverware."

Finnegan's battered Packard appeared at our curb precisely at 3 P.M. I was standing at the front window, my mother and father waited in the parlor, and Gramaw had taken Mary upstairs while Frank made himself scarce out back. My parents had put on their good clothes, as had I. For no good reason, I was nervous about all this.

Finnegan got out of his car and I did a double take. He had come in his Sunday best: ice cream slacks with very wide cuffs, a white shirt and broad blue tie, a Palm Beach jacket, white shoes, a straw skimmer. Coming around the huge nose of his Packard, he removed his tobacco cud and dropped it curbside. Without dirt on his face he looked pale.

I had the door open when he reached the porch, hat in hand, mopping his forehead with a silk handkerchief. "Hello, Mr. Finnegan!"

"Good afternoon, du—dear boy. Am I to understand yer parents will be seein' me?"

"Yes sir! Come right in!"

We went into the living room. My mother and father were on their feet. Finnegan approached Pop with deference. "Ah, Mr. Riley, it's fine to see ye again after so long!"

Pop shook hands like a man mindful of his wallet. "Mr. Finnegan, it's been a long time."

"Yes sir! It was at Cartigan's shop in 'twenty-seven, I figger."

"May I present Mrs. Riley? Dear, this is Mr. Finnegan."

Finnegan made a sweeping and not altogether uncourtly bow. "It's a rare pleasure, madam!"

Color touched my mother's cheeks. "Sit down, Mr. Finnegan."

So we all sat, Finnegan in Gramaw's armchair, Mom and Pop on the sofa, me in Pop's usual place with Max sitting beside me, tail thumping. There was a moment of awkward silence.

"Wal, it's certain mighty hot," Finnegan assayed.

"Yes, it certainly is," my mother agreed.

"Hot at the yard," Finnegan added.

"I imagine it's really hot down there," Pop said.

"Air is hot even in a car. Ye git no relief even drivin'.'"

"That's so."

"Past ninety out there right now."

"Is it now!"

"Yes, indeedie. Past ninety."

"And humid."

"Ah, the humidity is fierce."

Finnegan rolled his eyes toward me as if for help. "Ye have a good boy here."

My mother smiled. "Yes. We know."

Finnegan looked around. "An' a nice home. A real nice home."

"Thank you."

Silence again.

"Wal," Finnegan said with the look of a man about to go down for the third time.

My mother asked, "Would you like some tea, Mr. Finnegan?"

He jumped. "Tea? Say! Thet'd be mighty nice. Thank ye."

My mother got up and left the room. Finnegan looked around some more. He spotted the ukelele. "Ye play, Mr. Riley?" he asked.

"A little," Pop said.

"I used to play the mandolin."

"Did you, now."

"Yessir. Couldn't ever git it right, though. By the time I got all them strings in tune, it was time to git back to work." Finnegan held up a work-gnarled paw. "Some hands are made fer music an' some fer work. These're workin' hands."

"I know what you mean," Pop said.

Mom came back with a tray holding the tea, cups, saucers, napkins, and a little dish of cookies along with sugar and cream. Finnegan took two of everything except the cup. "Say, thet's fine tea!" he exclaimed, balancing saucer on one knee and hat on the other.

"Why, thank you, Mr. Finnegan."

I reached for an extra cookie and got a dirty look. Max, seeing he was going to get nothing, ambled disgustedly out of the room.

"Wal, now," Finnegan said. "I suppose I ought to be tellin' ye why I dropped by."

"Good," Pop said, watching him.

"Wal, yer boy here has told me a little of yer problem. He's a fine boy. An' you, Mr. Riley, was always a good, hard worker before yer illness. An' the idea of some two-bit loan company givin' good people like yerselfs trouble, makin' 'em worry, it sticks in my craw, so to speak." He cocked his eye at my father. "If ye catch my drift?"

"I think I know what you've said so far, sir."

"Yes, sir. Wal, sir. The lad here is a good worker. It wouldna be good business fer me to have an employee worryin' all the time about his home. So I got to thinkin' about all this. I think I've got a good business proposition."

"Business proposition?" Pop repeated, and his left hand actually stole back to check for his wallet.

"Yes, sir. Yer boy makes a decent wage. Not a great wage, but adequate. I try to pay an adequate wage. Good help is hard to find. I figger give this lad a year or two an' he'll be fine help. So. Wouldn't it make good sense fer me to try an' guarantee the lad's help over a period of time? Yes, sir. It would."

Finnegan paused and almost upset his teacup, snatching it as it teetered on his bony kneecap. "Now. What, I asked myself, if I was to give the lad a guarantee—a year's wages in advance? Thet'd be four hundred an' sixteen dollars, don't ye see. At the same time, I'd be guaranteein' myself the boy's work, an' the family here would have that additional cash money to help try an' settle with those da—blasted loan sharks over the house."

"*You* want to lend *us* four hundred dollars?" Pop gasped.

"Not a loan," Finnegan said quickly. "Nary a loan! Call it a business investment. I'm guaranteein' myself the boy's services fer at least a year at his present salary. I don't *do* favors."

My mother's hand went to her throat. Pop appeared stupefied. I was the first to react openly. *"Gaw!* That would give us more than seven hundred dollars! Those guys would *have* to—"

"Wait a minute, wait a minute," Pop said. "I don't get this."

Finnegan was sweating heavily. "I'm a working man. Yer a working man. The lad is gonna be the same. Seems to me the working men of this country had ought to better stick together right now. He promises to stick with me, I promise to—"

"But he's got to go back to school next month!" Pop said.

Finnegan went blank. "Eh? What say?"

"I said," Pop repeated, his face coloring with anger directed at me, "he goes back to school next month. *Didn't he tell you that?"*

Finnegan's good eye rolled around toward me. "Boy?"

"I don't have to go back next month," I said miserably. "We *need* the money. I've got to do my part around here or I'm not worth anything! I can go back to school some other—"

"He's going back to school next month," Pop cut in icily, watching Finnegan. "I ordered him to make that clear to you, Mr. Finnegan. It looks like he deceived you. I want to apologize for that."

I stared, crushed and unable to protest. I had imagined I would be a hero. But instead of that, I was only a liar—a kid trying to take on too much.

Finnegan shakily put his teacup on the floor. "Wal, now. This is . . . a surprise. He's a good worker, sure enough." He heaved a big sigh. "I suppose the lad wanted the job awful bad, an'—"

"Which is no excuse for lying," Pop said tightly. "Mr. Finnegan, I want you to know that this family appreciates your offer very, very deeply. It was kind of you. Very kind. I thank you. But you can see that it's impossible. Kenny is going to get his education."

"Even if we lose the house?" I cried.

"Even if we lose everything we own," Pop snapped.

"Pop—!"

"You should be ashamed of yourself," he told me sternly. "You disobeyed me and you deceived Mr. Finnegan. That's flying under false colors. A man is only as good as his word, and you've made your word absolutely worthless."

My mother said, distressed, "He was only trying to help—"

"I know what he was trying to do," Pop snapped, getting to his feet. "But the ends don't always justify the means." He glared at Finnegan. "I'm sorry he lied to you. We thank you again, very, very much. But under the circumstances, it's impossible."

Finnegan too rose, his skimmer twirling in nervous hands. "Yes, sir. I understand. Without an education, a man ain't worth a flip." He looked at me. "Yer daddy is right, boy. Git yer education. Make something of yerself."

"What about my *job?*" I asked, fighting tears.

Finnegan sighed again. "Ye can finish out yer time till school starts." He looked at my mother. "Madam, I'm sorry."

"Mr. Finnegan, it was wonderful of you to come see us this way."

"Wal." My father was walking him to the door. "Maybe it'll all work out. About the house, I mean."

They shook hands again on the porch. I stood beside my mother, my whole world crashing down around me. Pop stayed on the porch until the hollow engine note of the Packard and a slight grinding of gears signaled Finnegan's departure. Then he came in like a thundercloud.

"I *meant* to tell him!" I pleaded.

"You lied. And you would have gone right on lying—right on working down there—despite what your mother and I want. That man went way and the hell out of his way to try to help us, Kenny. Only to find out he was trying to help a damned liar!"

"Pop—"

"You'll go to school. You'll *learn.* You'll go further than I ever did. That's *final.* Now go to your room and stay there until I tell you different."

"Maybe—" Mom began.

"I'm handling this, Mrs. Riley," Pop snapped.

I fled up the stairs. My feeling of humiliation and failure was extreme. I knew, even as I threw myself across my bed, that there was no dream left. With Finnegan's "advance salary," we might have had a chance. My father had just thrown that chance away for the sake of blind and stupid faith in education—schooling in a society that put its best men out of work and discarded its sick like so much garbage. He was, I thought, not only cruel and arbitrary, but a fool. And so my last article of faith disintegrated.

September came with a heat wave. President Hoover said conditions were starting to improve. More For Sale signs went up along our street, and hobos coming to the back door asking for work or a handout became normal. Frank put a picture of Wiley Post up on the wall of our bedroom to commemorate his circling of the globe earlier in the summer. The newspaper said they were starting a grand new RKO Building in New York, and that would put some construction workers there back on payrolls. On his good days, Pop went around whistling "Barnacle Bill the Sailor," but there were not many of those. Kids in the neighborhood, including us, got new stick-ons—gluey pasteboard halfsoles—to press on the bottoms of our shoes in anticipation of school. Frank, Mary, and I got tablets and pencils. Jimmy Doolittle's picture went up beside Wiley Post's the day after he flew from California to New Jersey in less than twelve hours. Frank had gone airplane crazy, and almost every day we saw one fly over.

On a Sunday morning I discovered an envelope in our mailbox. It had no name on the outside, and no stamp.

"What in the world?" Mom said when I handed it to her. Then she opened it, read the pencil-printed message, and handed it to me with the strangest little smile, showing me three one-dollar bills folded inside.

I read:

> FOR THE GROCERIES. I GOT A JOB. THANK YOU.

"Gaw!" I said.

"Yes," Mom said, still smiling. " 'Gaw' indeed. I wonder where he found work."

We never found out.

A day or two later, Mr. Caldwell and Mr. Emmer appeared at our door again. I was at work. My parents were grim about it that evening. Our lawyer's letter seeking an extension of time or continuation of the existing mortgage agreement had been denied.

"Then what *now?*" I demanded.

"Next week we go downtown and meet with the president of the company," Pop told me. "We decide then and there whether they'll take what we've saved and sign a new agreement with us, or. . . ." He did not have to finish it.

"You better take our lawyer!" I told him.

"Oh, we will," he said with a bitter smile. "But I don't know if it would do any good if we took an army."

"What *happens* to us if they say no?" Mary asked me later that evening when we were alone in the backyard near the grape arbor.

"Look out!" I said. "There's one!" And caught another lightning bug to slip into the Mason jar she was holding, already alight with the captured insects.

"What *does?*" she pressed.

"I guess we move," I told her.

"I don't *want* to move!"

"Who does? Look out, watch it. Got him! Here."

"Mama says we'll move over there on Clarendon or Wheatland or one of those streets and they're not *nearly* as nice as Terrace Avenue."

"I know, sis. But we'll just have to make the best of it."

"Gail will *never* come home now, if he has to live over there!"

"Gail has to stay where he has some work."

"I miss him. He's nicer than you, and he'll never come back if we move!"

"You heard his last letter. He said we all have to do our best. He said he wanted to come help us move, but it would risk his job. That's the only reason he's staying away right now."

Mary was silent a moment. I seemed to have won a point. Then, however, she said, "People on those streets over there have infantile paralysis and everything else! We'll probably all get sick and die!"

I sat down beside her and put an arm over her shoulders. "Come on, now. You know better than that."

"They do. They *do!* Lots of people over there have infantile paralysis!"

In those times the words usually used to describe polio were enough to send chills down anyone's back. All of us knew the facts: the disease struck children far more often than adults, and with no evident pattern. It was worse in summer, but people said the germs were not carried by insects, so there was a theory that you might catch it if you got too overheated and then lay out too long in the cool evening air and got a chill. Trying to be clean and always washing your hands before meals was supposed to help, but a little girl a block south on our street had gotten it in the spring and everyone knew she was among the cleanest people in the world. She was dead now. Not just sick, not merely hobbling on hideous steel braces and canes or in a wheelchair, or lying in one of those ghastly great iron lungs with everything immobil-

ized and only her head sticking out, the way they showed children in *Our Catholic Messenger* sometimes, but *dead*. The fact
that Mary now saw the specter of polio in a move from this house
told me how frightened she really was.

"Well, now, look," I told her. "You're not going to get infantile paralysis if we have to move, and neither is anyone else.
Maybe we won't have to move. And if we do, what we have to
do is just try to be good soldiers about it."

"But it will mean we're so *poor!*"

"You don't go to hell for being poor, Mary. Not even Sister
Leocadia says that's a sin, and she's sure got almost everything
else in there."

"Well, I don't want it anyway. I like the way we are."

"We all do. But whether we stay here or move, we'll still
have each other. That's what's important. And it's up to us, if we
have to move, to try to act real cheerful to help Mom and Pop
and Gramaw get through it okay."

"The way *you've* been cheerful about daddy making you
quit your job and go back to school?"

"That's different."

"You don't even like daddy anymore."

"That's an awful thing to say!"

"It's true, isn't it?"

I looked at her small oval face in the faint starlight. "That's
all different and you're not old enough to understand," I told her.

She rubbed her knuckles across her eyes and got up.

"You want some more lightning bugs?" I asked.

"No, thank you," she said, and marched into the house.

I wondered what it was about little sisters. I thought I had
been doing a magnificent job of telling her to believe things
about moving that I did not totally believe myself. But she had
seen right through me. As usual. I sat there awhile, the cool wet
of the earth soaking through my britches, wishing I could have
a profound insight or something.

The day came when my father got up and put on his good
suit and sat uncomfortably at the breakfast table, smelling of lint

and mothballs, and Mom came in wearing her good church dress and a white hat. They were due downtown at the mortgage-company office at ten, and were ready hours early. Gramaw served us cereal and toast and coffee, and I took my lunch bucket and went off to work.

It was a cloudy day, but very hot. I tried to go about my work. Ten o'clock came, eleven, noon. My mouth was so dry I couldn't eat all of my catsup sandwich. *By now it had been decided,* and I knew nothing. But by God I would do my work. And I had only the rest of this week and next remaining before I had to go back to the classroom and be a parasite again.

A little after two, I was struggling to get a tire back on a rim. I became aware that someone was standing over me. I looked up and it was Finnegan, chewing thoughtfully.

"What?" I said.

"Yer not worth a flip today," he told me.

Angrily I worked harder, barking my knuckles open. Flecks of red splattered as the tire tool slipped again.

"Yer jus' worryin' about what happened downtown," Finnegan said.

"Wouldn't you be?" I fired back angrily.

"Gawan home an' find out," he told me. "Yer no good to me in this condition. Go! Git! Do ye need a road map?"

I didn't even wash my face or hands. I ran to the streetcar stop and had to wait an interminable ten minutes. Then the car seemed to stop at every intersection all the way out to the Hilltop. Finally I got there, running up the street. I burst into the house. It was as silent as a tomb. I rushed into the kitchen. My mother and father sat there at the table, and Gramaw was at the sink, but doing nothing. One look at their faces told it all.

"What happened?" I demanded, knowing.

Pop did not meet my eyes. He was mortified. "Well, son, it . . . just didn't . . . work out."

"They're taking our house?"

"I'm afraid so."

"*Why?*"

"We just didn't have enough cash money . . . times are hard

. . . we couldn't show them enough future employment potential—"

"But we even sold our *radio!*"

"Child—" Gramaw began, reaching for me.

I pulled away from her. "You saw the boss?"

"Yes." Pop still would not look at me.

"Our lawyer was there?"

"Yes. We explained everything."

Mom stirred, looked at me with awful eyes. "It's just the way
they do business—"

"Business, hell! What did they *want?* We did everything we
could!"

"Kenneth, calm down."

"I won't calm down! Did you see the president himself?"

"Yes. Mr. Fletcher was very nice. But there was just nothing
he or anyone could do."

"We ought to go to court! We ought to sue them!"

"You're talking nonsense," Pop told me coldly. "We don't
have a leg to stand on. Now just shut up about it."

"Did they give you our money?" I persisted.

"What? *What* money?"

"*Our* money. The money we've got in the house. We own
over half of it. They can't just take our house and not pay us for
our part!"

"Son," Pop said slowly, "they don't have to pay us anything
at all."

"How can *that* be?"

"That's the way business is. In business—"

"You keep talking about 'business!' What *is* business? A li-
cense to steal?"

"I don't want to hear that kind of talk."

The warning note was in his voice, but I was too far gone to
heed. "What kind of crooks are in charge of this country, anyway? Somebody needs to be shot! Maybe Gail was right, boy!
Maybe what we need is just a whole lot of riots in this country,
a lot of people with guns—"

I got no further. Pop's hand cracked across my face, staggering me backward.

"I said that's enough!" he snapped, his eyes terrible with anger and pain.

"You should have let me keep my job. That might have made the difference!"

"I said that's *enough!*" He came half out of his chair.

My mother moved between us, her arms going around me. "Kenny! Come on! Go to your room—that's it—come on with me."

Blindly I let her lead me out of the kitchen. I was crying now, passive, the force of my fury suddenly gone as if it had never existed, the sting of my father's slap sharp across my face. She guided me up the stairs, down the hall to my room.

"You have to be strong now," she whispered, still holding me. "You have to be brave."

"I hate him," I sobbed through my teeth. "I hate him! I *hate* him!"

"No, you don't. No, you don't. It's going to be all right. You'll see, little boy."

"It's just not right, Mom! It's not *fair!*"

"I know," she crooned, holding me. "I know." Through the rocking motion of her body, I could feel the tumult of her heart.

It could have ended there, as far as my disillusionment was concerned, but it did not. In the morning I went back to my job like a robot. But in the night, telling no one, I had come up with a wildly improbable scenario by which I still might somehow save the day. My mind was filled with my idea as I dragged into the yard and found Finnegan standing in the middle of it alone, waiting.

"Wal?" he demanded, hands on hips.

I told him what had happened.

He spat. Then he took off his cap and hurled it to the ground. Without a word, he trampled on the cap and kicked it away. Then he looked up at the cloudy heavens and started cursing. I listened with mounting amazement and admiration. I had never heard a performance anything like it. He called down deities I had never suspected might exist. He discussed the parentage of businessmen in general and mortgage men in particular, and then he shifted his attention to Herbert Hoover in terms that turned the air blue and my ears red. He began to talk about where the mortgage men should go and the things that should be done to them on the way and after they got there. Then he stormed off into the machine shop and threw something heavy against the wall.

I followed him.

"Wal?" he demanded again.

"I'd like a half-hour off about nine o'clock this morning?"

"*Why*, dumb boy?"

"I want to go down to that mortgage company office myself."

"Ye got a gun?"

"No. But I want to talk to that boss myself."

"Yer crazy. They'll throw ye out."

"I want to see him—talk to him myself. Maybe if he sees I'm grown—"

Finnegan had begun to calm. He sighed heavily. "Yer wastin' yer time."

"I've got to go. And try."

"Yer parents did everything. Ye must know that."

"I can't do anything else until I talk to him myself. Don't you *see* that?"

Finnegan threw his tobacco chew against the wall. "All right, then. I'll drive ye."

"I couldn't ask you to do that! And I don't want anyone else fighting my battles—"

"I'm not fightin' yer battles fer ye, dumb boy! I won't git outta the car at the curb! But if I drive ye, ye won't be away from work fer so long, thet's all! Ye think I'm some sentimental fool? I'm as hardheaded as they come. Ye got to be, when yer in business!"

So we left the yard a little after nine o'clock. Drizzling rain pelted the car as we crossed the river and drove along Front Street. I was in a daze and did not quite know what I really hoped to accomplish. I simply could not . . . quite . . . give it up.

We found the address, a five-story office building with a cigar store on the lower level. I left Finnegan behind the wheel of the car and entered. According to the name plates, Allied National was on the second floor. I walked up a staircase rank from old cigars.

The second floor had many opaque glass doors. One had our firm's name on it. Expecting a grand large office, I entered. Instead I found a small, dingy reception room with four doors leading off it. The names on the door were Emmer, Caldwell, Cline and Fletcher, a name per door. Mr. Fletcher's door was directly behind the reception desk, where a girl not much older than I was on the telephone.

She hung up and gave me a smile. "Yes? Delivery?"

"My name is Riley," I told her. "I would like to see Mr. Fletcher."

The girl got up, went to Fletcher's door, rapped softly, and went in, closing the door behind her. I looked at the Carborundum calendar on the wall.

In a moment she was back. "I'm sorry, but Mr. Fletcher is in conference."

"How long?"

"I'm sorry. He's going to be busy all day."

I hesitated. But I was too far gone to be cautious. Before the girl could move, I was around the desk and at the door. I pushed it open.

"Wait!" the girl cried.

The office was not large, and the desk and filing cabinet, plus two straight chairs, were the only furniture. There were no curtains at the window, which looked out onto a narrow alley.

Fletcher was behind his desk. He looked up, startled, and our eyes met.

I understood instantly.

"I'm *sorry*, Mr. Fletcher!" the girl said, bustling in behind me. "He just barged in—!"

"It's all right, Milly," Fletcher said, still staring at me.

I turned and stumbled out. Downstairs, Finnegan took one look at my face and drove me back to the yard without a word. I walked in numb all over, all my new truths soaking in.

I knew now why our possible settlement had been turned down so summarily—why we had had no chance—why Pop had not wanted to talk about it or look me in the eye.

There was a great deal that I now understood, although it would take a long time for me to come to terms with all of it.

For I had recognized Fletcher immediately, despite the fact that now he wore a business suit in contrast to the dress he had affected those times he had appeared on our front porch. There was no mistaking him. He was our Klansman.

19

Often in September or early October we had a cool snap, even first frost, with periods of miserable rain. Then the weather would moderate magically, bringing nearly cloudless days, cool sunlight, and balmy, windless afternoons: Indian summer.

It was a day in Indian summer when Uncle Bob brought the rented truck and we carried our belongings out of the house on South Terrace Avenue. Our radiator-shop sign was gone from the yard, already replaced by the For Sale placard. Pop, his color ghastly, carried small boxes along with my mother and Gramaw Prater. Uncle Bob, Frank, and I wrestled the heavy stuff. Aunt Sal and her two girls came to help, and Aunt Helen. It was the biggest gathering of our family since Uncle Jack's funeral. Our voices and footsteps echoed through the house as we made our last trips outside, leaving behind us bare wood floors and staring, immaculate windows. Pop sat on the front porch steps, catching his breath. Mom and Gramaw stood nearby. Frank and I hefted a box of towels and sheets onto the back of the old Ford truck. Bob climbed aboard and we handed up Mary's old tricycle. We were all but loaded.

Adult neighbors had drifted by throughout the morning, but we had seen few of our childhood friends. Now I turned from the truck to see a delegation of them approaching us across the parkway: Jack and Hugh Rayburn, Terry McCall, John and Sylvester Smith, Billy Anderson and George and David Vincent.

"What's this all about?" Frank muttered.

"I guess we'll see," I said.

Since it was a Saturday, everyone in the gang took pride in looking terrible: cutoff pants, knickers with the knees gone and the elastic torn out, tennis shoes that let the toes show through, or no shoes at all. They shuffled across the street and up to us, standing at the back of the truck. They all looked a little sheepish, and it dawned on me that they had come to say good-bye.

"No giveaways, boys," I said, trying to be funny. "We're taking it all with us."

David Vincent nudged Hugh Rayburn, who took a half-step forward. "Well . . . we know we'll be seeing you around and some of us at school and all like that, but we just wanted to say so long." He traced a pattern in the dusty pavement with his bare big toe. "We'll . . . uh . . . miss you, sort of."

"Aw, we'll come back to play," Frank said with phony cheer.

"We'll miss you guys, too," I told them.

"Maybe we'll get together all the time anyway," Billy Anderson said. "And anytime we have war with the guys over on Eldon Avenue, we want you guys to be on our side."

No one spoke. I realized the adults were watching us, overhearing. I knew I ought to have something meaningful to say, but words did not come.

Frank finally said, "I guess I'll see if anything is left inside." He turned and fled into the house.

There was another silence. Then Terry McCall said, "We're gonna watch who moves into your house. If they don't take real good care of it and they've got kids, they'll be sorry."

"And on Halloween they'll *all* be sorry if they're not careful," Jack Rayburn added.

I swallowed a lump in my throat. "Thanks, you guys."

They came forward solemnly to shake hands, one by one.

"I'll see you at school, Kenny, right?"

"If anybody gives you trouble over there on Wheatland, you let us know."

"Don't take any wooden nickels, pal."

"Watch out for yourself."

"We're gonna miss you around here."

David Vincent came last in the line. We shook hands and he said something I didn't catch, and then he thrust a small, heavy cloth bag into my hands. The group started back across the park, shoving each other and acting the fool to break the tension, and I looked down at the bag in my hands. It had a drawstring at the top. I pulled it open. Inside, it looked like all the marbles he had ever won from me.

By nightfall we had everything moved into our new home, the north half of a cream-color double near Broad Street on Wheatland Avenue. The house had a long, narrow living room, a tiny dining room, a kitchen at the rear, and a curving staircase going up to three bedrooms and a bathroom upstairs. There was a dank, cavernous basement. Nothing was very clean, and we stacked boxes and shoved furniture against walls and pitched in with buckets, mops, and rags. We worked until past midnight, the darkness standing gaunt at naked, dirty windows.

In the morning we went to ten o'clock mass at St. Aloysius, went home, resumed work. Pop had a spell in mid-afternoon and had to lie down. We got the upstairs and the kitchen pretty well cleaned and straightened up. There was an ice house right on the

corner behind the gas station, so we had our ice box in good shape
and Gramaw made a roast for supper, acting like it was a festive
occasion. The only one who acted normal was Max, tied in the
backyard until he got used to his new surroundings, and he ran
around and around in circles, yipping endlessly and pausing his
frantic running only now and then to dig a small hole. Normal
for Max was insane.

We all turned in pretty early, Mary bedding down in the
room she would now share with Gramaw. Frank went to sleep
almost at once, but I couldn't. I lay awake listening to the creaking of this strange house, and the faint sounds of a radio coming
through the wall from the people in the other half of the double,
the Slaters. They were elderly and had no children. I could already see that we would be shushed every time we raised our
voices, "because of the Slaters."

Later, still wide awake, I heard the Slaters' radio stop, then
heard their gentle voices upstairs, through the bedroom wall.
Then it was still. The house creaked and groaned some more like a
living thing. I felt like it *was* a living being, a beast, and I hated it.

After a while some sharper creaking of floorboards caught
my attention. I sat up in bed. A nearby streetlight flooded the
room with silver. I could not see anything. The sound changed
—became that of someone definitely on the stairs.

Swinging bare feet out of bed, I crept out to investigate. The
stairs made no sound under my weight. I went downstairs and
cautiously peered into the living room. Pop, in only his pajama
bottoms, stood at the front window, looking out.

I must have made some sound. He turned. "Kenny?"

I went into the room. "I didn't know who it was."

"Having trouble sleeping?"

"Some."

"You need your rest. Big day at school tomorrow."

I said nothing. He always spoke as if every day was a big day
at school when in reality most were sheer boredom.

"Well," he said after a pause, "I think we'll do just fine here,
don't you?"

"If you say so," I told him.

"Yes, sir, just fine." He looked out the window again. "We'll get used to it."

I said nothing. I still loved him, but he was talking like a fool again. If it had not been for my fear, I think I would have lashed out.

"When I got sick," he mused, "I thought I was going to die. I was a pretty scared so-and-so, I'll tell you. But I've gotten a lot better. Things will improve. Most things happen for the best, even though we can't understand the reasons at the moment. We've got to go on, Kenny. Do our best. Trust in the Almighty."

I still refused to speak. His words sounded completely hollow to me. I almost wanted to feel sorry for him; how could anyone say these things after what had been done to us?

He turned to look at me. "Like I like to say, every cloud has a silver lining."

I stared at him.

"Right?" he prodded.

"If you say so."

His tone flattened. "But you don't believe in any of it."

I didn't reply.

"You're tough," he said.

"I'd like to be," I told him coldly.

"Tough and mean and don't believe in anything."

"I'd like to be," I repeated.

"And then what have you got for yourself, when you're just a cynic who doesn't give a damn?"

"Maybe a gun," I said. "To start a war."

"Go to bed." His voice was now tight with anger. "We'll talk when you start to grow up."

I obeyed him.

That night signaled the beginning of a long war between my father and me. In actuality I was at odds with the world. In school I kept quiet and did assignments grudgingly. At home I performed my chores, but found no pleasure in them. Pop put up the radiator-business sign in our new front yard and sometimes there was a customer, but even when I helped him with the work in the evenings we did not say much to one another. Sometimes I caught him looking at me, but he did not prod.

Max gave me some trouble. The first time he vanished, he was gone a day and two nights before it dawned on me where he might be. I hiked out to South Terrace and found him lying on the front steps of our abandoned home, tail thumping gladly as I approached. I put a leash on him and dragged him home. A few days later he was gone again, and I had to go collect him again.

"He's stupid," I told my mother. "He doesn't understand we live *here* now."

"Yes," she said, watching me. "He's a little like a certain young man I know."

A hot reply came to my mind but I choked it back.

October came and summer was truly over.

"When are we going hunting?" Frank asked me one day.

"I don't know when you're going," I said.

"When are *you?*"

"I'm not."

"Gaw! Why?"

"I don't feel like it."

"You act like you don't feel like *anything* anymore!"

"Maybe I don't. Leave me alone."

"What's the matter with you, anyhow?"

"Nothing! I don't feel like hunting and I don't feel like horsing around. Now is there anything else you want to know?"

He slunk off, angry with me again.

I hated everything about the new house and everything about my life. We lived so close to Broad Street that traffic noises were constant, night and day. You looked out the side window and saw the ugly back of the ice house. The latticework on the back porch was rotten, and smelled. Whenever I went to the dank basement at night and flicked on the light, glittering black waterbugs scampered for the drain. It was impossible to do anything in the barren backyard because Mr. Slater sat out there all the time, aged flabby arms like sagging pie dough in his undershirt, and then when it was colder with a muffler around his face and neck so that he resembled a putty figure in a museum. There were no boys our age in the neighborhood, only several little ones and one older boy named Hankins who carried a knife and struck me as the most sinister person I had ever seen. Sometimes in the night there was a fire somewhere, and the trucks rolled out of the fire station across Broad Street, startling us with their sirens and bells. Frank thought this was exciting. I took it as only another proof that we now were trash, in a trash neighborhood.

I carried my rosary beads to mass every Sunday. You could move the beads around in your fingers and look like you were paying attention when in fact you were only waiting for all the mumbling to stop so you could go home. My grudge against God —if there was One—ran deep.

Finnegan came to call one Sunday early in November.

"So how are ye, du—dear boy?" he asked, balancing his teacup on a bony knee.

"Fine," I said.

"An' yer school?"

"Fine."

"I imagine yer learnin' a lot?"

"Oh, sure. Just this week we learned how many cows they've got in Switzerland."

Finnegan blinked. "Wal, ye never know when ye might need information like thet."

"Right," I said sarcastically.

"Wal, things are about the same at the yard. Berg is as lazy as ever, an' I have to watch Stein ever' minute. McGiver's gut hurts all the time. I told him the other day what we might have to do is strap a toilet on his back so he could maybe git some work done now an' then."

"Hum," I said.

"So do ye ever miss the ole yard?" Finnegan prodded.

"Sometimes," I admitted.

"Wal, mebbe ye'll come back to work fer me next summer."

I looked at him. He was smiling—a very rare thing for him —and watching me closely. It occurred to me that his visit might be a put-up job to cheer me up, and the idea made me furious.

"I don't need any charity," I snapped.

"Nobody ever accused Finnegan of doin' charity," he replied. "Had ye forgot? I'm the mean so-and-so, right? Ye done good work fer me. If ye want to do more next summer, it'll be grand. But don't think I'll be easy on ye, or like ye, or anything like thet. Strictly business, I am. Remember it!"

"Well," I said, flustered, "I'll sure think about it."

"Ah, the ladies," Finnegan said and grinned as my mother and Gramaw entered the room. He got to his feet. "An' Mr. Riley. Howdedo, sir!" So we all sat there and Finnegan told outrageous jokes and lies, and after a while even Pop was chuckling at him. I watched in amazement: how could they all act like we were not in disgrace—had not *failed?*

"Kenny, are you feeling sick?"

"No, sis. I'm just fine."

"You don't *play* anymore."

"Mary, I'm busy."

"Daddy told Mama you're mad at the world."

"Oh, he did, did he?"

"Yep. I wasn't supposed to hear it, but I did. *Are* you mad at the world, Kenny? Why?"

"I'm not mad at anybody. I just don't care."

"*Why?*"

"If you don't care, you can't get hurt."

Mary studied my face. "Kenny, that's a terrible thing to say!"

"Wash my mouth out with soap," I suggested.

A few days before Thanksgiving, Gail came home. He simply appeared at the door on Saturday afternoon, a lank, sunburned stranger in an ill-fitting dark suit with the same battered suitcase in his hand. Mom, who had answered the doorbell, cried out in surprise when she saw him.

"Joe! Everyone! It's Gail! Gail is home!"

We all rushed into the living room and everyone talked at once. Gail hugged me fiercely. He was taller, gaunt as a skeleton, so dark he looked like an Indian except on his nose and forehead, which had never tanned and always just blistered and peeled over and over again. He smelled of dust and tobacco.

"But you didn't even write to tell us you were coming!" Mom exclaimed.

"We got laid off," Gail said, shrugging. "We looked—there wasn't anything else. We just didn't see any sense in hanging around out there."

"You're home for good?" Pop asked.

"I'm going to look for a job. If I can find anything around here, I'll stay." Gail scowled. "But now listen. I know you're sort of cramped here. I'll find my own place in a few days."

"Son, there's always room for you with us."

Gail's shoulders heaved. "It's . . . good to be home."

"What was it like in Oklahoma?" Frank demanded. "You never said a lot in your letters except it was hot."

"It was so hot you couldn't believe it," Gail said. "It was still hot when we left Tulsa the day before yesterday. That whole part of the country is a dust bowl. It's not so bad in eastern Oklahoma because it rains every once in a while, but the western part of the state is blowing away. Kansas and Texas are blowing away, too. You look up in the afternoon and here comes this cloud, like a black wall in the west, and pretty soon it's there and it's like night, but when you breathe you get this fine grit in your mouth and nose. It's terrible. A lot of people are leaving the western part." Gail shook his head. "We would have stuck it out. But oil prices have just gone down the drain. They can't afford to drill. It's folding up."

"Well, we're glad to have you back," Pop said with feeling. "You'll find something here."

"I hope so," Gail said. He looked around at our faces. "I want you to know . . . I'm sorry. If I could have done better—sent more money—maybe this thing wouldn't have happened about the house."

"Honey, it wasn't your fault!" Mom said.

"It really wasn't anybody's fault," Pop said. "Except maybe mine."

"No," Gail said, "I should have done better."

I was astonished. So he, too, felt guilty. *And Pop felt guilty.* When in fact the fault was mine, and I knew it.

"Things happen," Gramaw said. "Sometimes there is no one to blame."

No one replied.

Mom suddenly startled us by clapping her hands. "That's enough of that kind of talk! Kenny—Frank—show your big brother the room upstairs. We'll get the cot out of the attic. Mary, you can help your father do that. Gramaw and I have to get into that kitchen. This calls for something special for supper!"

And special it was: fried chicken, mashed potatoes and cream gravy, slaw, green beans, carrots, hot rolls, milk and coffee, and two steaming cherry pies just out of the oven. Gail told us everything about the work he had done in the oil fields, including stories that made us laugh. He had grown up and there was an air of sadness about him, as if he had left something—or someone—behind in Oklahoma. But we were festive and glad around the table.

We stayed up very late, trooping to bed past one o'clock in the morning. Gail's cot was set up temporarily between my and Frank's beds. The three of us chattered away while we undressed, took our turns in the bathroom, and turned in. With the lights out and the house quiet, the mood changed. Our voices lowered to whispers.

"Is Pop really okay?" Gail asked.

"He's about the same," I said.

"He had a spell the other day," Frank added.

"He's going to have those," I pointed out.

"Mom looks fine. Gramaw looks older."

"Well, she *is.*"

"Mary is sprouting like a weed. She's going to be pretty."

"She's pretty already."

Gail lit a cigarette in the dark. "I guess it was tough. The moving."

"Bad enough," I said.

"I guess everybody is used to it by now."

Frank said, "Well, like Mom says, it was just a house."

Gail sighed.

"Just a house," I added bitterly, "that Pop practically killed himself to get for us."

"Maybe we'll be able to buy another house sometime," Gail said.

"Fat chance."

"You've got to hope, anyway. Plan."

"Why?" I asked.

"Why, because there's always a silver lining. Things could always be worse."

"No," I said. "Things couldn't be any worse. Our house was stolen from us by a bunch of thieves. Pop is never going to be any better. We're trash now."

"I never thought I would hear you talk like that," Gail said, his tone shocked. "*I* was supposed to be the cynical one. But even I know you've got to have faith."

"In what?" I demanded.

"In the future. In things getting better. In . . . God."

"God!"

"Yes, God."

"I thought you were the smart one," I told him.

"Listen! Out in Oklahoma I saw people that were *really* poor. You just don't know how much we have here. I'll find a job if it kills me, and things will be a lot better. You wait and see."

I did not reply. Sure enough, Frank got the subject around

to hunting. Gail said they would go soon. It didn't matter to me. Nothing mattered to me, I assured myself.

I didn't know that it would be only a matter of days until our final crisis would show me how wrong I was.

20

On the Tuesday after Thanksgiving, Pop was out for a walk when I got home from school. I went to the basement after changing clothes. The dampness here made regular oiling of the tools mandatory, and it was a job I kept at slavishly, regardless of how disillusioned I might have become.

Perching on the stool, I oiled a cloth and began rubbing some of the wrenches. Max came kerflopping down the stairs to join me, and behind him came Mary.

"I got a new reader!" she told me brightly. "It's got lots of good stories in it!"

"Great," I said without much enthusiasm.

"It has stories about Germany and China and *everywhere* in it!"

"That's nice."

"And we're going to get a Bible history book, too. Sister said it has stories in it about Moses and Jesus and everybody. We'll get that next week. I saw one sister had. It's real thick. It has a blue cover."

"That's great, Mary."

"Did you have a Bible history when you were in my grade? Sister says before long I'll probably have to have a bookcase of my own, I'll have so many books. I'm really getting to be a good reader. Don't you think I'm a good reader? When I get the Bible history, I'll read it to you."

"Terrific."

"Would you like to see my new reader?" She started for the steps.

"Mary, I'm busy here," I snapped.

She looked back, her face falling. "I thought you would want to see it."

"Well, maybe later, okay?"

She came back over. "Okay. I'll stay here and keep you company."

"No, just go on," I said grumpily. "I said I'm *busy.*"

"Well, I didn't want to stay down here anyway."

I looked down at her. She was barefoot. "It's no wonder, running around on this wet concrete in bare feet. Are you stupid or something? Get upstairs and get something on your feet!"

She ran and I thought no more about it, absorbed in my own thoughts.

At supper, it was my mother who noticed Mary picking at her food. She said something about it. Mary said she wasn't hungry. Pop felt her forehead and shrugged to indicate that she didn't have a fever.

The next morning she *was* feverish. She came to the breakfast table in her robe, and pale. The decision had already been made to keep her home from school on this gray, sleety day. Touched by guilt for having been short with her before, I kissed her on the way to the door. Her skin was hot and dry and she seemed listless.

"A little camphorated oil on your chest and some hot tea, and you'll feel better in no time," Gramaw was telling her as I went out into the white, hostile world.

I thought little more about it during the morning and lunch hour. About two o'clock, during my math class, someone from the office came to the door and signaled the teacher. After a brief consultation in the hall, she came back in. "Kenneth, you have a visitor in the office. You're excused."

I followed the secretary down the hall. Standing in the office, his coat powdered by sleet, was Gail. A glance at his face told me something had happened.

"Pop—?" I said huskily.

"It's Mary," he said grimly.

"What happened?"

"She's sick. *Real* sick. Mom said to come get you and Frank and have you come on home."

Nothing like this had ever happened before. "You mean she's worse than this morning?"

"I told you she's real sick. She's burning up and vomiting and now she says her legs feel funny."

The cold that went through me was like nothing I had felt on the way to school this morning. *"Infantile paralysis?"*

"I don't know," Gail said. "We called the doctor and he's supposed to come over as soon as he can."

"Have you got Frank yet?"

"I came for you first. I'm heading there now."

"I'm going straight home."

Gail nodded and left the office. I ran for my coat and burst into the cold winter afternoon with only one arm through a sleeve and my stocking cap still in a pocket.

There was a Buick parked in front of our half of the double when I got home. When I rushed inside the living room, I found my father pacing up and down.

"How is she?" I demanded. "Is the doctor here?"

"He's with her now," Pop told me somberly. "Your mother and Gramaw are waiting outside the room. Take off your coat. Hang it up."

Without thinking how crazy it was to worry about a coat at a time like this, I obeyed. I went back into the living room. Pop was lighting a Chesterfield.

"Can I have one of those?" I asked shakily.

"You don't smoke," he told me.

"The hell I don't."

He stared at me a moment, then tapped a cigarette partly out of the pack and extended it to me. I took it. He struck a match and I inhaled raggedly.

"I guess you do, at that," he said quietly.

"Is she better? Worse? What?"

"Son, we don't know a thing. Her fever kept going up all morning. About eleven she threw up. Then she had chills: bad, hard chills. Your mother tried to get some tea and toast down her at noon, and she threw up again. She says she hurts, especially in her legs."

"Maybe it's nothing serious," I said. "Maybe it's the flu."

He seemed to consider something. Then he said it: "She says she feels a little numb."

I didn't say anything. *Would you do this to us, too?* I thought.

"But there's no sense borrowing trouble," Pop added, although the havoc of his expression said otherwise. "We'll just wait and see what the doctor says."

Upstairs we heard low voices, then footsteps on the stairs. Dr. Edwards appeared, carrying his medical bag. He had grayed since his last visit to attend my father. He came into the living room, Mom behind him.

"Well," he said slowly, "there's just no way to be sure yet. She seems to be a mighty sick little girl."

"What's her temperature?" Pop asked.

"One hundred and four."

"Good God!"

"Well, children can run a very high fever and then bounce right back. At any rate, I've given her something to try to bring that down. I left a thermometer by the bedside. I want you to take her temperature every two hours. If it rises more than another degree, I want you to let me know immediately."

"We understand. What else?"

"Keep her warm. I expect the chills to abate as the fever goes down." Dr. Edwards handed Pop a small white envelope. "Give

her one of these pills every four hours. I noticed her grand-
mother go in when I came out. That's good. It's common for a
person to have some delirium with this high a fever, especially
children. The family needs to keep someone with her around the
clock tonight in case she gets frightened."

"We will," Pop said.

"Doctor," my mother said, her voice quavering, "what is it?"

"I'll be back in the morning, assuming there's no significant
change that brings me back sooner. We ought to have a lot better
idea by that time."

"Is it infantile paralysis?" I blurted.

The doctor studied me a moment. "It's too early to tell. Any
number of things can present this sort of picture early on. All we
can do right now is watch her closely for changes. Try to get her
to take lots of liquids."

"She vomited earlier," Mom said.

"Yes, but I think that's a thing of the past. The medication
will help." He found his heavy overcoat and hat on the chair and
put them on. He smiled. "Try not to borrow trouble. It could be
quite minor."

Or major, I thought.

We stood at the door and watched the doctor go out to his
sleet-encrusted car, the tires spinning as he drove away. Then my
mother and father turned and went upstairs. As I started to
follow, I saw Gail and Frank running up the street. They
pounded onto the porch, blowing great clouds of steam from
their chests. I let them in and told them what the doctor had said,
verbatim. Of course they were as upset as I was.

"Let's go up," Frank said at once.

"We have to wait till we warm up a little," Gail said. "We
can't go up there and give her more cold."

Gramaw came down the steps carrying a water glass and
what looked like a roll of soiled bed linens. She shook her head.
"She's feeling quite poorly, boys."

"The doctor said it could be anything," I told her. "He said
it might not be serious at all."

She nodded. "I'm going to make some more tea for her. He said that would be all right."

"Do you think we could go up?"

"I think you could wait outside the room. Your mother and father are in there right now, and if everyone goes in at once, she's going to think she's sicker than she is."

How wise grandmothers were! "We really ought to take turns," I agreed. "And be real casual about it."

"I'll help Gramaw," Gail said, "and you and Frank can go first."

Frank and I didn't argue. We went upstairs and waited until Pop came out. When she saw us in the doorway, my mother came out, too.

"Only a few minutes," she whispered.

A small light burned on the bedside table. Mary's toys and books were put away neatly on the shelves—Mom, even in her worry, had cleaned the room before the doctor came. Mary lay in the bed very still, the covers up under her chin, her eyes closed.

Frank and I approached the bed, he on one side, I on the other. One of us must have made a sound because our sister's eyes opened. She seemed unfocused as she looked at us. She was flushed, her skin dry, and the covers showed her effort in breathing.

"Hi," she said huskily.

"Hi yourself," I said, forcing a smile.

"I'm sick," she said.

"We know. But the doctor says you're going to get better."

"My legs feel funny."

"They'll be better tomorrow."

Her eyes focused and clung to me. "Have I got infantile paralysis?"

"No! Of course not!"

"But my legs feel so *funny!*" Tears appeared in her eyes.

"You're going to be all right," I said. "The doctor gave you medicine. He left some more. You mustn't get upset. You need your strength."

"I don't want to get infantile paralysis! I don't want to walk funny...or be in one of those iron lung things. I don't want to *die.*"

"Don't be silly! You're not going to die! You're going to be just fine!"

Mom came back into the room with Gramaw following her. "You boys better leave now. We'll take care of everything."

I bent and kissed my sister's cheek. Her skin was dry, burning up.

"She's going to die," Frank said when we had gone down to the living room.

"Don't say stuff like that!" I replied sharply.

Pop and Gail came through the living room to the stairs and went up. Frank and I sat silent. The sleet had resumed outside, sifting like cat's claws against the windows. The house was chilling. I went to the basement and checked the furnace. Pop had just put in some coal. Going back upstairs, I found Gramaw in the kitchen, starting the evening meal.

"Can I help?" I asked. I had to do something.

"You can peel the potatoes," she told me matter-of-factly.

I took potatoes to the sink. "She's *so* sick," I said.

"She'll get better, child."

"We don't know that. I've never seen anybody so sick!"

"There are times, Kenny, when all we can do is place ourselves in the hands of the Lord."

And how can I do that when I have no faith?

"She's always been a healthy child," Gramaw added. "That stands in her favor. It's up to us to be calm, and watch over her, and pray."

I looked at her. Her face was pinched, gray. *You're so old,* I thought suddenly. *I never saw how old. Soon we'll lose you, too.*

We got through the evening meal, and night came. I took a turn sitting by the bedside. My sister slept, sometimes turning her head this way and that and murmuring, as if tormented by bad dreams. I was so upset I could not think in a straight line about anything. Mom and Pop said they would take turns sitting with her through the night. The rest of us wanted to, but they said they would not sleep anyway.

By midnight there had been no discernible change. Mary had awakened for a while and sipped tea and water. Gramaw hugged each of us boys and made a bed for herself on the living room couch. Gail and Frank and I had some coffee and whispered conversation in the kitchen, and then there was nothing to do but try to sleep. Pop was in the room with Mary and she was sleeping. Mom was in her bedroom, a light shining underneath the door. Mechanically we took turns brushing teeth, undressing, getting into our beds. The sleet continued to whisper periodically at the windows.

"I'll never get any sleep tonight," Frank said.

Neither Gail nor I answered him. We lay silent, and in a few minutes Frank's even breathing announced that he was asleep after all.

A long time passed.

"Still awake?" Gail whispered finally.

"Yes," I whispered back.

"I'm going to try to sleep," my older brother told me. "It's been a long day. We can't do anything anyway."

"Right."

So I lay awake, staring at the ceiling, and after another long time Gail, too, was breathing with that depth and regularity that said he had found sleep.

This could not be happening, I thought. Mary could not have *that* disease. But instantly my overactive imagination saw her hobbling on horrid steel braces . . . encased in an iron lung . . . lying waxen in a coffin. Sweat broke out all over my body and I felt ill. Was *I* getting it, too? Were we all going to get it?

I sat bolt upright in bed, shaking. I listened to my body. No, I was not sick . . . not physically. But I had been mean to my sister and had thought of no one but myself, and if there *was* a God, what better way to punish me than this?

What had I said only days ago? *"Nothing worse could happen. We've got nothing more to lose."* Something like that. Something so brilliant, so bitter, so intelligent, that I cringed in recalling it. Had there *ever* been anybody as stupid as I?

Out in the hallway I heard my mother and father in whispered consultation. Lights flashed briefly as doors opened, closed. Boards creaked. Then it was still again, except for the faintest groaning of boards in Mary and Gramaw's room. I recognized the sound. It had to be my mother in there now, rocking . . . rocking.

The sleet had finally stopped. Sitting up, I could look out through the wind at a still, lovely, icy-white world. The traffic light on the corner flashed red and then green, red and green, signaling to empty streets of silver. I lay down and closed my eyes and the images of Mary, dead, came back instantly.

It was just impossible. I had to do something. Slipping out of bed, I silently found my robe in the closet and put it on. I had no slippers. Barefoot, I crept down the hall. A faint seam of light showed under both the other bedroom doors.

Going downstairs, I first thought I could sit in the living room, but then remembered Gramaw sleeping there. I padded into the black kitchen. If I turned on a light here, it would shine into the living room. I opened the basement door, reached inside, and flicked on the switch that sent black waterbugs scampering. Max looked up at me from his rug at the foot of the steps and his tail thumped.

I went down. The concrete floor was icy under my bare feet. Perching on the workbench stool, I wished for a Chesterfield and thought how my sister had wanted to show me her new reader. *"Too busy,"* I had said. Too busy!

I sat looking at the tools. Ever since my father's first attack, I had come to this workbench and these tools as if to an altar. I had imagined that by working somehow I could make things right. But nothing was right, and my bitterness was gone in a wave of sheer confusion.

There was nothing I could do. This was the fact that over-whelmed me. I saw that all summer long I had only imagined that I could have an impact on our destiny. I had been helpless then and I was helpless now, and it was a very bitter pill to swallow. Was there *never* a time in life when one controlled his own life?

Max's tail thumped vigorously, as it had when I started down the steps. I looked toward him and saw Pop standing partway down from the kitchen. He wore his flannel bathrobe, very faded, a gray and tan pattern, and house slippers. His bare legs and ankles looked skinny and pale. He was studying me with a sober, questioning expression, and his hair stood up as if from fright.

"Son?" he said softly.

"I'm sorry if I bothered you," I said. "I couldn't sleep."

He came on down the steps and to the bench. "Well. I couldn't sleep either."

"How is she?"

"Sleeping."

"The fever?"

"Just about the same."

"It just kills me to know she's so sick and is having bad dreams and everything! I wish it was me. I could handle it. But she's so little!"

"I know, Kenny. I know."

I looked at him, seeing. "You *do* know."

He smiled faintly, as if in amusement at himself and the strange ways of the world. "I think so."

"Pop—it was my fault we had to move."

"No, it wasn't, son."

"It was. You know that Mom and I lied to those Klan guys when they came to the house. But I did more than that. I popped off—got smart. I told them I had a picture of the Grand Dragon or somebody in my bedroom. That's what made them sure we were lying, so that's why they got even with us."

Pop's eyes were dark and intense. "What do you mean, got even?"

"That's something else I never told you. The day after you were turned down on the new loan, I went down there."

"*You?*"

"Yes. I barged right in—saw the guy. Mom must have told you. He was the one that was the leader of the guys on our porch that night."

"She told me," Pop said grimly. "But you went down there? Good lord! *Why?*"

"I don't know . . . But I went in and recognized him, and that was when I knew they would *never* let us keep our house if they could help it, because I had shot off my mouth and made them mad."

Pop put his arm roughly around my shoulders. "My God! You've known that? You've carried that knowledge? What a terrible thing for a boy to have to learn!"

"And it's my own fault."

"No!" He shook me gently. "Kenny, boy, listen! I would give anything if you hadn't had to go down there. Most people are good. When you're older, you'll understand that; you can . . . sort things out."

"You don't have to tell me people are good." I told him. "I know the truth."

"But they *are!*" he insisted. "Maybe we wouldn't have kept the house anyway—and it doesn't matter."

"It was all my fault!"

"No! Listen! You made fun of them on the porch? Good!"

"You're not mad?" I asked in astonishment.

His eyes were wet. "I'm proud of you. Just don't let one or two experiences make you bitter, son. We have to believe in people. Because it's through people that we experience God."

"God," I said hollowly.

"God," he repeated firmly. "Oh, I know I don't go to church. I suppose your priest would say I'm a heathen." A smile quirked

the corners of his lips. "But I know about God. I believe in God.
And I know you do, too."

"Even when Mary is up there, so sick?"

"Especially then. What do you think I've been doing? I've
been sitting up there, praying. I know we're all praying. And
that's what's going to pull her through."

"I wish I could believe that!"

"You can." His face grew stern. "This family is going to
endure."

"I hope so," I said passionately.

"We ought to talk more about this," he said. "But do you
know what time it is?" He took out his watch and examined it.
"Holy mackerel, Andy, it's three o'clock."

"I don't know if I'll ever sleep," I said.

He yawned, an elaborate stage yawn that didn't fool me.
"Well, I'll tell you. I think I'll turn in. You ought to think about
it, too."

"Maybe I'll just stay down here another few minutes," I said.

He nodded, patted my shoulder, and started to the stairs. He
climbed a few steps slowly, then looked back at me. "I love you,"
he said softly.

"I—love you," I said.

He smiled and went slowly upward and out of sight.

Pulse thudding, I stared again at the tools. His tools. I saw
suddenly that I was his son in ways I had never thought about
before, in ways neither of us could ever deny.

And he *prayed!*

I thought of Mary. Then, closing my eyes, I decided to try
to pray.

The words would not come in the ways I had been taught.
I tried repeatedly, but my mind and heart were too full. Finally
in a mixture of desperation and exhaustion I gave it up: I simply
thought of God, and all at once it was as if something inside me
opened. There was nothing I could say—no formula, no promise,
nothing—that meant much to God.

Here I am, I thought, and somehow in ways I despair of ever making clear, it seemed the most profound and simple moment I had ever known. Whatever happened would happen, and *I did not have to be in charge of anything.*

I put my head down on the workbench. Sleep came.

In the morning they found me asleep at the bench. Every bone in my body ached from the cold of the basement. Gramaw hustled me upstairs and into bed. Everyone was puzzled and upset with me except Pop, and he said nothing.

"What were you thinking of, child?" Gramaw scolded.

"I was just dumb," I told her.

Frank grimaced. "You sure were."

The doctor came early. Mary was a little better. He talked to her and my parents, and then came in to look at me. A thermometer was stuck in my mouth.

"How's my sis?" I asked around it.

He smiled wearily. "Better. Probably not as sick as you at the moment."

"She doesn't have . . . ?"

"She has the flu, and her fever is down." He removed the thermometer. "Very nice. One hundred and two. Are you going for her record?"

I grinned at him idiotically.

He took out a wooden tongue depressor and gagged me with it. "Say ah."

I was in bed longer than Mary. She brought me soup the last day before they let me get up. I felt weak and achy, but happier than I had in a very long time. Frank could not understand it; he *knew* I should feel disgraced for having made myself sick.

I didn't try to explain it to him or anyone else. What I had found, I could only hope that somehow I might hang onto. I think Pop understood. He came in a couple of afternoons and sneaked me a Chesterfield, and we smoked together. Mom would have killed us. Maybe we would always grieve for our lost house. But *we* would endure.

The first weekend after I was all better, we went hunting. Max ran around like crazy. Pop could stay out only an hour or two. He shot three rabbits with three shots and Gail was two for two. Even Frank got one. I fired and missed six times. It didn't matter. Even Max forgave me, eventually.

21

We lived on South Wheatland for another five years. When the war came, Gail, Frank and I all went into the army. We survived. Pop died peacefully in his sleep late in 1947 and we lost Gramaw only months later. My mother lived for many more years, the last of them with my wife and me in a new house farther west on the Hilltop. The education Pop had wanted so badly for me finally took me to Ohio State, where I ended up teaching English.

Old Max lived to be seventeen. The last time I saw Finnegan, he was in his eighties and still bullying the men who worked in his yard. He hugged me and got tears in his eyes and called me a dumb boy, and offered me a chew of tobacco. It made me a little sick, but I never let him know that.

In all those years I never went back to the house of South Terrace. Then in retirement we moved to where we live now in Arizona, not far from where Mary's husband has his small tool firm . . . and where Mary dotes on two grandchildren.

Only a year or so ago, though, my wife and I were back in Columbus to visit Gail and Frank and their families. I found myself driving on a much-changed Broad Street near Terrace. On impulse, I watched the signs and turned south.

"Where are we going?" my wife asked. Then she, too, saw the street sign. "Oh," she said quietly.

"Just a peek," I said.

She smiled uncertainly and nodded.

We drove along the first block and I saw that the houses seemed the same, not run-down as I had feared, but undergoing a neighborhood transformation as new people, young people, moved in and lovingly restored the old homes to the way they had been when I was a child. At the corner, the little grocery store was no longer there. The building was still there, but it was boarded up, vacant.

Beyond the intersection, the street forked as it always had to enclose the park. The trees were very old and large now, shading the grassy parkway, which was somehow much smaller than I had remembered it. The city had put up a sign on a pole that said NO BASEBALL PLAYING. Six small boys were playing two-a-cat. Good.

We passed the Vincents' old house and there were small children on the porch. The Rayburn house was changed, painted a different color, and it looked like the tree where the tree house had been was removed.

I looked ahead, and there it was.

Our house.

It was just fine. The lot was much narrower than I remembered. But someone had very recently done a lot of work on it. There was a fine new green shingle roof and fresh white paint with dark green trim. The sidewalk was new, but just like the old one, and the grass had been cut. The windows gleamed from a fresh washing.

In the front yard was a For Sale sign.

I turned at the next corner and drove back by on the right side of the street, going very slowly, gawking through the windshield as we passed. There was a lump in my throat. "You know," I said, "we were awfully happy here."

"You're all awfully happy now."

I sighed. "Old, but happy. Yes."

"We could stop," she suggested.

I slowed further, considering it.

"Look in the windows," my wife added. "Walk around to the back?"

"No," I said quietly, and drove on by. For my mother, I saw now, had been right all the time. I would never forget this place, but it was as she had said: only a house.